FROM THE CASE FILES OF
STEVE ROCKFISH

THE PINE BARRENS Stratagem

KEN HARRIS

Black Rose Writing | Texas

First printing

ISBN: 978-1-68433-871-9
PUBLISHED BY BLACK ROSE WRITING
www.blackrosewriting.com

Printed in the United States of America
Suggested Retail Price (SRP) $19.95

The Pine Barrens Stratagem is printed in Book Antiqua

*As a planet-friendly publisher, Black Rose Writing does its best to eliminate unnecessary waste to reduce paper usage and energy costs, while never compromising the reading experience. As a result, the final word count vs. page count may not meet common expectations.

Praise for

The Pine Barrens Stratagem

"Amazing novel by a great writer with a tremendous background in the subject matter! Ken Harris's *Pine Barrens Stratagem* was an exciting, fun, and captivating read that kept my attention for hours at a time. This will be the first book of many, I'm sure! Ready to see the movie!"

–Larry Karl, Retired FBI Senior Executive

"Harris stands out from other authors in the genre, shining like a star upon a midnight sea of mediocrity. Fearless, full of heart, loveable characters, and twists and turns that will take you to the very heart of darkness."

–Ben Eads, author of *Cracked Sky* and *Hollow Heart*

"As a retired police detective I found the storyline spot on and compelling. The author tied together past and current day stories seamlessly, making it easy and enjoyable to follow."

–Michelle Cyr, retired Detective

"In Ken Harris's fast-paced, can't-put-it-down thriller, Steve Rockfish takes his place in the PI pantheon alongside Philip Marlowe, Sam Spade and Jim Rockford."

–John Hazen, author of *Fava and Beyond Revelation*

"*The Pine Barrens Stratagem* is a fantastic blend of classic detective storytelling with modern elements, making for a fun and thought-provoking read. You'll laugh at the character interactions, and then you'll get mad when you realize the conspiracies that unfold are probably very close to real life. I demand more stories about the adventures of Private Eye Steve Rockfish!"

–Brent Michael Kelley, author of
Keep Away from Psycho Joe, Cruce Roosters* and *The Chuggie Series

"Details of missing pregnant teens in the 1940s hint of murder and child kidnapping. Using his own experience with the FBI child exploitation task force, Harris weaves the decades' old mystery into today's pandemic with a private investigator you can like."

–Val Conrad, author of *Signal of Guilt*

"Ken Harris takes you on a trip through history, tied to the present and hidden by police corruption, mob influence and church secrets."

–Stephen W. Briggs, author of *Family of Killers, 'Memoirs of an Assassin'*

"A private detective thriller in the same vein as the great detective shows of the '70s, '80s and '90s, but as up-to-date as the global pandemic. The sort of story you'd love to share with your father or son — both of you reading it at the same time and talking about it between readings."

–Ben Sharpton, author of *The Awakening of Jim Bishop: This Changes Things*

For my wife Nicolita and children, Kenny and Riley

Mom & Dad - Wishing you were here to see this - Miss you

THE PINE BARRENS Stratagem

PROLOGUE - FEBRUARY 1943

The sun began its afternoon descent and dusk brought with it a bone-numbing cold. The gusts of wind that accompanied it just added insult to injury. The cold crept between Kathleen's ribs, caressing her heart, her lungs. Those same gusts whistled through the dilapidated shed's walls as if made of cardboard and tar paper. The smell of smoke and moisture hung in the air. It all signaled the impending nor'easter was on final approach and there would be no rest this evening for the weary. The primary task would be to keep the small wood stove stoked through the night and well into the dawn hours. It would require more of Kathleen's attention and fuel than the previous two nights, but the stove was her only source of heat and light in the cramped shed. Add in the expected steep drop in temperature tonight, her infant daughter, Evelyn, would need both to survive.

Kathleen lugged firewood in from the outside pile over the late morning hours. The pathway took her around the large pig pen, then along the backside of the barn and to the opposite corner where wood deemed not worthy of burning in the main house was discarded. The ground was hazardous, uneven in most spots and filled with mud ruts frozen in place. The route was too treacherous to navigate for someone who had given birth less than forty-eight hours ago. Kathleen then spent the afternoon trying to shore up the uneven boards that made up her home's walls. She searched the old barn for newspapers, rags, or anything else she could find to fill the large cracks between the planks of half rotted wood. She addressed what areas she could reach and said a prayer that the snow the incoming storm brought would not collapse the roof.

Kathleen's living space was only eight feet by eight feet and that, she thought, was being generous. The day's work had resulted in a stack of firewood that took up most of the wall to her left and for the moment was close to chin high. It would shrink considerably during the night, and force Kathleen out into the snow the next morning to replenish it.

It should do for the night, Kathleen thought. *That is all I can concern myself with now. There will be time between chores in the morning to worry.* Her right hand unconsciously reached up and gripped the silver cross that hung from her neck and gave it a tight squeeze.

As for the rest of the living space, against the far wall, opposite the door, sat an army cot with an old wicker baby bassinet perched atop it. The paint was peeling and the side strips were beginning to fray, but like the shed; it was part of their temporary home. The constant cries of hunger and cold that emanated from Evelyn served as a reminder of why the upcoming storm could only take up so much of Kathleen's attention. She had to stay strong for her daughter.

A few more days, she kept repeating to herself, reaching down to pull Evelyn close to her chest. *A few more then we can be on our way, away from this godforsaken place and town.*

****

Kathleen's tears had long dried before the storm hit and she promised herself, no more crying, even if things continued in a downward spiral for her and baby Evelyn. Kathleen would fight back the tears with all she had. Her agreement with her emotions was one where it was okay to feel sad from time to time, but there would be no nightly self-pity parties. She had made her bed willingly, and slept in it, figuratively.

No one pushed me into that car's backseat, Kathleen thought. *It was my decision to bring Evelyn into this world, an act I would repeat one thousand times, knowing we'd end up in this shed. But I need to stay strong and persevere. For Evelyn.*

Kathleen's eyes were on the endgame and that was to provide her daughter with a good life and loving home like her parents had raised her in, before the great shame caused them to throw her out on her pregnant bottom.

Kathleen had grown up in a small house with her parents, the middle child to an older brother and younger sister. They had it all, the white picket fence, a Cocker Spaniel named Woody, and plenty of toys. Her parents doted on each child as if they were the only one, and all three siblings got along so well, most times no one could remember the last time they fought. As they'd grew older, Kathleen and Gertrude drew closer, especially after Tim graduated high school and enlisted the day after Pearl Harbor.

Kathleen's trip to the shed had started the previous May, coincidently after the Mother's Day dance at the school. The irony was lost on no one. That evening David McCutchin sweet-talked her into the backseat of his father's Ford with talk of his own enlistment and impending boot camp at Fort Jackson, outside Columbia, South Carolina. Ten hours by car, but a lifetime to a teenager in love. Things only got worse on July 4th when Kathleen had smacked her mother across the face when she suggested a particular doctor across the bridge in Philadelphia could put an abrupt end to the shame. Shame that would eventually be bequeathed on the entire family by their so-called friends and neighbors. That slap had prevented Kathleen's mother from even mentioning the second and more palatable option of adoption through a contact in the church and an eventual, faster return to normalcy. But with the slap and the aftermath, it was full speed ahead with no options remaining on the table.

Kathleen's parents had let it be known this outcome was her decision alone and they wouldn't hear differently. Both parents reinforced the point with each conversation until they essentially washed their hands of what they called 'the entire mess.' The swelling in her mother's face had not yet receded when they calmly informed Kathleen that she and whatever was inside her was dead to them. Dead as their loving son Tim, who passed the prior April from a stumble in the Philippines during the infamous Bataan Death March. Lest the two be confused, her father reiterated, Tim's death was the only one for which they would hold their heads high. And with that, he firmly closed the front door and locked the deadbolt.

Kathleen and her future baby were now alone, and it terrified her. She'd remained on the front porch for a couple of minutes, unsure where to go and what to do when she got there. The small suitcase slipped from her hand and she collapsed next to it, sobbing uncontrollably.

****

The shed and its ramshackle condition were courtesy of Mary D'arnaud, the midwife that assisted in Evelyn's birth, but it wasn't Kathleen's first destination after being kicked out of her girlhood home. With the sound of the deadbolt sliding into place and her father's ultimate words still careening around between her ears, Kathleen had eventually gotten up. She knew she couldn't stay there and hope someone inside would have pity on her, so Kathleen composed herself, picked up her suitcase and had walked down the driveway. County Route 538 lay ahead.

The entire world lay ahead for me, she thought, but it only emphasized her loneliness and with the recognition the tears had flowed freely again.

Kathleen's initial thought had been of the church. All she learned each Sunday, since she was a young girl, was God loved her no matter what and would always be there for her, although he had been darn silent the past two months when she reached out before bed each night. Doubt had soon crept into that option, and along with the possibility of having to see her family each week at Sunday mass, Kathleen instead took a left turn onto Evergreen Drive. She would consider the church a fallback plan, only should her second choice not welcome her in with open arms. David's house became the destination and in Kathleen's mind, there was no way his parents could turn away their son's unborn child.

What were the odds that the second set of grandparents would be as unforgiving as the first? She thought.

After all, the McCutchins were Methodists, so there was absolutely no chance of Kathleen coming across her parents every Sunday and making a scene. Most of all, the McCutchins had their only child about to head off to war. By God, they would need somewhere and more importantly someone to focus their love and attention on. Kathleen was partially right in the long run, but it took more convincing than she ever thought in order to get David's mother to open the front door. Sadly, it wasn't long before Kathleen realized that the primary concern of what others might think was not an ideology lauded solely by her parents.

Once she crossed the McCutchins foyer, Kathleen spent almost all of the last two trimesters confined to David's childhood bedroom. She slept in his bed, read his collection of Hardy Boys books, and even wore his old shirts when hers became too tight. David soon graduated from basic training and only to Kathleen's surprise, did not come home prior to shipping off for the European theatre. Kathleen never received so much as a postcard from Ft. Jackson or anywhere else in the world, but that did nothing to dissuade her from diligently writing her future husband daily during the entirety of her seven-month stay. In the end, Kathleen absolved David of any guilt, and instead solely blamed Mrs. McCutchins.

I know she's keeping David's letters from me, she thought. *Hidden away in a box somewhere I'd never find them.* Kathleen's mind then went one step farther. *What if she had never mailed my letters, instead just walked outside and dumped them in the trashcan?* She fought back the tears at this thought.

There came a point in time where nothing exemplified the commonalities shared between the McCutchins and her own parents regarding grandparental disdain than when the contractions started. In less than six hours, Kathleen was fittingly packed up and driven to Mary D'arnaud's farmhouse with Mr. McCutchin having spoke the only words during the trip. He stated to never contact them or their son again. Kathleen died inside but gritted her teeth to not show how deeply those words had hurt. She didn't say a word in response and hoped that her silence had not been taken as agreement. She remained quiet and slouched in the back seat, staring out the window as the world she knew flashed by.

The drive had taken Kathleen through a part of Elk Township she was unfamiliar with. Soon she would be alone and lost. Here, the panic started. It churned deep within and came close to rising to the surface when they passed a police car parked off the side of the road. Kathleen needed to alert him and she instinctively reached for the door handle. If the door opened, Mr. McCutchin would have to hit the brakes and come to a stop. That would be her cue to jump out and run for help. She had debated the idea a minute too long. Before she could act, the car then turned onto a winding dirt road that led to the D'arnaud farm. Her opportunity disappeared before her mind and body could agree on the plan.

Prior to this late-night introduction, Kathleen had not heard of Mary's name while growing up or seen the woman walking around town. When Mrs. McCutchin knocked and the front door opened, Kathleen understood why. She had been dropped off in the part of town her father had referred to as The Lawns. You see, Elk Township in 1943 was as segregated as the rest of the country, and never the two parts shall meet. A large man ushered Kathleen and Mrs. McCutchin inside, where Mary D'arnaud waited at a small table. Kathleen could still hear the engine running, so she didn't expect a long, tearful goodbye. After all, it was wartime and gasoline was heavily rationed.

Once Kathleen was inside and seated, they exchanged pleasantries. Not to mention, cash. Mrs. McCutchin removed a wad of bills from her purse that Mary accepted without counting. Mary placed the money in a Maxwell House coffee tin and with a nod, Mrs. McCutchin was out the door without so much as a farewell.

Mary then turned her attention to Kathleen and tried to make her feel at ease. Mary said she was the loyal friend of the unwed and unwanted mothers of the area and a midwife for when it was time to deliver the baby. But what Kathleen didn't know, and would never learn, was that there was so much more that Mary was involved in.

The McCutchins had simply paid for this woman to deliver Kathleen's baby and to get the young woman on her way, far away, once back on her feet. There was a small shed out back where Kathleen and baby could stay. Mary would bring meals out to the shed and Kathleen was permitted to stay until she recovered her strength. Or unless the next paying unwed mother showed up and at that point, Kathleen would be expected to vacate the premises.

Mary shuffled her chair closer to Kathleen and draped an arm across Kathleen's shoulders. "Don't you worry your little head none, I got a hunch you won't be leaving before you're ready. You just focus all your worrying on that little bundle you're going to have and let old Mary take care of the rest."

****

The night the nor'easter landed was only Evelyn's third day on the planet and Kathleen was drop-dead exhausted. Tired of it all. Tired of the crying, the cold, the chores to survive, and especially the loneliness. So much so, she had already convinced herself that as soon as the weather broke, she would head out for home. Her real home with the suitcase under one arm and Evelyn under the other. Her proper home. On bended knee or whatever it took for her father to reopen that door, her mother to take pity and sneak her in through the cellar door, or her younger sister to leave a window unlocked.

If I can just get back inside, I'm dropping anchor and they'll never get rid of us, she whispered to Evelyn. She kissed her baby on the forehead and swore on it.

Unbeknownst to Kathleen, only half her plan would be executed and there would be no waiting for the snow to cease. That night would be her last night in the shed, but it would also be her first at the bottom of an old well on the far end of the farm. A place where her body would be kept company by the three previous residents of the shed. As for Evelyn, within twenty-four hours she would be handed off three times and renamed Yola. By the time the sun set and the wind picked up again the next night, she would be safe and warm. Yola would be tucked into her new crib, within her own room, on the second floor of a three-story row house in South Philadelphia.

CHAPTER ONE

This is Steve Rockfish. At the tone, leave your name and message. I'll get back to you. [Beep]

Mr. Rockfish, this is Charles Nelson from Capital Financial Recovery and I'm calling about your 2015 Dodge Challenger auto loan. You are currently three payments behind and I am letting you know that...

The sound bounced off the wood paneling of the single-wide trailer and added to Rockfish's anger. He didn't need to look down. Muscle memory knew where the trashcan icon was and he deleted the message before Mr. Nelson could make his not-so-veiled threat or plea for payment. Experience led Rockfish to believe Mr. Nelson would surely threaten repossession.

It's too goddamn early in the day for this shit, he thought. *Another consequence of COVID-19 coming back to continually bite me in the ass. The perfect start to another pandemic day.*

The repo man would soon come for Lana. She was his pride and joy, the only luxury he allowed himself on a private investigator's tight budget. He named the Challenger after the character Lana Kane on the show *Archer*. Both were smoking hot and powerful under the hood.

Rockfish would need to figure out a way to either sweet talk Mr. Nelson into giving him a week or two to come up with the funds for at least a partial payment, or it was time to run the car out to Luke's Blueberry Farm. Luke was an old client who still owed Rockfish a favor or two, due to lack of payment for services rendered. He could always work around the occasional non-paying client. But add a dash of COVID-

19, and the financial shortcomings were a million times harder to overcome. As a last resort, Rockfish could hide Lana in an old barn on the far end of Luke's farm, in order to keep the repo man at arm's length. The game of hide-and-go-seek worked twice in the past, and Rockfish didn't see it failing again. Of course, an influx of cash would solve the problem and prevent the drive out to Luke's in the first place.

Goddamn, I just want to stay one step ahead of the bill collectors, he thought. *Maybe a couple so I can get out of this trailer and into something a bit more respectable.* He had sworn that if the Ravens could make it to another Super Bowl, he'd buy the biggest TV he could afford, but that wouldn't be a stretch in the narrow single-wide.

The governor of Maryland had the entire state in full shutdown because of the skyrocketing number of positive cases being reported on a daily basis. The state was in its third month of quarantine and who knew how long it would last with President Trump getting on television each day telling the American public not to adhere to mandates issued by governors across the country. *Everything is going to be all right*, he kept saying, despite slipping more than once and saying "*all white*". At least Rockfish hoped it was a mistake, but looking at his base, it probably wasn't.

Mixed messages aside, Rockfish's business model had firmly taken it in the ass. Potential clients remained planted on their couches streaming Netflix with their so-called loved ones, after a hard day of Zoom meetings and pretending to work from home. No longer were they leaving the office after work, crossing the street to their favorite bar, and meeting up/hooking up with that co-worker they admired from the confines of their cubicle. What it came down to was spouses didn't have the opportunity and weren't cheating on each other like the good old days. That meant no one was hiring Rockfish to get it all on video and audio for the divorce proceedings. No cases, no money. No money and Lana is forced to hide out at the farm.

On the average, Rockfish Investigations carried a caseload of between six and eight clients, but 2020 was not average. The government's complete screw-up on handling the pandemic had shrunk those numbers to a solid two. And lucky for him, one of those had the potential for a big payout. A windfall that Rockfish hoped wasn't too far away, based on recently received information.

The Reeceworth case was his temporary golden ticket out of debtor's prison. Gordon and Ginny Reeceworth looked like the perfect married upper middle-class couple. Rockfish had gone to high school with both, playing football with Gordon and crushing on Ginny. They had stayed in touch through the years, but over the course of the last few, it was obvious to Rockfish and his private investigator instincts that things weren't exactly what they seemed.

Gordon ran a slew of laundromats and self-service car washes across northern Baltimore. The good news was that both industries were primarily cash businesses, ripe for money laundering, and Gordon could wash with the best of them. The bad news was the dirty money he collected and cleaned belonged to the Marini Crime Family. Worse was after a particularly nasty fight, Ginny flew the coop with a quarter million dollars in Marini cash. Rockfish was the first call Gordon made. There was no way he could call the Baltimore Police Department or drive over to Angelo Marini's with his hat in his hand. Gordon had limited options and Rockfish welcomed the work.

Gordon hired Rockfish to find his wife, like yesterday, and signaled he would pay above Rockfish's daily rate plus expenses. In addition, Rockfish negotiated a ten percent finder's fee, and he was on the case. That was six days ago, and through some stellar PI work, Rockfish had tracked Ginny to the Drifting Sands Motel in Kill Devil Hills, on North Carolina's Outer Banks. It seemed like the perfect place to hide out during the pandemic or if you were on the run. Rockfish learned that the reservation ran through the end of the current week. He had called Gordon immediately after locating her and relayed the information. She wasn't going anywhere for the next couple of days, and Rockfish would get on the road as soon as he could to scout out the place. His plan was to surprise and pick her up on short notice, or more like no notice. Both men laughed and Rockfish hung up after letting Gordon know he'd call when he had eyes on her.

Life being what it was during a pandemic, two days passed before Rockfish got his shit together. His father Mack had a couple of medical appointments that couldn't be missed, and Rockfish didn't think twice about the delay as Ginny's reservation ran through the weekend. He expected to finally be on the road shortly after dinner that evening. Once on site, Rockfish would smooth talk whoever was manning the front desk and surprise Ginny in the middle of the night when she'd be half asleep and he, twenty-five thousand dollars richer. Rockfish would have Lana's account back in the black and then some. He could pocket that marker from Luke for when the second or even third wave of COVID-19 hit.

Rockfish had stopped counting the money in his head and begun packing a small bag for the trip, when there was a knock at the door to his trailer. He glanced at his watch and nodded to himself.

"Door's open Dad, come on in."

Mack Rockfish was a seventy-year-old retiree from the local Exxon Mobil Oil Refinery, and the old man still wasn't sure what to do with all his free time. His fishing hat, lures dangling off the side, and coveralls let you know he'd rather be fishing, but if that wasn't an option, Mack was willing to roll up his sleeves and help with any chores needing done. But today, coffee over a simple lunch with his son was the one standing appointment on his calendar.

"Morning, sonny," Mack said as he opened the trailer's flimsy front door.

"Hey, Dad," Rockfish yelled from the back bedroom. "You know where everything is, put the coffee on and I'll be out in a minute." He tossed his Glock 23 in the bag, on top of the extra change of clothes, and stopped short of zippering it. Odds were he would not need anything other than a fake business card and his way with words to sweet talk the night manager into giving him a key to Ginny's room. After all, he'd arrive at the motel as Stevie Taggert, Bounty Hunter, and if he didn't get that key, well they'd have to bust that door clean off its hinges and Code 37, subsection 20 clearly stated that the damage would be the responsibility of the property owner. The ruse worked nine out of ten times and ten out of ten when you were dealing with some Southern rube, short on sleep. But in the end, he took the gun. The drive back to Maryland was going to be long, with a handful of pee stops. Combine that with the quarter million in cash hidden somewhere in Lana, and there was a decent chance he would end up needing the added protection.

Mack was sitting on the couch watching the coffee brew when Rockfish walked out of the back and tossed his bag on the couch, opposite his dad.

"Going somewhere?" Mack said.

"Business, short drive tonight and back before sunup, if all goes well."

"You got a case you're working on?"

"Yeah, Dad, one of the few that haven't dried up." Rockfish hated answering questions about his work and rarely told the old man anything about it. But his dad was supportive and desperate to talk to anyone, so Rockfish humored him with an occasional detail.

"Hey, speaking of sun up, did I ever tell you about the time Rocky and I were working overnights in the Coker unit at the plant and listening to the O's on the radio. Eighteenth inning and Eddie Murray comes up to hit that grand slam to beat the Yankees?"

"A few times, Dad," Rockfish replied. "I know you're missing baseball with this damn pandemic, but I've got the '83 World Series on my DVR." He motioned towards the small entertainment center in the corner as if Mack had never been inside the trailer. "ESPN4 aired it a couple weeks back and I made a point to record it. If you want to hang out here tonight, keep an eye on the place and watch the clinching game, I should be back by ten or so. I'll grab us a couple of breakfast burritos."

"Appreciate it, Son, but I'm hanging out with Rocky tonight. He's making me dinner and I'm going to work on that damn garbage disposal of his that keeps jamming up. Hey that reminds me, did you look at today's paper?"

"Afraid I haven't, I've been running around trying to clear up a few things before I have to head out. Why, what did I miss? Did the President finally test positive?"

"No, Stevie, nothing like that," Mack said. "That girl you chased throughout high school Ginny what's her name..."

"Reeceworth now, Scarpa then. What about her?" Rockfish's entire body was suddenly at attention.

"This morning's Baltimore Sun reported she was found dead in North Carolina—"

Rockfish stopped listening and lunged for his phone on the table. He quickly pulled up the Sun's app. Not that he didn't believe his dad, but in this one case, he was really hoping for the first signs of dementia. His bank account was counting on it.

The headline wasn't front page above the fold, like Mack implied, but Rockfish found the story buried towards the bottom of the Metro Section.

Local Entrepreneur Killed Execution-Style in Outer Banks; Husband Missing

Rockfish quickly skimmed the article for all he needed to know, which ended up being all of it. The story leaned heavily on the theory that Gordon had killed his wife and was on the run. What it failed to mention was more important, at least to Rockfish. There was no mention of a large suitcase overflowing with cash, so either Ginny stashed it somewhere before meeting her untimely death, or the Marini boys, who ended up getting to her first, were currently returning it to its rightful owner. Rockfish guessed Gordon wasn't on the run. He most likely suffered the same fate as his wife, but his body was probably in a fifty-five-gallon drum headed out to the middle of the Chesapeake Bay, never to be found. There would be no finder's fee for Rockfish, no daily rate of six hundred dollars a day plus expenses and no happy thoughts of avoiding the drive out to the blueberry farm.

Rockfish quickly filled his Dad in on how the story not only affected his now missing old friend, but more importantly, how it fucked over his tardy finances.

"Well Stevie, I know you ain't much for the church these days, but it's like they say, when one door closes, the good Lord opens another."

"Who in the blue hell are *they*, Dad?" There was more to that thought, but his cell phone on the table vibrated and skidded towards the napkin holder. Rockfish reached down and picked it up. The message was from his now only client.

hey steve u got a sec for a zoom? shit's gone sideways not in good way

"So Dad, did *they* ever say anything about when it rains it pours?"

gimme 5, Rockfish texted back.

****

The video call went about as shitty as expected. *Rockfish Investigations was officially now open to any and all offers,* he thought. *Shit, ain't no such thing as a small job now. Cat in a tree, I'll take it. Husband Zooming with his secretary during odd hours, I'll jump in feet first. I need a payday to turn this ship around.*

It had been a few years since he was completely unemployed, and like that last time, there was a bottle waiting to crawl into. There was always a bottle, deep in the back of a cabinet, on standby and willing to help ease the pain. Rockfish was glad he forced Mack to head back home, despite promising the old man he wouldn't do exactly what he was about to. But never having a kid, Rockfish wasn't familiar with a father's ability to read a child like an open book.

When the sun rose the next morning, Rockfish's head felt like it was about to split in two, yet there was Mack standing in front of the stove. Eggs, bacon and potatoes were all doing their thing, patiently waiting to be brought together in one of Mack's famous breakfast dishes.

Rockfish staggered through the trailer, closing blinds and curtains as he went. The breakfast, grease and a handful of Tylenol would help, but darkness was what he needed most at the moment. With Mack's encouragement, Rockfish went back to the bedroom and tossed on a t-shirt and shorts. He didn't think he looked that bad in his Fruit of the Looms, but it had been a while since he'd been on a date. *Father might know best,* he thought.

"Coffee's on, put a shot of whiskey in, if that will help with whatever mental gymnastics you need to get straightened out."

Mack was full of sunshine and roses this morning, Rockfish thought. *God, I hope that comes with age.*

Rockfish grabbed his favorite oversized Baltimore Ravens mug and poured the coffee all the way to the brim. He sipped in silence, occasionally turning his head to the near empty bottle of Irish whiskey next to the sink, but held his sober ground. Hair of the dog was a quick fix, but Mack's breakfast would be more sustainable.

"I really appreciate all this, dad," Rockfish finally said. "It's been a rough last couple of months and worse twenty-four hours."

Mack grinned and shook his head. "What else are retired dads for? With your mom gone, I got nobody else to dote on. Now here, eat some more." Mack reached for the large frying pan in the middle of the table and heaped more onto his son's plate.

"Well, if you're in a doting mood," Rockfish said. "There's some shit under and behind the couch that needs swept up. Not to mention I've noticed a fine layer of dust throughout the place."

"Sonny, I didn't tuck my junk between my legs, put on this apron and make you the best damn breakfast East of the Patapsco River to audition for the role of your maid," Mack said with a grin.

"I'm sorry, Dad, I shouldn't bust your balls about cleaning this place. Listen, shit's really gone sideways for me since Governor Hogan shut the state down. I mean really, really, really sideways. I ain't sure where my next check is coming from, let alone how I can pay the late bills piling up on the desk." He shrugged his shoulders and with his right hand knocked a pile of envelopes to the floor. "That text yesterday, when I kicked you out, the client bailed on our arrangement, so I'm fucked. I've got no clients, leads for potential clients, or even a referral from Decker down at Baltimore PD. The only way I'm going to keep my head above water is if Trump ever gets me another one of those stimulus checks. It'll help, but I'll still be bailing water with a bucket. One with a hole in it, but you get my point."

Mack nodded but said nothing. Neither one spoke for a minute. Forks scrapped against paper plates and coffee mugs raised. Eventually it was Mack who broke the silence.

"Are things bad enough that you'd think about going back to the refinery? I mean, I can call Bobby and he can check with the shift work supervisor, see if they're hiring. That whiskey bottle can't be deep enough that you'd forgotten everything you learned there before quitting to play Barnaby Jones. Please tell me I'm somewhat right." Mack's eyes were wide open and his head tilted.

"You know what they say about desperate times, Dad? But no matter how bad I look, I ain't giving up yet. Can't do it. Won't do it." Rockfish vehemently shook his head. "There's gotta be a way to take advantage of this goddamn pandemic and squeeze people for cash. Some way to make it work for me and this business I've built. It's not like I suck. Look at my RateYourPI.com and Google reviews, not a one under four stars. I got something here, something I won't let a bump in the space-time continuum fuck up. I just gotta figure out my angle. It's all about angles."

"You play with your protractor till you're blue in the face," Mack said. "But don't you forget that your old man is here to bail you out, like I've always been."

"I know Dad, I appreciate it, but more importantly screw you."

For the first time that morning, the trailer filled with laughs.

****

They enjoyed an hour more of coffee and grease before he could get Mack to a place where the old man felt comfortable enough to leave. The woe is me act works well when you're drinking, but Rockfish was working towards the tail end of this hangover and with a big fat zero on the official PI list of things to do today. There was more than enough around the trailer that could keep his mind occupied and off the runaway train his anxiety had booked him on. Rockfish decided that today's chores would start with venturing out into the restricted quarantine zone known as Catonsville. First up would be Strickland's Home Hardware. Unlike the big box stores, Hank Strickland would extend some store credit Rockfish's way. The collateral was based solely on Strickland's friendship with his father and Mack's stellar history of covering outstanding markers when Strickland called them in.

The trailer door's deadbolt had taken some damage from an unsatisfied customer a tad more than a month ago and needed to be repaired. You'd be surprised at what a Karen could accomplish with a decent sized pry bar and her three bills of weight behind it before succumbing to pepper spray. Rockfish would never hit a woman, but he sure as hell would capsaicin the shit out of one that was trying to break into his home. It wasn't as if Rockfish was the one fucking around on her. He was just the bearer of bad news. And not to mention video.

Rockfish had no urgency to do the repair, as he firmly believed there was nothing in the trailer worth stealing. He knew it, and any potential thieves in the neighborhood probably did too. He wondered if Strickland had one of those fancy smart locks he could use to keep Mack out of the house when he wasn't around. He could never bring himself to ask the old man for his key back, but it would be nice to drag a dancer from

Delilah's home after a hard-fought night and not have his old man on the couch watching goddamn Fox News at 3:00am.

At the hardware store, Rockfish parked Lana at the far end of the parking lot. He aimed her in between two Hertz rent-a-trucks that you could get from the business next door. If a repo man had followed him from the trailer, he was fucked, but if the grim reaper was cruising around on the lookout, odds were that Lana would be safely out of sight until Rockfish got through the checkout line. He grabbed his mask, shut the door, and chirped the key fob.

Rockfish pulled open the front door and hadn't made it past those fake Amish heaters that you see advertised in the Sunday newspaper magazine section, when he encountered his first mask denier.

"Hey bud, that chin diaper only works if it's over the important bits on your face," Rockfish said. "I got an old man at home who covers an awful lot of my bills. I really don't want him to die."

The man in the Lynyrd Skynyrd long sleeve concert t-shirt said nothing in return, nor did he pull up his mask. Rockfish thought about stopping and pressing the point, but he wanted to get in and out of the store as quickly as possible. Going viral on YouTube or TikTok wasn't high on the list of things to accomplish today.

He turned away and headed off towards the area where they made keys, assuming that was where the locks would also be. As he made his way over to aisle seven, he stopped counting the number of customers flouting the state's mask mandate. If you were teleported here from your couch and had no idea where you were, odds are you would assume Strickland's Home Hardware was actually a Home Depot in the middle of any southern state. Pick one. There would be a Walmart on one side and a combination Pizza Hut Taco Bell on the other. But here in Catonsville, the lack of open carry AR-15s outed these Mason Dixon role players for the brainwashed keyboard warriors they most likely were.

"I swear to God, on the Raven's last Super Bowl victory, I know Lord this is probably the fifteenth time, but I gotta move further north," Rockfish swore under his breath. "Sooner rather than later."

Aisle seven was vacant. Not a customer or employee was in sight. Old man Strickland once spouted aloud in a drunken stupor with Mack that he had installed dummy cameras throughout the store for show and that the only ones operational were those by the front door and above the cashiers. So, Rockfish made his money-saving move. He didn't have any coupons, but there was a discount angle he was willing to work. *Just until he got his next check*, he thought. *Then I can settle up with old man Strickland and make things right.*

Rockfish grabbed a basic forty-dollar Yale deadbolt from the shelf and hooked a fingernail beneath the bar code sticker before returning it and walking further down to where the smart locks were stacked. In a matter of a minute, he pressed the Yale bar code over one on the smart lock, and he was the potential recipient of one hundred and forty-nine dollars in savings. Unfortunately, this side hustle had one sticking point. Strickland Home Hardware was small enough that the self-checkout craze never took hold. In this store it was honest to goodness, person-to-person interaction with every purchase. Rockfish would have to make it past the cashier, but he knew exactly which line to get in.

The young cashier manning the express lane had hair that was half a dozen colors and enough metal in her face to set off the cheapest, half-broken metal detector. She snapped her chewing gum loud enough that Rockfish heard it before he saw her. The name tag read London, and her apparent pride in an attentive job well done was clear. Rockfish knew she'd scan his 'purchase' and not think twice.

By the time he tossed the plastic bag on Lana's passenger seat and she roared to life, he really thought things might finally be looking up for him. All he needed now was an easy install so he wouldn't have to call his father for help and not listen to his questions on how he could afford such a fancy lock. If everything went to plan, he could sit outside with a beer afterwards and debate sharing the entry code with his old man.

****

The next morning Rockfish awoke to the cold hard truth that came with problem free lock installation. Unlike the previous day, Mack wasn't in the kitchen rustling up a big breakfast. The only thing waiting on Rockfish this morning was store brand frozen waffles and a cold linoleum floor.

Maybe I should have called and pretended I was having trouble installing the lock, he thought. *He'd have come over this morning and had it installed before I got up. Probably would have brought breakfast too.*

Mack had spoiled him yesterday, and no amounts of butter or syrup this morning would change that.

Rockfish picked up his cell phone from the nightstand charger, half expecting to see a missed call from Mack, but instead there was a notification he wasn't familiar with. A red number one sat firmly upon the rarely opened and less used Facebook Messenger icon.

Angel Davenport: Mr. Rockfish, I've read through your 57 reviews across various social media and web platforms. I'm not sure if you know this but you have three reviews on Yelp, two of which are not very flattering. Either way, I would like to discuss your rates and possibly hiring you to help dig up some information for a project I am currently working on. The job would take you out of state, and with the current state of affairs within our country, I hope that is not a deal breaker. Please respond here with your new cell phone number, as the ad I saw listed one that is no longer operational, and a time that is convenient for me to call.

Potential paying client? Check. A case that would take Lana far from the repo man until said paying client's check cleared? Check. Rockfish fired off his reply and then headed down the short hallway to load the toaster oven and put the coffee on. *Them waffles might not be so bad after all,* he thought.

Ding

Rockfish picked up his phone, but there were no new notifications. He shook his head and put it down.

"Jesus Christ," he said aloud and to no one in particular. The toaster oven was what he had heard. The waffles were done. He sat back down and slathered them with butter and blueberry syrup before reaching over to fill his coffee cup.

Well, sweet little sista's high as hell, cheating on a halo

The opening riff and vocals from Thunder Kiss '65 filled the trailer and Rockfish again reached for his phone as Rob Zombie's voice faded. The song was an adrenaline kick in the pants and had set his mood for client calls since the day he left the refinery for the last time. Granted, he was currently on a losing streak, but with Rob's help, together they'd turn it around. Rockfish pushed his plate to the side and reached for a pad of paper and pencil before picking up the call.

"Good morning, you've reached Steve Rockfish. What can I do you for?"

"Mr. Rockfish, this is Angel Davenport, we communicated earlier via FB Messenger."

"Please, Mr. Davenport, call me Steve."

"And me, Angel then," Davenport said. "Steve, I'll cut to the punch. I'm a producer out in Los Angeles and I'd like to hire you to assist with a research project I'm undertaking, but this whole lockdown situation has put a cramp in my traveling plans. If you don't mind traveling, I'd like to do business. Are your rates still $600 per day plus expenses?"

"Yes, they are, and I'm available. You've done your homework," Rockfish said wondering how Davenport found out about his rates. He didn't advertise them anymore.

"That I have. Your reputation is in high standing amongst those I've reached out to and spoken with. If you don't mind me saying, you could really use a professional-looking website to take advantage of your reputation and promote your business. Having an ad on Facebook Marketplace with the wrong cell number really is only going to get you so far, and most people aren't as tenacious as me."

"Websites cost money, Angel, and can be hacked," Rockfish replied. "Facebook is free, and if someone wants to fuck with my ad, it's basically Zuckerberg's problem. But enough about how I may or may not correctly market my services in your eyes, you mentioned the job is out of state? So which way would I be headed, if we were to come to some sort of over-the-phone-verbal-handshake agreement?"

"Yes, I did. I'm currently quarantining here in Southern California, but the work is in southern New Jersey, right outside Philadelphia. What I need is for you to run down some leads, dig up additional information on a particular event, and do some straightforward interviews with an individual I've identified. Also, check out any other points of interest that your investigation might turn up. Not very exciting PI work, but I need someone who can dig and pull information out of people. Like I said, your reports will help feed a project I'm trying to get off the ground and produce in the near future."

"Seems like a lot of work that could easily be done sitting at a computer or over the telephone," Rockfish said. "Not sure why paying me to drive two hours north to do this makes any business sense, not that I've got any myself." Rockfish smirked to himself. Angel Davenport wanted to call him out on how he advertised, Steve Rockfish would give as well as he got.

"Touché, Mr. Rockfish. But you see, most people familiar with what I am interested in lived through these events and are elderly. We're talking eighty-plus years old. They're not thrilled with some Hollywood-type calling them out of the blue or worse yet, Zoom. While you're not exactly kin to them, I think they'd be more receptive to someone sitting across from them in their living room or assisted living facility and chatting over a hot Ensure or whatever old people drink."

Rockfish cracked a smile at that line. *This guy got jokes,* he thought.

"I need these people relaxed and their memories firing on all cylinders. Additionally, I was able to get some confirmation on what one woman told me from an old online Philadelphia newspaper article, but apparently across the river in Jersey, they are slow to digitize older records and articles. That is why I need someone to be on the ground. And with COVID-19, I'd prefer to stay out here in LA and direct the action."

Rockfish could feel the fish hook just inside his cheek, but he had one more question to ask before he let this guy set it.

"Why not a PI closer to the action," he asked. "Someone local that won't run up the expense account?"

"Steve, what I need is a tenacious investigator and you, sir, fit the bill. I want someone unfamiliar with the players I've identified so far, someone coming into this with a fresh set of eyes. You know, not a local guy whose vision or way of doing things could be tainted by a story a relative or friend told over cocktails or at a cookout."

"Totally, get it," Rockfish said. "Let's start with the story you know, what rumors you want me to confirm or shoot down, and the information gaps you need filled in. Basically, what you're paying me to accomplish on my end."

"Steve, back in the 1940s in a small Southern New Jersey area called Elk Township, there was prolific, ah, what we could call now child trafficking, going on. People then referred to it as some sort of illegal adoption scam, but in this case the young mothers who had given birth were never heard from again."

****

Three days after the initial call with Davenport, Rockfish pocketed an advance on his expenses and guided Lana across the crest of the Delaware Memorial Bridge. The entrance to the New Jersey Turnpike started at the bottom of the bridge, right at the border of the two states, and Rockfish was getting off at Exit 2. From there it would be a short drive to the Marriott Courtyard in Glassboro. There wasn't much in the way of decent hotels in that college town, with the only other available option being a Motel 6.

Rockfish chose the Courtyard mainly because it wasn't his money and he had an expense report he would make sure not to scrimp on. He was spending Hollywood dollars, and while they were not bottomless; it was more money than he normally had to conduct his work. He didn't know how long he'd be in the area but figured on a week as a good starting point for an advance from Davenport, but made sure he could extend the reservation if needed. With a little luck, he'd wrap this puppy up in a nice bow and have some time on the back end to do a little Philadelphia historical sightseeing on the client's dime.

Davenport came across on all their phone calls as a big shot Hollywood producer, and from what Rockfish could deduct from some additional Internet sleuthing of his own, the guy was an up and comer in the niche corner of true crime podcasts. A blue flamer is what the boys called them at the refinery, A fast riser, with eyes on all the big streaming video platforms. While Davenport bided his time until his big break, he clarified that Rockfish's work would result in a must-listen podcast that Netflix, Hulu or CheeseTV would lineup for the privilege to turn into the next big docuseries.

The one positive point Rockfish found through his mini background check was that Davenport came from money. His father was a studio executive at Warner Brothers and played a big part in producing many blockbusters over the past thirty years. For a welcomed change, it didn't appear that collecting final payment would be an issue in this case, and if it did, Rockfish had a feeling this wasn't the first time that daddy would cover his son's markers. That subject was a little something he knew too much about.

After digging up what he could on Davenport, Rockfish looked into the area he was driving towards and the story that Davenport tasked him with flushing out.

Indeed, Elk Township and the surrounding areas had been home to ten or twelve missing pregnant and unwed women in the early to mid-1940s. What reports Rockfish could find differed on the numbers. During this timeframe, most of the township's competent police force had gone off to fight for Uncle Sam, leaving a bunch of local yokels to pick up the day-to-day policing and investigate the stories surrounding the missing girls.

Not to Rockfish's surprise, the police investigation seemed to end as fast as it began. The missing women were all unwed, and either disowned by their families, or runaways that no one cared much about in the first place. With no genuine concern other than gossiping over their wellbeing, the tales of these girls became just that, gossip, and public interest waned. With no one knocking down the temporary police officer's door to solve the case, it was shelved in place of easier crimes that required little to no actual police work. Even after the war, when Elk Township's men returned, it seemed as if the townspeople were more interested in forgetting about what had happened both at home and abroad over those years. Once Ike took office and the Fifties were in full swing, those girls were relegated to campfire scary stories in the likes of the Jersey Devil or never spoken of again.

CHAPTER TWO

Angel Davenport had learned of the story that he felt would save his career during an extended layover in Philadelphia. He was returning from a business trip in London to Southern California. On the trip, he had presented the most recent idea that was going to skyrocket his career beyond the next level.

From the day Davenport signed on as a producer for the All Things True Crime Podcast Network, he was convinced he was destined for bigger things. Streaming video services was where the money, fame and recognition were to be found. Davenport knew all he needed was an idea, perhaps even something established that he could reboot with little effort, in order to get out of the audio studio for good.

That's what I need, he thought. *Something to update a story with a killer hook to pull in the Netflix and Chill crowd. A story where the plot has already been laid out and all I need to do is add a piece of recent information on the tail end, set the hook and reel in those goddamn viewers. Like the blowjob old man from Fyre Festival or the even creepier hand job old man from Abducted in Plain Site.*

All he needed was for a minor scene to go viral, or better yet, a meme that would spread across the Internet and drive people to stream his work. His father, an executive at Warner Brothers, had other plans for his son's late blooming career. He had turned off the money faucet for any more of his son's harebrained ideas and insisted he work his way up the Hollywood ladder through experience and hard work. Davenport was in his mid-30s and his dad didn't let him forget it.

I don't have time to learn grunt work, he lectured his father the last time they spoke. *I have ideas. Ideas that will line my wall with awards and when the press speaks of me, it will be with a small mention of you as my dad and not the other way around any longer.*

This transatlantic idea involved the true story of a summer night in Northern Ireland where members of a popular cabaret band were ambushed and killed. An event unheard of in the States, but well known across the United Kingdom. Davenport's pitch revolved around updating a forty-five-minute grainy YouTube documentary into a full-fledged eight-episode docuseries.

The Miami Showband Massacre occurred on July 31, 1975, when on their way home to Dublin after playing a show in Banbridge the band's tour van had been stopped at a roadside checkpoint in Northern Ireland. Soon after the van was pulled over, the Ulster Volunteer Force, a loyalist paramilitary group, opened fire, killing three members. Local officials and the British Government covered up the events of that night for decades. The short documentary had been filmed in the early 1990s, and Davenport immediately knew he could update the story with his own flair and turn it into Netflix docuseries gold. Or even a full-length motion picture like the recent Freddie Mercury bio pic.

Davenport showed up for his meetings in England with attitude, an over-the-top précis and ended up entirely unprepared for the network executives' reactions to the subject. He was unaware of the long-harbored grudges that each country still held over the ensuing decades-long cover up by the British government. A fact that simple research prior to the trip would have flushed out, but in his production-oriented mind, he was way past that stage. The viral meme factory pump needed priming.

With Davenport's inability to read the room, the pitch meeting quickly dissolved in a barrage of "we'll get back to you" conversations as the investors and executives fled the conference room. He was left alone to pack up his handouts and carry the box back to his hotel room, where he immediately began to wallow in self-pity. Room service gin and tonics were the only item on the menu until his flight left in the morning.

Chalk it up to a learning experience, he thought, and crushed his first drink. *Can't half-ass it next time, I'm going to have to roll up my sleeves and not depend on the family name to open a door or green light a project.*

For the first time, Davenport admitted to himself there was hard work needed to be done in order to achieve the success he expected. It wouldn't be easy, something he would never admit to the old man. But in the back of his mind, that little voice was already looking for some wiggle room.

Maybe if I contract out the leg work next time, he thought and drained the next glass. *Not all of it, but a good portion since manual work just ain't my thing. I'm a director. I give orders. Find someone who can take orders and then disappear into the background and not care if I take most of the credit.* His head nodded and his throat swallowed after each line in some sort of drunken, self-reinforcement. His mental gymnastics continued well into the night until he passed out, and the front desk's wake-up call did just that.

****

Davenport flew out of Heathrow while Miami Showband songs played rent-free through his head. Ironically, listening to their music had encompassed all the research he did after watching the YouTube clip. He tried to counter the ongoing concert with the hair of the dog, but the music played on and his mind continued to dwell on negatives; returning to Los Angeles and what he deemed an unfulfilling career as an audio podcast producer. The vicious cycle continued long after landing in Philadelphia and discovering an unexpected layover before the six-hour flight home.

Exactly how drunk would I have to be for security to not let me board the next plane, he thought? *What would happen then? A night in the 52nd Precinct's drunk tank might do me some good. But like the President said, bad things happen in Philadelphia, but it would be ten times better than having to listen to dad's "I told you so."*

For the next hour, Davenport pondered that question and debated whether to get up from his seat at the gate and walk down to the closest concourse bar. Those thoughts quickly ended the second an elderly woman in a wheelchair crashed into the side of his seat at Gate B23's waiting area.

The old woman mumbled something that sounded like an apology, but her head was down and her voice clearly ashamed. Davenport shook his head. The right side of his brain wondered if the woman was a figment of his alcohol-fueled imagination and the left side wanted to reach out, push, and let her slowly roll away. He giggled to himself before hearing a group of people laughing. He glanced over and noticed four people. They stood on the concourse looking at him. One pointed directly at Davenport and then they turned, and speed-walked towards the bar.

"I'm guessing you're with them," Davenport asked after turning back around. He reached out and touched the sleeve of the woman's coat to make sure she was real. "And if so, are they planning on coming back for you?"

"I'm so sorry," the old woman said. "We just landed from Atlanta. With a little time to kill, they all decided they need one or two more for the road. A car service is coming shortly to drop me off in Jersey, and they're continuing on to Atlantic City."

"No problem," Davenport said as he extended his hand. "My name is Angel."

"Nice to meet you, Angel, I'm Gertrude. Gertrude Roberts, but you can call me Gertie."

Their conversation covered all the airport chat bases: hometowns, travels to and from. *"What do you do for a living, oh wait your husband's dead, my sympathies."* When a relaxed Davenport spoke his drunken mind of what he really wanted to do in life, Gertie nodded her head, leaned in, and asked a question.

"Are you open to suggestions, because I have a story you might be interested in, or not. I won't be offended."

Davenport nodded and wondered what kind of Stolen Pies and Other Tales of Sin from the Church Bake Sale he was in for. Half-heartedly, he again looked over his shoulder hoping to be saved by her family and maybe, just maybe, they'd take pity on him for the last-minute babysitting assignment and bring a drink.

"During the summer of '43, I turned thirteen and had my first kiss with a boy in a hallway coat closet during my birthday party..."

Davenport visibly winced and quickly regretted his decision to listen to Gertie's story.

"...My life went from a schoolgirl-high to the lowest of lows when three days later my parents kicked my pregnant, older sister out of the house and I've not seen her since."

Okay, he thought, *maybe this had some legs and would at least be worth a listen. Or am I going to be longing for the great pie caper in a minute?*

"Kathleen was four years my senior and was with child, because of a romp with a boy shipping off to war. My parents considered her an embarrassment to the family, but mostly to them. Once she walked out that door, they never spoke of 'it' again, but I never stopped loving or missing her." Gertie covered her mouth with her hand and shook her head. She continued after a few seconds. "The problem was while my parents never spoke of Kathleen again, my friends and most of the nosey old biddies in town tended to point and talk when we were seen outside the house. They always seemed to know more about what happened to her than I did."

Davenport noticed her voice cracked with the end of that last sentence. His heartstrings pulled for what the old woman felt as she spilled each word. It didn't matter what he thought of her tale so far; it remained extremely personal and painful to Gertie all these years later. He pulled a Virgin Atlantic cocktail napkin from his shirt front pocket and placed it in her hands.

"Here you go," he said, and Gertie softly dabbed her eyes with it.

"Thank you. What I could put together through the years, mostly by gossip, was that my sister ended up at this woman's farm on the black side of the county. The poor lived there, and our father had always warned us never to wander over there. If we were playing with friends, that section of town was to be given a wide berth. Looking back, our parents were extremely racist and I'm sure it wasn't as bad as they made it out to be."

Davenport noticed Gertie clenched the cocktail napkin tightly in her fist. Veins were visible on the backs of her hands and seemed to pulse with each word.

"The lady's name was Mary. She was supposedly a midwife that catered to those white girls that showed up on her doorstep with nowhere else to turn. Mary's business was booming with all the young men running off to war and dipping their wicks in anything they could before being shipped out."

"You think I could make a worthwhile show out of tracking down your sister's kid or her family for you?" Davenport said, but was getting the feeling Gertie needed the services of a private detective and not a failed media content producer.

"No sir, I would never ask such a favor of a stranger," Gertie said, shaking her head vehemently. "The point is that these girls all went to this farm, and here's where the mystery begins. Or ends, nobody was ever really sure. They and their babies were never seen or heard from again. People I spoke to always suggested that—"

Gertie stopped abruptly as her head whipped forward, and the wheelchair moved in reverse.

Thanks buddy, Davenport heard someone shout from behind.

He twisted around in his seat and could only watch as Gertie's drunk family pushed her down the concourse at what he determined to be a tad under light speed. He stood and considered giving chase, but it wasn't long before they were on a moving walkway and Davenport lost sight of them before he could decide.

****

Davenport thought about this strange and unexpected interaction during the flight home, but upon arrival at LAX, he was instantly up to his elbows in uninteresting podcast work and that took the pole position in his brain and to-do list. London wasn't the only thing quickly forgotten about and Gertie's mystery was regulated to a back burner, left simmering until he could give her story some attention. After all, this was the newly focused Angel Davenport, or at least he tried to convince himself of it.

One such mental argument went along the lines that if he burned the candle at both ends, he could prevent his brain from dwelling on London's epic fail. He wasn't more than two days into his new attitude when he regretted his decision and the old unfocused Angel Davenport began to infiltrate his way back into the work day.

I'm the brains, not the brawn, he would recount to any coworker that happened to walk by and into ear shot. *I'm the guy that puts the vision out there and those others are the ones that need to make it a reality. But don't get me wrong, I'm not against stepping in as a guest director in an occasional episode to show how shit needs to be done. I lead from the front like that.*

Gertie's move to the front burner finally came in the spring. The country was flailing in its attempt to battle the novel Coronavirus, and the Federal Government was content to microwave popcorn, sit back, and watch. California Governor Newsom boldly put the Los Angeles area on quarantine lockdown and unintentionally gave Davenport more free time than he'd had in years. Stuck at home, away from the studio, video games filled his days, but at night it was the muse of alcohol that nudged him closer and closer to look further into Gertie's story. Johnnie Walker Blue provided the final push and one night, long past dinner, Davenport fired his laptop.

This could be it, goddamn it, I'm due for a freaking break, he thought and pounded those initial keystrokes with force.

But his positive attitude was short-lived as the initial Google searches resulted only in him slamming the laptop closed, cursing local governments and pouring himself another hefty drink. The brick wall was most 1940s era records and news reports from southern New Jersey were not accessible online. Once the self-serving tantrums ended, he fell down a bureaucratic rabbit hole regarding local government's fiscal policy. He learned that every couple of years counties, townships and municipalities across southern New Jersey allocated funds for the digitization of paper records and microfiche conversion, but politicians nearing re-election would always divert those earmarked funds for hot-button issues to appease voters.

Davenport was less than halfway through the bottle and about to give up when he widened his fishing net and came across a link to a news article out of Philadelphia, dated June 1945. It detailed a woman who escaped from jail, fleeing a capital murder charge. Once he got to the end of the article, his mind was made up. Nothing could sway him that this didn't confirm Gertie's story and then some.

"Hot fucking damn!" he shouted over and over as he raced around the small apartment. The voice that had previously told him he was too good for grunt work, had returned to the forefront and at full volume. "There's something here. I never doubted it. I can smell a future Emmy Award-winning idea when I see one," he said aloud. He topped off his drink, pressed Control-P and stood at the printer waiting, hand on hip. When the second page printed, he grabbed the article and plopped down on the couch and re-read it half a dozen times.

In June 1945, Elk Township Police arrested a woman named Mary D'arnaud for swindling a man on the sale of a cow. While in jail, an anonymous tip claimed other nefarious crimes had taken place at her farm, and the county magistrate ordered a search of the property. Upon arrival, police found the farmhouse and several outbuildings in flames. A barn was untouched by the fire and behind its doors sat the patrol car of missing police officer Edward McGee. On the front seat, officers found McGee's badge, service weapon and baton. D'arnaud's charges were promptly upgraded to capital murder. Not long after, the jailer responsible for the evening headcount found D'arnaud's cell empty with no outward signs of an escape nor that she had any overt help in the escape.

Davenport's whiskey-fueled mind planted a flag in the ground and declared that Mary D'arnaud was the same woman Gertie had mentioned. *The anonymous tips had to be about the illegal baby adoption racket,* he thought. *Or the missing girls.* He was sure of it and pumped his one empty fist in celebration in his leap to judgement. He would die on this hill, but realistically in his mind he was already building the stage to accept his Documentary Producer of the Year award.

The only thing left to do was get boots on the ground digging up all the facts and information he would need, but with COVID-19 flaring up across the nation, he knew damn well those boots wouldn't belong to him.

CHAPTER THREE

In one thousand feet, follow the traffic circle and bear right onto Rowan Boulevard and then immediately turn left onto Redmond Avenue. Your destination is on the left.

Rockfish parked Lana away from the other cars in the lot and checked into the Marriott Courtyard. After unpacking, he pulled open the curtains and looked outside for a decent place within walking distance to grab a bite to eat. He spotted a sports bar, Chickie's & Pete's, catty-cornered to the hotel across Rowan Boulevard.

Looks like a decent place to run through tomorrow's plans over wings and a beer, or four, he thought. Being back on the clock, Rockfish planned to curb his daily adult beverage intake, but dealing with COVID-19 in an unfamiliar town caused him to fall back into his own personal safe-space and renege ever so slightly on that self-promise.

Four turned in to one too many and Rockfish ended up watching a couple of baseball games on the big screens instead of shoring up the following day's to-do-list. When he finally addressed this error, the page was a little harder to focus on and the pen did not work like he wanted.

Yeah, he thought, *I'm gonna have to chalk this one up to being a little rusty on the whole work-planning thing. Plenty of time in the morning to figure out the day's agenda. Lemme just set an alarm for a little earlier than normal when I get back to the room.* He thanked his lucky stars he picked a place close by and would only have to navigate a crosswalk in order to make it safely back to the room. *Next time, more wings, fewer Blue Moons.*

The following morning, the sun's rays filled the hotel room and Rockfish knew immediately that he shouldn't open his eyes. The sudden pounding in his head would only increase. Experience was talking, so he remained on the bed.

"Goddamn it," Rockfish said. If he had a dollar for every time he forgot to close the blinds during a drunken episode, he sure as hell wouldn't be stuck in New Jersey during a global pandemic. For the eighty-seventh time, he promised himself he would leave a note for drunk Rockfish to close the damn curtains before falling into bed.

Not one of my finer moments, he thought, and ran his fingers through his bedhead. *But, hey, I'm in one piece, hopefully no one's pissed off at me and I'm still employed.* He checked his phone to make sure he didn't drunk-dial Davenport, and promised again to cut back while working. The phone told him the only call he made was to his dad. *Whew, not like this is the first time I've probably sounded like an ass to him. Probably not the last either, but Dad knows that.*

Rockfish eventually made his way to the bathroom and drank straight from the faucet before filling a glass to take back to bed. A review of the day's plans would have to be virtual as he was in no mood to walk over and grab his notebook.

He expected to accomplish two things before heading back to Chickie & Petes for dinner. That was unless either of these points ended up leading him in a different, urgent direction. Then he might have to settle for room service.

The first stop was Davenport's airport buddy, Gertrude Roberts. She was ninety-one and confined to the Pitman Manor assisted living facility. Rockfish wasn't thrilled starting the day diving straight into an industry the media was describing as a hotspot for explosive COVID-19 outbreaks. He said a silent prayer for the extra mask he snagged from the hotel's front desk when he checked in.

If he left Pitman Manor unscathed, next would be the exciting world of research in the microfiche room of the Elk Township library. According to what Davenport told him, that would be where he could find the treasure trove of information that the Internet had failed to uncover for him back in Los Angeles.

For starters, he needed to build a profile of this Mary D'arnaud, an outline of her time in Elk Township and any corresponding events he could uncover. The same went for any information on Kathleen. Kathleen Roberts? Davenport couldn't even answer that one. Rockfish would have to ask Gertrude if Roberts was her maiden or married name. The detail was an important one, that could save him from going off on the wrong path and spending more time than necessary in the library.

He needed to start turning over some rocks. As soon as the pain dissipated to a point where he could open his eyes and get into the shower, that is.

****

Pitman Manor ended up being only a ten-minute drive from the Marriott. Rockfish pulled into the parking lot without calling ahead. He wasn't a relative of Gertie's, but this wasn't his first rodeo. He had turned an absurd ability to talk his way into any place, no matter the circumstance, into somewhat of a career.

A few years into a career that still didn't pay enough, and Rockfish was as cheap when it came to spending what little money he had. But he wasn't above padding the occasional expense report so that he could afford the benefits and toys that made the job easier and ultimately benefited the client. Maybe not the client that paid a little extra for the padded expenses, but the next one and the ones after that. Rockfish had invested in a high-quality printer, some software and costly card stock. Lana's backseat now doubled as a print shop. Once the laptop and printer were plugged into the car's auxiliary power outlet, Rockfish could have a business card for any occupation and occasion.

He blew on the new card and, with a few shakes of the wrist, it was dry and ready for action. Rockfish grabbed his mask, a professional-looking pleather portfolio, and walked across the parking lot and towards the assisted living facility's main entrance.

"Hi, good morning," Rockfish said to the woman behind the glass at the front desk. She was practically wearing a Tyvek suit, at least from the waist up, and her greeting sounded as if it came over a walkie-talkie, circa 1970s.

Ah Christ, this mask ain't gonna do shit for me today, he thought and swallowed long and hard before continuing with his opening spiel.

"I'm Tom Ridgewell, People's National Insurance Company, and I'm here to see a Mrs. Gertrude Roberts. I have some papers her son asked for me to run over here for her to sign." Rockfish handed the woman a business card.

"I'm sorry, Mr. Ridgewell, I don't see any visitor appointments for Mrs. Roberts on the calendar today. Do you know if her son called us in advance? Our policy with COVID-19 is that we receive, a minimum forty-eight hours' notice for any visit, excluding medical. There are no exceptions." She pointed at the sign to Rockfish's right and crossed her arms for emphasis. "We are essentially on lockdown because of our tenants being highly susceptible to this virus. Now please lean forward. I need to take your temperature, since you couldn't be bothered to read the sign on the door before bringing who knows what into our facility."

Rockfish wasn't surprised by her tone or the rules they had in place, but he wasn't close to turning around and walking back outside. He leaned forward and aimed his forehead for the small rectangle opening in the plexiglass.

"97.9," the receptionist said aloud to nobody in particular and marked it down in some ledger. "Have you experienced any of these symptoms in the last forty-eight hours..."

Rockfish firmly answered no to all, not really listening to what she was asking, but it was more about putting on airs that he belonged there and had vital business to attend to. After she finished with the list of questions, Rockfish adjusted his mask as a sign that he was ready as far as he was concerned. The receptionist's eyes never looked up and his entire little show was for naught.

Holy crap, how friggin thick am I going to have to lay this on, he thought. *Or can I just throw some money at the problem to get around this forty-eight-hour bullshit?*

In past situations such as this, there were always two things that gave Rockfish an advantage over the average minimum wage employee. He could act as calm and persuasive as if he really was Tom Ridgewell and needed her to believe as strongly as he did that he belonged there. If that didn't work, he moved to phase two, which was that the average low paid clerical employee hated confrontation or be overwhelmed. Matter of fact, they would work harder and longer just to avoid any situation that could cause someone to 'call corporate' or leave a scathing review on the Internet. One resulting in 'corporate' calling the employee out on the carpet. Truth be told, Rockfish could 'Karen' with the best of them. That was the route he chose to break this logjam.

"You mean Lawrence, from our Familial Remuneration Bureau didn't set this up? I do apologize ma'am, you see Pam, she's the administrative assistant to Mr. Maxwell, and she's been going through a pretty tough time of her own." Rockfish leaned in towards the plexiglass hole before lowering his voice. "She lost her husband last year and her twin boys, well they just done gone wild on her these past six months. You know, that marijuana, the Internet porn and one of them was volunteering for the Bernie Sanders campaign. Poor thing, she's at her wit's end."

Rockfish paused for a second. The receptionist looked somewhat concerned, somewhat interested, but not annoyed, so he continued on and ratcheted it up a notch.

"I apologize again for the mix-up, but Mrs. Roberts' brother-in-law recently passed, and she was his lone heir. We are really under the deadline with the end of the quarter rapidly approaching to close as many of our pending files as possible. Sometimes those pending ones are never closed, and the monies end up with the damn Government." Rockfish picked up the sign-in pen and signed his name in the visitor's ledger. He gave his hands a squirt of sanitizer and continued. "To be honest with you, Mrs. Roberts is due for a rather large distribution, and I bet you and me don't want to see the damn liberals in charge of this here state get their hands on Mrs. Roberts' money. Now ethics and our company's procedures prevent me from saying exactly how much, but the sum is large enough that I would be willing to bet once it's in her bank account she'd upgrade her conditions here, if you know what I mean. This isn't a guess, I do this for a living, and I'll make plenty sure I drop that hint to her." He winked for added emphasis, but still couldn't get a read on this lady. "Now you don't want to take that income out Pitman Manor's pocket before it even gets there, do ya now? That money would trickle down to you and the people who do the actual work."

He paused again to see if she was going to even try to unscramble all that. At the same time, he didn't want to take a chance and slid a folded hundred-dollar bill beneath the protective glass. Rockfish would either be marching right back out the door he came in or talking to Gertrude in a matter of minutes. But the only thing he was sure of was that he'd be out a hundred either way.

"That's a lot of information, Mr. Ridgewell," she said while looking back and forth from the business card to his face and then back down. "I wouldn't want to delay Ms. Roberts ability to upgrade to one of our Flowering Dogwood level suites. She should have the best, if that's what she really wants. I'll tell you what, looking at her schedule, she should be back from the Granny Aerobics class by now. If you promise to keep it quick and quiet, I can wheel her out to our atrium to meet with you..."

She paused to point out the sign and directional arrow for the atrium, but what Rockfish noticed was that the hundred was now conspicuously absent from where he slid it.

"...as long as you can maintain your social distancing and be able to conduct your business without putting her or any of our other residents in harm's way. You understand these directions are the complete opposite of your actions when you came through the door without reading the large, posted signs. The ones in red ink, surely you couldn't just ignore them, but you did." She stopped and paused for what he took as her attempt at dramatic effect. "Let me just zip around the corner here and get an orderly to go find Ms. Roberts for you."

The receptionist disappeared and Rockfish headed off in the atrium's direction. He silently wondered how long he'd have to sit there watching everyone and their half-dead mother walk by before admitting he was played. He couldn't help but shake the feeling that with her parting shot, the receptionist was now sitting in the breakroom bragging to the other mopes how she took this clown out front for a crisp hundred. The worst part would be having to walk back past her again to get to his car.

After ten minutes of those thoughts, an orderly pushed a wheelchair to the spot across from him and locked its wheels atop the blue square on the floor. Rockfish bet it was the mandatory six feet marker and gave her the old once over. Gertrude was appropriately masked up and dressed as if they were headed for a night out on the town. It differed from the bathrobes most of the other inmates wore. He said nothing until the orderly left, but by then, Gertrude Roberts had beaten him to the punch.

"It's nice to meet you, Mr. Ridgewell, I don't have a brother, but you already know that."

Rockfish noticed Gertrude now held his fake business card in her presumably Parkinson's hands.

"But what I do have is a monumental loathing for sitting in my room and staring out the window or at Drew Carey all day. So, while I'm going to assume you are not here to talk about some imaginary inheritance, I am going to enjoy this conversation and drag it out as long as humanly possible," Gertrude said with a slow wink and Rockfish caught the meaning.

"You would be correct on all points, Mrs. Roberts," Rockfish said with a wink of his own.

"Call me Gertie."

"And me, Steve," Rockfish replied. "Steve Rockfish is my legal name. Do you remember meeting a man by the name of Angel Davenport in the Philadelphia airport roughly a little more than a year ago?"

"That fancy man from Hollywood? Of course, I do. He was the best part of the trip home. When you're my age, you can't always get away from your family, but he gave me a well-deserved break."

"The same. It seems his interest in the story you told him that day has grown exponentially. He's stuck in California, with this awful virus situation, and he's reached out to me to stop by and to see if you would be interested in talking more about it."

"To you?"

"Yes, through me to him, I guess you could say."

"Well, if you recall our conversation two minutes ago, you're not a window or Drew Carey. Steve, you had your answer at hello." Gertie laughed but it came out more like a smoker's cough and Rockfish hoped her mask wasn't a cheap one made by child labor in some faraway country.

If I can get the fuck out of dodge without the 'rona all over me, he thought, *this might be a damn worthwhile chat.*

****

"I remember the day like it was yesterday, July 13, 1942. Kathleen wasn't even showing when she left. We all knew she had ended up at the McCutchin's, but never talked about around our table. Word passed from parents to daughters then to me was that she wore out her welcome at the McCutchin's, too, she was a handful," Gertie said and clasped her hands together. "But I loved her. By the time the contractions started, Mrs. McCutchin had well enough too, and word had it Kathleen was shipped off to the colored side of town. You don't mind me saying that, do you, Steve? It was a different time and well, some habits are just damn hard to break." Gertie raised her eyebrows and Rockfish thought she wanted him to concur.

"Anyway, there was this woman who would handle the births of the unwed, runaways or those looking for help, off the books, if you get my drift."

Rockfish held up a hand and stopped her there. He wanted to congratulate her on being the oldest living MAGA member, but instead pulled out a copy of the Philadelphia Record news article Davenport found.

"Can you take a look at this and tell me if you think it's the same woman," Rockfish asked. He stood up and handed the paper to Gertie. She held the paper roughly an inch away from her glasses before dropping it onto her lap. "And you can keep that copy, I've got another in the car."

Gertie nodded. She pulled a tissue from her sleeve, reached up under her mask and blew her nose. It took her a minute to readjust the oxygen tube before continuing.

"Yes, that is her, Mary D'arnaud. I once overheard my mother crying that Mary killed Kathleen and stole her baby. My father told her not to believe a word of it. He claimed it was all rumor and hearsay, but I could tell that my mother believed it. Father chalked it up as a way to scare kids from going to that side of town and keep teenage girls from being curious with all the local boys going off to war. Looking for something they weren't getting at home, if you know what I mean. People weren't very tolerant of the races mixing back then. Not sure it's gotten any better, but the papers say it has."

Rockfish could see the tears welling up in the corners of her eyes. *She can't dab those eyes with that dirty snot rag,* he thought. He spotted a tissue box on a table to his right. He walked over and brought it back to where they sat and placed it on the small table next to her. "We can take a break anytime, if you need to."

"Thank you, very much. I'll be okay," she said and readjusted her oxygen again. "Everything came to a head when that policeman went missing. They never found a body, you know. The same voices that claimed Mary was the devil incarnate soon started whispering that she killed him too. Of course, the police wouldn't say anything and then 'poof,' Mary's gone from jail. Pulled a Harry Houdini right in front of the guards. My father believed a mob came to the police station and pulled her from the cell. A mob..."

Gertie stopped and looked around in all directions. She lifted her mask and mouthed the word 'mob' and for emphasis, took her index finger and pushed the tip of her nose to the side.

"Gotcha," Rockfish said and mimicked the gesture. A mob equaled THE mob.

That makes a hell of a lot more sense, he thought. *If a mob of townsfolk stormed the jail, you bet your ass that would have made the news. But if THE mob greased palms and made a person disappear before she could start talking and naming names, well, that's straight out of the La Cosa Nostra playbook.* Rockfish bet that Mary was likely wearing a pair of seventy-five-year-old cement shoes wherever she was. He nodded and held up a finger. He needed a second to catch up on his notes. "Okay, I'm good now," he said.

"Mary was never seen 'round here again. And then the Catholic Archdiocese of Camden donated enough cash for Underwood Memorial Hospital to build its own maternity wing for the underprivileged. That's fact, you can look it up. I dwelled on these coincidences as I grew older.

The timing was damn suspicious. A mob..." Gertie stopped and raised a finger to her covered nose again. "...and the Church in cahoots? My mother threatened to slap me if I brought it up. But my father, when he was older and less in control of what came out of his mouth, would say they were the same. Two sides of the same coin. And I know you'll find this hard to believe, but no one else was charged or even arrested in the case of that poor policeman." Gertie reached for another tissue and dabbed her eyes. "Gimme a second, will you, Steve?"

"Of course, Gertie, you take as much time as you need. Do you need me to get you anything, water, an orderly to get you something from your room?" Rockfish's professional response was the polar opposite of his emotional one. *Goddamn,* he thought. *Davenport actually knew what the fuck he was talking about, and this woman's gonna play a large part in it.* There was a powerful part of him that wanted to step over, wrap his arms and console her, COVID-19 be damned.

Three minutes passed before Gertie continued. "I'm not sure how long Mr. Davenport is having you run around town, but the policeman's family has stuck around these parts. Matter of fact, his great granddaughter is here from time to time. I'm not sure what name she goes by, if she ever married, but I remember her coming here one day and fixing the computers in the Internet room. Ethel, God rest her soul, was the one who pointed her out. Said the poor girl was running a computer repair shop out of her parents' garage in Westville. You can probably narrow that down a little, but our Internets are down right now. Or so they keep telling us..."

Just when you think it couldn't get any better, wham, she points you towards the next person you need to talk with, Rockfish thought. He wanted to do a little victory dance, but that would be the quickest way to get thrown out on his ass. Speaking of which, the internal clock in his head told him it was close to closing time. *Better get going before she tuckers out or more likely, someone higher on the authority food chain than the receptionist stops by and starts asking questions.* No scam was endless.

"Hey Gertie, I wanted to say thanks again for sticking around and talking this morning. I greatly appreciated every minute, but I need to head out to my next appointment."

She raised a shaky hand and pretended to crack a whip. "Mr. Davenport got you on a short leash?"

"Something like that," Rockfish said. *She's got jokes,* he thought, and stood up. The hell with social distancing and he stepped forward and stuck out his right elbow. The old woman wasn't sure what do to at first but tried to imitate the move. Rockfish bent down to get their elbows to touch and by this time he wasn't sure the coordination was worth the effort.

"Well, Steve, it was my pleasure," she said. "I hope I was of some help and please stop by anytime. I will be sure to let my caretaker know that Mr. Ridgewell needs to be added to the guest ledger. I'm sure there are many more papers my son needs signed regarding my brother-in-law's estate." Gertie awkwardly winked at Rockfish.

"The pleasure was all mine and if you remember anything else, no matter how small, here's my real contact information." Rockfish pulled one of his actual business cards from his wallet and she tucked it into the little bag attached to the wheelchair. "Do you need me to get anyone for you, I don't want to leave you trapped here."

"No, you go on to your appointment. I'm going to sit here with the sun on my face until someone wanders by and pushes me back to the darkness of my room."

They said their goodbyes again, and Rockfish walked out toward the reception area and front doors. He stopped at the front desk and waited for the receptionist to make eye contact before tugging down his mask.

"Better get your cleaning crew ready. Based on our conversation, I'm betting she's going to want the penthouse suite." He winked and grinned as he pulled up his mask.

Two minutes later, Lana roared to life and Rockfish made a mental note to update Davenport later, perhaps after meeting with McGee's relative. One of his rules was, once hired, Rockfish appreciated minimal contact with the client. Less opportunity for them to become involved and offer 'suggestions.'

They don't call it a final report for nothing, he thought. He didn't need to be micromanaged; he could perfectly do that himself.

In the back of his mind, he contemplated if Davenport's initial thought of a serial killer might be a little on the cautious side. Unless

Rockfish was reading too far into it, this was a case of missing and presumed dead girls, 1940s child trafficking, a dirty thin blue line, local mafia goons and perhaps the Catholic Church doing God knows what to these kids after they were born.

"Yes!" he exclaimed over the roar of the engine. "Gonna be a whole lot more involved with this job than a handful of interviews and a library microfiche review. Finally, the 'rona doing me a solid!" He punched the passenger seat with exhilaration and didn't care if anyone could see through the tint. This opportunity had the chance to be one hell of a ride, and if Rockfish could put any actual evidence behind Gertie's ramblings, Davenport's planned show would blow any incarnation of 'Making a Murderer' out of the water.

CHAPTER FOUR

Rockfish sat at the small desk in his hotel room and sipped coffee. His laptop had pinpointed the address for McGee Computer Repair and Refurbished Sales on only his third try. He was getting better at this Google stuff. The business in question, coincidentally, also had a Facebook Marketplace page. Its visuals were better and provided more pertinent information than his, but Rockfish was always a firm believer in coincidence. According to the ad, the 'open' sign on the door had been flipped a few hours ago and it wouldn't close until 5pm. Rockfish gathered his things and walked down to his car. He put the address into his GPS and looked at the display for a place close by to eat beforehand.

He burped the last of the fish tacos a few minutes past 2pm and drove past the shop to give himself a lay of the land. Thirty Avon Avenue was a Cape Cod, and the business was run out of the attached garage. A Scion xB sat in the driveway and a young woman, probably late twenties he guessed, unloaded boxes from it. He street parked, popped a couple of breath mints to cover the smell of halibut and walked back down the sidewalk. What stood out to him was the knit hat and Ruth Bader Ginsburg t-shirt.

Looks like I might finally meet one of these hipsters I've heard so much about, he thought.

"Hi, Ms. McGee?"

"That, depends who's asking," she said. "If you don't mind grabbing that last box for me, I might answer that question."

Rockfish reached into the back of the Scion and grabbed an old dusty bankers' box and placed it on the ground next to the others. A cloud of dust shot back up towards his face as the box settled and Rockfish stood up too quickly. He wasn't sure what was worse, the light-headedness that he blamed on the three-whiskey lunch, or the sneezing fit he ultimately couldn't fight off. His mask had slipped under his nose at some point.

By this time, the woman had propped open the door with the one box she carried. She looked back at Rockfish as the sneezing fit continued.

"You okay, Mister?" She said.

"Oh, just fine, how old were those mold spores I inhaled? I'm beginning to doubt the return on investment with this cheap mask."

"Close to seventy-five years and I got a better one you can have, inside."

"Hopefully, the antibiotic to fight off whatever is swimming around in my lungs has already been discovered. And thank you for the offer."

"I couldn't tell you. I'm also not sure what you're selling, Mister," she said. "But if you'll grab those last two boxes and bring them inside, I'll at least listen to your sales pitch. No promises." She shrugged her shoulders and tilted her head towards the door.

Rockfish nodded in her direction and gently piled the boxes atop one another. He stood back up slowly and followed her inside.

"Put them on the floor behind my desk," she said and pointed to an old faded green metal desk against the far wall. To Rockfish it looked more like something a 1953 Soviet bureaucrat would sit behind and not a young, hipster business woman. Rockfish put them down gently and then walked back to the other side of the desk. The 'business' took up most of the two-car garage. Various standing desks and tables were spread throughout the space, with computers and laptops stacked atop each one. Some looked as if they were in mid-dissection and others looked brand new. The woman cleared her throat and Rockfish took the cue to start his 'sales pitch'.

"Ms. McGee, my name is Steve Rockfish. I'm a private investigator from Baltimore and my client hired me to dig up what information I can, regarding events that occurred here in South Jersey during World War II."

"So, you're not a salesman," she said. "The alcohol coming off your breath or out of your pores would say otherwise. I'll agree with you on the cheap mask," she said as walked around the desk, opened a drawer and tossed him a new one. "My name's Jawnie, Ms. McGee was my mom, and I'm not one to believe in coincidences, but is what happened to my great grandfather one of those events? Because if it is, this is some seriously fucked-up timing." Her sentence ended hands firmly on hips. Rockfish realized he hadn't yet won her confidence.

"Oh, I for one, very much do believe in them and for your second question, I can give you a maybe? I think he's on the peripheral of what I'm looking into. I mean his name has come up a few times in my initial research and discussions with others. That is why I wanted to talk to you."

"Like I said, Mr. Rockfish, you sure have some timing," Jawnie said. "You see, these boxes you helped me carry in hold the contents of my great grandfather Edward's old police desk. After he was officially pronounced dead, the Chief of Police asked his wife if she wanted to come down to the station and collect his personal effects. She declined and offered to do it after some grieving time."

"Totally understandable," Rockfish said. He noticed the furrows in her brow had relaxed. They were all he could see above her mask. *I might be establishing some credibility here,* he thought.

"She wanted to get her head straight, so she wasn't seen collapsing at his desk while she packed it up. Of course, if those idiots had manners and half a clue, they would have done it for her and dropped everything off at the house. But like I said, the PD at that time consisted of dolts and those that had any brains were dirty as those mold spores you breathed in."

"I'm sorry to hear that," Rockfish said. "Some cop just packed up his desk and they've stored the boxes ever since?"

"Something like that. Maybe it was the cleaning woman, who the fuck knows. From what the new Chief told me, they've gathered dust in the back of the evidence room this entire time. I've tried to get custody since my mother first mentioned them. Everyone else in the family wrote them off."

Jawnie stopped and took a breath and sat down. She obviously had a story to tell, and he for one would not interrupt or try to prompt her to continue. He was thrilled he hadn't stepped in his normal pile of dog shit after the success with Gertie yesterday. Rockfish pulled up a black folding chair from against one of the computer workbenches and handed Jawnie one of his cards.

"Yeah, that chair will do. I have a couple of minutes I can give you right now, because I kind of fancy myself as a part-time investigator. The Edward McGee case always hit a nerve with me ever since I was a young kid and that nerve twitched more and more the older I got and the more I understood. Since opening the shop here, it's been a hobby of mine for the past two years. I've never gotten far, but once I learned about the boxes down at the station, I started reaching out trying to see if I could claim his stuff. I never got nowhere until today."

"Well, from one private investigator to another, glad to meet you," Rockfish said. "I don't want to take up too much of your time, dropping in out of the blue like this. Perhaps if you are free later, we could meet up. But based on what you've said, I have one question. What changed after a couple of years that you could acquire them today?"

"Election year," Jawnie said. "Scott Ringle was the previous Chief. If the name sounds familiar, you might have run across his dad Chuck during your research. Chuckles was the Chief back when great granddad went missing. When I first asked Ringle about the boxes, he blew me off. I'm not sure if it was because all this was actual cold case evidence, as he claimed, or he was more worried I'd find something that would embarrass the PD or his own relatives' legacy." She stopped and put her feet up on the desk. Rockfish took it as a sign of Jawnie becoming a little more at ease with his presence.

"The guy is a real redneck prick, and thought he was going to ride the President's dick to another term as Chief, but he didn't. Make Elk Township Great Again, my ass. An outsider, a guy by the name of Ned Hasty, ended up winning. And I've been on Ned's ass about these boxes since he took his hand off the bible."

"Okay, so Hasty didn't have the same concerns, or was he too new to care?"

"You see, a lot of things around here are inbred to hell," Jawnie said "It's small town living at its finest."

"Small town, but pretty revolutionary if you ask me," Rockfish said. "Hiring an African American man onto the police force in the early 1940s was damn progressive."

Jawnie closed her eyes and shook her head. Rockfish's complement landed with a thud.

"That's a good one," Jawnie replied. "Edward McGee was a cracker and probably a racist one at that, seeing it was all the rage then. It doesn't mean I don't love the memory of him or what he was doing when he died, any less. Edward's son, my grandfather and his son, my father were the true progressives, as you say. They both married strong African American women, and the result is the tenacious and intelligent woman you see before you today." She pointed both thumbs at her chest.

"I apologize," Rockfish said, back peddling. "I meant nothing derogatory. Seriously, no offense."

"None taken. I can see the road you were headed down, wheels spinning in your head. Don't sweat it."

"I appreciate you understanding, but back to the small-town thing. You were making a point until I waylaid you."

"Right. Elk Township finally elected a police chief that wasn't born and raised there. Ned isn't related to half of Lakeview Trailer Park and doesn't have a dog in the fight regarding a man's personal effects and work ledgers from a lifetime ago. Past is the past, and he's looking towards the Township's future. That was actually part of his campaign that appealed to most voters. Now, granted, he would be interested if I turned up something and the new Chief could be known as the guy who finally closed the books on a seventy-six-year-old unsolved homicide."

"And from what I've learned, they never found Edward's body? Just some of his personal belongings at Mary's farm?" Rockfish said.

"You have done your homework," Jawnie said. "And that was the hardest for my family, through the years, not being able to give him a proper burial." Her voice cracked and chin dropped to her chest.

"I'm sorry to hear that, but with the new Chief being available, that is very fortunate, or should I say coincidental for both of our investigations. Circling back, what's a good time for you to continue this conversation. I'm not a paying customer and I don't want to take up anymore of your time," Rockfish said. "Perhaps we could further discuss all this over a drink? I'd like to tell you more about what I'm looking into and if you've heard or come across anything regarding it. Hell, I'd even help you go through the boxes if you'd like, but that is one hundred percent your call."

Jawnie crossed her arms. "I don't drink, Mr. Rockfish."

"But, I do. I do some of my best interviews when my tongue isn't as tight as it normally is. You might have figured that out already. Could I convince you to meet at my hotel so at the very least, I'd only have to crawl back into the elevator. I've seen both *First Blood* and *Deliverance*. The last thing I need is to be pulled over by a local cop on some dark back road." That finally got a small audible laugh.

"I could have an ice tea with you," Jawnie said. "Is dinner involved? I understand real PI's have expense accounts and as you can see, a lot of my money is tied up here in inventory," She waived her hand at the piles of computers and laptops spread throughout the shop.

"Dinner it is. Praise the lord for expense accounts and gullible clients," Rockfish said with a nod of his head.

"I'll actually be over in that area later this afternoon and can call you. In return for the boxes, I agreed to some pro bono IT work for Chief Hasty. He's still friendly with his ex, and her new step kids fucked over her laptop. Her new guy has some anger issues, so she asked Hasty if he could get someone to figure it out on the down-low."

"Kids love online sketchy porn sites. Who doesn't't?" Rockfish said, and Jawnie laughed again.

"It's been riding around in Hasty's trunk for a week, when the lightbulb went on during our conversation. I'm going to power it up and look at it this afternoon and if necessary, wipe the hard drive and reinstall Windows. I told Hasty I'd have it back to him by six at the latest."

"Copy that, see you around 6:30, or earlier," Rockfish said. Jawnie agreed and he walked back out towards Lana.

****

Jawnie pulled her Scion into the hotel's small parking garage and sat behind the wheel for a minute.

You could turn her back on and reverse out of this, she thought. *No harm, no foul, and if he calls, just come up with some lame excuse. Or let it go to voicemail.*

Jawnie had been having second and third thoughts about continuing their discussion ever since the private investigator walked out of her shop. It's not that she didn't appreciate the offer to help. Jawnie could only benefit from someone having experience in solving shit like this. But the timing ate at her.

It was too perfect. He had called it coincidence, and she wanted to call bullshit. Jawnie was twenty-nine and she could count on one hand the number of times in her life that things dropped out of the sky and went her way. Was Rockfish the exception to the rule, or was he somehow involved in the nagging feeling that she had over the past couple of weeks that someone was always around the next corner, watching and waiting? But instead of peeping, this someone decided to walk out of the shadows and confront her?

It played on her worst fear, that someone in the Elk Township department had it out for her. She had ruffled a lot of feathers over the past two years with all her questions and demands. That place had been a good old boys' network for how many decades now? If someone had something to hide in relation to what others might have done, would they try and scare her way in this day and age?

It's all anxiety and fear of the unknown, Jawnie always concluded when this same discussion left her with no actual answers. Tonight, was no different, and she made a promise to herself that she would go into this conversation guarded and on her toes for anything this guy might say that would raise a red flag.

Rockfish was waiting for her inside the small hotel bar. The televisions blared SportsCenter and the air smelled of grease and hamburger. Her stomach felt queasy from both anxiety and the smell, but she forged ahead and slid into the booth. She immediately noticed he still wore the sport coat that looked as if hadn't seen the inside of a dry cleaner's in a long while. *Has to be single or long divorced,* she thought.

On an evening like this, the pandemic was actually a good thing. The booths on either side were cordoned off, giving the pair the privacy that wouldn't hinder any of their conversation.

"Glad you could make it. How did that freebie job you threw Hasty go? Get all that porn off the laptop?"

Jawnie nodded, picked up a menu and noticed the empty rocks glass on the table.

"Nothing exciting from a work standpoint. I ended up wiping it. Not really heavy lifting. I typed a few commands and waited. Put in an install DVD and waited. But I have my doubts it was her step kids. You ask me, the ex-Mrs. Hasty is a nasty freak and that's all I'm going to say about that."

Jawnie looked back at the menu and saw that her vegan options were pretty much nonexistent among the standard burgers, chicken wings, and bourbon salmon. *House salad and water with lemon*, she thought. Every place had them, so it became her go to order when she didn't have a say in choosing the eatery.

"Mr. Rockfish, I'd like to get straight to the point if you don't mind. If I appeared a little weary of you and your coincidences this afternoon, see it from my point of view. The day I get my great grandfather's belongings, you just happen to show up and help me carry them into the shop, of all things. I'd be lying if a large neon sign flashing 'set up' wasn't still going off in my head." Her bullshit detector kept an eye out for what facial tics she could spot around the mask. She hoped being blunt caught him off guard.

"I totally understand," Rockfish said. "Look, if it will put you more at ease, I can give you a rundown of what I know and what I'm here to find out. Granted, there is client investigator confidentiality, but I can dance around that. Gimme a few more of these and I might spill the whole thing." Rockfish picked up the empty rocks glass and held it up to get the waitress's attention.

"That would be a splendid start," Jawnie said.

At that moment, the young girl appeared and took their orders, her standard and his burger, fries and another whiskey sour. As the waitress walked away, Jawnie pulled a small notebook from her backpack.

"Do you mind if I take notes," she asked.

"Not if you don't mind me doing the same later," Rockfish said, and he wove his tale.

Jawnie listened intensely, and her eyes rarely looked up from the notepad as her left hand struggled to keep up with Rockfish. He covered his client's interest in the case of the missing girls and his intention to dig up enough additional information that Angel Davenport could spin it into a true crime podcast and then a television docuseries. Jawnie put a couple of stars next to the producer's name. This could be a good thing if the guy was what Rockfish said he was. Big wigs in the entertainment industry might have a way of getting doors open that your average ITT Technical Institute grad couldn't even get up the courage to knock on. It surprised her that Edward didn't play a major role in the PI's research. To Rockfish, he was considered more of a minor side character. Jawnie believed the complete opposite.

How does he believe that the killing of a law enforcement officer is not the main issue here? Everything else must revolve around that action, she thought. *Maybe we're looking at the same thing but from different sides?*

Rockfish moved on to his meeting with Gertie Roberts and how the old woman wished to have some sort of closure for her sister before they would eventually move her up to Pitman Manor's third floor.

"The third floor?" Jawnie said.

"It's the assisted living facility's medical wing. Gertie said when they move you up there, you don't come back down. Ever."

"Gotcha. Do you know if her sister's last name was Roberts or is that Gertie's married name?"

"Matter of fact, I do. That was one of my first questions for her," Rockfish said. "Roberts is the family name. There's a story there about how shitty her marriage was and when her husband finally croaked, she couldn't run fast enough down to the courthouse to revert to her maiden name." He laughed and smacked the table. Jawnie caught her fork before it skittered off the edge.

"Have you tried looking up a Kathleen Roberts?" Jawnie asked. If he hadn't, this could be a starting place for her once she got back to the house. Jawnie fancied herself an Internet sleuth and was already anxious to get home and see what she could pull up based on her notes.

"Nope, haven't had a second to myself since I finished talking to Gertie." Rockfish continued with what few assumptions he had drawn since his meeting. The more he talked about substance, the more Jawnie felt at ease and let her own informational guard down.

"There's a whole kettle of bad going on here, back in the day," Rockfish said. "I figure we've got a woman doing some evil shit to young girls and babies on behalf of someone, and that someone eventually shut her up for good. Gertie said there were rumblings of the Catholic church doing more than watching from the front pew and I'd bet my trailer that Edward was putting all the pieces together, before someone stopped him. I'll bet it was the same goons that took care of Mary."

Jawnie watched as Rockfish pushed the tip of his nose through the mask with his finger.

"Huh?"

"The mafia," he whispered.

"Why are you whispering? The booths on either side are empty."

"Sorry, picked that up yesterday," Rockfish said. "If you want to talk about the mafia, without actually saying it, the finger to the nose is a telltale gesture. You can Google that."

You learn something new every day, Jawnie thought. "If you're talking mafia, then you're talking about the Provolones," she said.

"The what? I ordered cheddar on my burger."

Jawnie laughed and went over what little she knew about the offshoot of the Philadelphia mob that ran South Jersey going as far back as prohibition.

"A woman heads the family now, Annetta Provolone. Girl power, I guess. I only know because a few of her soldiers, I think that's what they're called, were busted like six months ago down in Cape May trying to sell counterfeit asthma inhalers. Could have killed somebody with that shit if the Feds hadn't busted them. Based on that arrest, the local news did a special half-hour investigative report on the family and all the shit they've been involved with over the years."

"Do you have an idea who headed the family back in the day," Rockfish asked.

"They mentioned it on the show, but I can't remember," Jawnie said and picked up her phone to search.

Heads of the Provolone Crime Family

"According to MafiaDons.net, it was a guy by the name of Julius Provolone. I'll take a chance and assume that he's probably the grandfather of Annetta. But I can do a deeper dive later."

Rockfish nodded, and Jawnie continued aloud with her previous thought.

"Steve, I gotta tell ya, I agree with everything you've said so far. It's always been my line of thinking that the same people that got to Mary, killed Edward. From what you said, he got too close to uncovering something that tied Mary, the missing women and their babies to someone or something. And after he 'vanished' she became a liability to the same people."

"Didn't I just say that?

"I wanted to let you know we actually might be on the same page, now." Jawnie said, but she wasn't sure he had caught on.

"We're both gonna go on record its most likely the Provolones?"

"That's where I was headed," Jawnie said.

She watched as Rockfish clicked his pen, closed his portfolio, and stuck them on the bench.

"Then I'd like to make the offer again to help you run through the contents of the boxes, in the morning, if you're agreeable and up for it. I don't know how busy you are, but if I can get one of those desks, I can start doing some inventory and laying the contents out."

"I'll have the shop open around seven," Jawnie said. "You can swing by any time after that but knock because I'll have the closed sign up and the door locked." It wasn't like she would lose a lot of walk-in business, the pandemic was already doing that, but keeping the door locked would at least make her feel safer. Maybe if Rockfish hung around for a bit, she could lose that feeling of being watched and followed.

Jawnie said her goodbyes and slid out of the booth. Rockfish followed suit and shuffled out towards the elevator when she called him back. Jawnie felt comfortable enough to ask one more question of the private eye.

"Steve, how do you know you're being followed, or like someone is watching you? Not every move, but too often for it to be part of your imagination. Unless, of course, you have a very active imagination."

"If you're asking if they teach classes on it, that'd be a negative. I'm betting the FBI does, but at my level, I've always considered it a sixth sense thing, something you develop through trial and error. Why?"

"No reason, I'll see you in the morning. Please thank your client for dinner."

Jawnie let out an enormous sigh of relief as she slid into the driver's seat. *I'm a decent judge of character, right?* She thought. *I think I can trust this guy. It's a gut feeling, but I'm gonna go with it.*

****

Jawnie got up that morning a little after five and tried to keep busy. She had promised that they would go through the boxes together, but with each tick of the clock, she wanted to dive in. They belonged to her, after all. What kept her from doing that was the fear of overlooking something, maybe a nondescript item of minutiae that Rockfish would pounce upon as an 'aha' moment. She planned to use the time with him as a learning experience. So instead, she fiddled with the stack of Chromebooks that had come over from the local middle school with heat sync issues until her new partner showed up.

That knock came earlier than expected, especially after watching Rockfish sway side to side on his trek back to the elevator last night. She glanced down at her phone, 7:47am.

"I brought breakfast, but sadly they don't have a breakfast salad on the menu, yet," Rockfish said as the door closed.

Jawnie thanked him anyway and put her small grease-stained bag down on the desk. She walked around, relocked the door and pulled the shade. *If somebody's watching today, they're out of luck,* she thought.

"Here's a mug and the coffee pot's over there," she said and pointed towards the computer desk to Rockfish's right. "I hope you like a medium Yirgacheffe roast."

"Is that the one made from monkey shit," he asked quizzically. Jawnie could tell he was a gas station brew kinda guy.

"No, just regular beans, no primate digestive juices included," Jawnie replied. "We can use that standing desk over there where I set up the laptop. Let me grab the first box."

Jawnie could read his expression that Rockfish wasn't expecting them to actually work together, side-by-side.

How the hell am I going to learn a damn thing if we're not joined at the hip, she wondered? *Partners work together, but I guess we'll do it his way for now.*

Rockfish was meticulous with each item as he removed it from the box. Jawnie stood to his right, manning the laptop where she inventoried each item, along with any notes or follow-up actions they both agreed needed to be taken. By the time they were onto the second box, Jawnie thought it surprised each of them how well they worked together. The defining moment was when Rockfish called time out and headed out to Vegan Treats. Then she knew she had won him over and he considered her one of the team. He also brought himself a second breakfast from McDonalds.

As she finished eating, Jawnie thought she could really get used to this expense account. That is as long as he continued to hit two different cafes. She glanced over at the untouched bag of a McGriddle and hash browns on her desk. He would definitely need to stop twice.

They finished up with the third box as the clock clicked past two in the afternoon.

"Do you want to pull those documents up so we can both look at 'em?" Rockfish said. "I want to make sure we agree on what we both deem important and worthy of moving forward on."

Jawnie swiveled the display and increased the zoom so that eyes both young and old could easily read the font. She had one spreadsheet for Edward's personal items, such as his wallet, desk photos and badge, all of which she would give her mother and grandmother. Her grandmother's only memories of her father were as a toddler and Jawnie believed Gram deserved these items back before she was to meet her dad on the other side.

The second spreadsheet had several items that were listed in the order they were found with the team's typed thoughts on priority in the adjoining column.

Most of the information came from two, what was known today as day planners. Each book covered a ninety-day window, totaling six months prior to Edward's presumed murder. Handwritten notes filled both volumes, detailing daily administrative and investigative duties.

Jawnie and Rockfish came to the same conclusion after finishing with Edward's logs. The man was clearly on to something. He had all the pieces of what Rockfish called a vast *criminal conspiracy*, but had Edward put them together and fully understood what he had stumbled on to?

Most of the entries came from surveillance he conducted. The strange part was that a lot of his entries appeared to document work long after he had clocked out for the day. He had several locations that he watched at night after normal patrol duties throughout the day. Edward's own words suggested the reasoning behind it was to keep out from underneath the chief's prying eyes.

"Okay, let's go through these again, top to bottom," Rockfish said.

Items Requiring Further Investigation

New Hope Catholic Charities Orphanage - Listed the most times throughout either ledger and the site of numerous stakeouts by Edward. Note - Way out of his jurisdiction.

Julius/Monsignor - listed only one time. Could this be referencing agreement/relationship between the Provolones and the Church?

Mary's farm - The scene of Edward's largest number of surveillances and where he identified:

-Cars tied back to Provolone front companies seen coming and going at all hours.

-Mary's income from more than only farming - purchased 1942 Pontiac Streamliner,

Hickory CI - An informant of Edward's?

Baltimore Outfit - possibly mafia related. Note - Rockfish to check with Baltimore PD sources.

Chief Ringle - Edward references spotting chief's wife and family car at Mary's farm, usually late at night.

"Why in the blue hell did no one follow up on any of this?" Jawnie exclaimed. "It's all right here in blue ink and bad handwriting."

They were both in agreement that Edward was definitely on to something. But that's where the mutual understanding stopped.

To Jawnie, Edward's handwritten notes told the exact story she and Rockfish were trying to piece together. All they would have to do was cart their findings back down to the Elk Township police and her family could finally have closure. Jawnie pressed this point and lobbied to take what they had found to the new Chief. He could decide the next steps, ones that she hoped would lead to re-open the investigation into Edward's disappearance and flush out what Mary D'arnaud was involved in at that farm.

I can't believe he doesn't see it. It's all right there on the screen, she thought.

To Rockfish, Edward was the king of off-duty surveillance, but his written notes were jumbled and mostly non-sequiturs. He felt Jawnie was making some large leaps from the notes. Rockfish had more questions. He wondered, had Edward been in such a hurry, worried that someone was onto his personal investigation, that he never had time to put all the pieces together in a place other than his mind? Was he worried, rightfully so, what would happen if he brought any of his findings to the Chief? The same man who constantly rode his ass that there was no case and that Edward needed to cut the shit before it cost him his badge? In the end, Rockfish pushed to veto the idea of taking anything to the new Chief.

"What evidence do we have?" he said. "Evidence is backed by facts, indisputable, in the eyes of a prosecutor. So when laid out before twelve citizens, they will all come to the same conclusion. What you have here is hearsay, plain and simple. Edward McGee won't be able to take the stand and guide a jury through his notes as to what he saw, let alone be cross-examined. Any first-year public defender would have this deemed inadmissible, even if it made it to any kind of trial." He pounded the table with an index finger after each point. "Not to mention the biggest point is that none of these people are alive anymore. More importantly, despite readily turning over these boxes to you, do you trust this Hasty?" Rockfish picked up one journal and shook it. "After all, didn't you say he beat out a Ringle in the election and that last name is all over Edward's notes? A lot of loyalists on the force, election results or not, would want to make life miserable for you after sullying the good name of who they believe to be a long-dead honorable relative of their previous boss."

Jawnie crossed her arms again. "I've spent more time with him than you have. Meet the man and then offer to tell me I'm wrong." Rockfish nodded, and Jawnie hoped she had made her point.

"If we wagon-wheeled all these snippets he wrote about—"

"Wagon what?" Jawnie said.

"Created a link chart. The orphanage has the most written entries. Put that in the center of your paper and draw lines, or spokes, out to all the connections we've found or heard about. Mary, unwed mothers, babies and now a Catholic orphanage. It seems like a good starting point. Have you heard of this place, the New Hope Catholic Charities Orphanage? Next link would be Mary's farm. There was a ton of surveillance conducted there, but not as many written notations. All roads, at least from Edward's view, led from the farm to the orphanage."

"Never heard of it. But this idea makes sense once you draw it out for us slow people," Jawnie said. She opened a browser window, did a quick Google search while Rockfish kept talking. What she found was compelling enough to interrupt and make him look at the screen.

"Now this is interesting. The place opened in 1937 and operated by the Sisters of the Holy Name, some offshoot from the Catholic Archdiocese in Camden. It closed in 1966 because of funding issues. This is weird. The church built it in the middle of the Pine Barrens, which is now Wharton State Forest. It's famous for a few things, some of which you might have heard of, amazing rivers to canoe, camping and the Jersey Devil. But definitely not your first thought when wanting to adopt a kid."

"I haven't heard of any of those, although hockey comes to mind for some reason," Rockfish said.

Jawnie dismissed the sports reference and her eyes lingered half-way down the page of search results on the orphanage. *Now this one result was curious,* she thought and tapped the keys a few more times before hitting enter. She wanted to make sure she understood what she was reading before saying anything to Rockfish.

"You gotta hear this," she finally said.

"Shoot."

"When I searched on the name of the orphanage, the fifth result on the page is for Propublica's coronavirus bailouts database. It's a site where you can search to find out if a company received Paycheck Protection Program loans from the Government."

Jawnie could see the confusion on his face, she could almost smell it.

"Okay, now I'm the slow one," Rockfish said.

She laughed behind her mask. *I know I shouldn't make fun of his cluelessness, but damn, this stuff is in the freakin' headlines every damn day.*

"Remember last month? We all got twelve hundred dollar checks from the President. He made a stink about signing the letter? Well, companies were given a shitload more through access to Federal loans in order to help them meet payroll and other obligations that they couldn't because of COVID-19."

"The Catholic Church is scamming the Government through this loan program? You know what else, nobody knows a good scam like the mafia," Rockfish said. "I think I'd be willing to make the leap now and assume the church and the Provolones have a long-standing agreement to work together when it's financially beneficial to both parties. Bookmark that shit and we can dig further when we get back."

"Get back?"

"Yeah, all roads lead to this orphanage. Hopefully, it's still standing, like you see on a lot of those ghost hunter shows. I'd take a chance and see if we can find a full filing cabinet somewhere in an administrative office that might give us something to go on. Hands-on evidence, it's worth a try. The drive will give me time to think and sort all this out. This box review and logging it on a computer is fine, but sometimes I make better progress rehashing it all in my head." Rockfish tapped his temple with an index finger.

"Not a computer guy, huh," Jawnie asked.

"ESPN and a few risky sites now and then, although I learned how to use this really good print shop type program recently. But back to the road. More importantly, I'd like to lay eyes on this place in the daylight, especially if that Jersey Devil you mentioned is eating people at night. But we could also be screwed in the daylight, as Paulie and Christopher never caught that Russian. He could be running around out there too.

"I haven't heard of any of those, although HBO comes to mind for some reason," Jawnie pulled her mask down and showed a shit-eating grin. "Let's go."

****

Rockfish sat in the Scion's passenger seat while Jawnie drove. He wasn't thrilled with the decision, but she was adamant that some of the dirt roads, deep within the Pine Barrens, were no place for a Dodge Challenger. Plus, she didn't feel like playing navigator. In the end, Rockfish decided not to put up much of a fight, considering Jawnie was more than a little familiar with where they were headed, although he had second thoughts with the four cases of whiplash he had suffered before even reaching the highway.

"Do you drive with two feet," he asked. "Because my head can't keep jerking forward and slamming back much more. Unless you're running an insurance scam, and if so, what would be my take?"

"Enough with the backseat driving, and can you put your visor back up? That late afternoon glare off the mirror is killing me."

"Make a deal with you. You drive how you want, I'll keep an eye on our surroundings the way I want. Speaking of which, can you move this right-side passenger mirror a little more to the right, all I'm seeing is the rear fender."

"You got it," Jawnie said, and she played with the mirror control until Rockfish let her know it was right where he needed it. He could monitor anyone approaching from behind without having to turn around.

"I do want to fill you in on something I learned before we left," Rockfish said. "When you went into the house to fix those sandwiches, I reached out to a guy I know in the Baltimore PD, Dan Decker. He's an old friend and helps me out when he can. He's going to have one of their academy cadets do some research for us and see if there is anything more than a current history between the Marini and Provolone families. The Marini's have run Baltimore as long as the Provolones have this area. If Edward's notation of the two factions working together has anything to it, Decker will let us know. He said currently both families have worked together when it was profitable to do so. Sound familiar?"

"Yeah, same M.O. as our knuckle draggers and kid touchers," Jawnie replied.

Rockfish was happy to learn Jawnie's disdain for organized religion matched his own. "Well put. But if there is a history there, what are the odds that some wealthy, non-fertile Baltimore Catholics would be willing to pony up some cash to right the situation. And Edward was witness to it all?"

They drove in silence over the next twenty minutes, Rockfish trying to figure out exactly what he expected to find in a fifty-four-year-old decrepit building in the middle of the woods. He hadn't arrived at a conclusion yet when something very familiar came into focus.

"Remember when you asked me about knowing when you're being followed?" Rockfish said.

"Yeah, I just chalked it up to anxiety and paranoia. It comes standard on the Millennial base model."

"Guess what? We are," Rockfish deadpanned. "Don't do a damn thing different and let me think for a second. There's a Jeep Grand Cherokee, right now, two cars back that's been with us since we pulled off the highway when I was telling you what Decker said."

Rockfish pulled out a scrap of paper and jotted down the license plate.

"I'll ask Decker to run this, if they end up sticking on our ass the whole way. I could be a tad paranoid, but I'd rather err on the side of caution. Just keep doing what you're doing, and I'll tell you if evasive actions become necessary. We'll start you slow and work our way up to the infamous private eye J-turn."

Ten minutes later, the Scion crossed the Hammonton City line and Rockfish lost sight of the Jeep. He had Jawnie drive a couple of concentric circles around the downtown area, before heading out on County Route 542 which, according to her, would point them towards the southern part of Wharton State Forest and the abandoned orphanage.

Rockfish spotted the Jeep, only a second or two after it turned on Route 542 from a side street.

"Company's back," Rockfish said. "I guess when we hit these dirt roads you mentioned, we'll see how serious they are."

When the Scion's tires soon left the asphalt, and began rolling down the slightly larger than single lane dirt road, the Jeep's true intentions came to light. No longer concerned about being spotted, the Jeep's speed increased until it was only a few feet from Jawnie's bumper. Rockfish's head swiveled from the Jeep and back to his pilot. He needed to stay calm, but Jawnie looked petrified, and while her hands had a death grip on the wheel, they were also visibly shaking.

"Jawnie, listen to me and we'll be alright."

She didn't say a word, but Rockfish could feel the car slowing down. *Screw her feelings,* he thought and began giving orders.

"Put your foot back on the gas. You need to keep a constant speed." And then a minute later. "Stay in the center, don't give them space to get alongside of us." Lastly, he shouted. "The center I said!" His voice gave out with that last outburst and he knew she heard the fear in it.

Rockfish swore as the Jeep slammed into their back bumper.

"That a girl, keep her straight! Gas, give it some—"

The rear windshield exploded, shards of safety glass like small pellets peppered the interior of the car. Jawnie screamed and instinctively yanked the wheel to the left. Likewise, Rockfish now yelled in order to be heard.

"Foot off the gas! Steer into it!"

Rockfish wasn't sure how he got through to Jawnie, but she listened, and the Scion straightened back up and they were rocketing straight down the dirt road once again. But before he could congratulate his pupil, the Jeep was now angling to get alongside; the Scion drifting dangerously close to the right shoulder, or lack thereof. Rockfish turned and looked out the driver's side rear window. He could clearly see the Jeep's front end.

In the next instant, they were sliding again, Jawnie's foot slammed on the brake and the Jeep's right fender nudged the Scion's left rear. Brakes squealed, and tires howled as dirt, dust and burnt rubber filled their lungs.

"Hold on, hold on, hold on!" It was all he managed to say, but her eyes told him she was a million miles away. Rockfish closed his and braced for impact.

The car spun violently to the left, a hundred and eighty degrees, and his head whipped left and then right, slamming against the window. The seatbelt dug into his chest and he had trouble breathing. A second later, the earth beneath the car's right side began to give way and the Scion slid into a ditch before coming to a stop.

By the time Rockfish opened his eyes and turned around, the taillights from the Jeep had disappeared into the distance.

****

"That settles it, I'm going to the police now! They, someone, fuck I don't know who just tried to kill us!" Jawnie said. "Look at my car! Who's going to pay for this? Not like we're exchanging fucking information with them!" Her mask was around her neck and Rockfish could see the tears.

Rockfish took a second before he replied. His partner was still in shock, borderline hysterical, and he didn't want to push her over the edge, unlike the car they pulled themselves from. The Jeep had performed a textbook pit maneuver and Rockfish bet Jawnie wasn't a big fan of Cops or Live PD. Hence, her jumping straight to attempted murder.

"Now hold on Jawnie," Rockfish said. "You're not hurt, right? That seatbelt and airbag did their jobs?"

"Of course, but—"

"No buts about it. Your chest might be a little sore tomorrow from that belt, your eyes swollen from the air bag, and more importantly, you'll never forget your first chase. But seriously, no one tried to kill us. If they had wanted us dead, we'd be bleeding out from gunshot wounds. Your rear window was the victim of a warning shot. When we were in that ditch, no one walked up from behind and pumped a few slugs into the back of our heads."

Rockfish stopped and looked at Jawnie, he needed to make sure he was getting through. Her breathing had slowed down quite a bit and that was a start.

"This was a warning, pure and simple. All this tells us is that someone thinks you might be sticking your nose somewhere it doesn't belong. Obviously, it pertains to those boxes. I haven't been in town long enough to piss someone off yet, at least, I hope. But if they were staking out your place, they'd have my license plate number and know who I am."

"But I've only dealt with Hasty on this," Jawnie said.

"Look. You might have worked out a deal with Hasty, but odds are he wasn't the one that went into the very back of the evidence room and pulled those boxes for you. He's probably recounted your conversation to a few of his 'trusted' senior men, and God knows who else might have been in the room when those conversations took place. Was there anything else you mentioned either to him or anyone else at the station that might cause a reaction like what just happened?"

"I d-d-did tell him I had hoped to t-t-take what I found in these boxes, scan what I could, and create a website. One that would ask the public for tips. Anonymously, of course. It would be a way to get the word out and maybe get someone's attention who might remember something. Hasty asked his secretary to check and see if he had the authority to put the PD's logo and tip line on this site. He was only trying to help."

"So, he's got a secretary. Old bird, I bet?"

"Yeah, Betty Lou Sommers. I'm guessing she's logged more than a few years there."

"There's your problem. Old Betty Lou sees all Hasty's business that comes and goes out of his office. I'd lay odds her loyalties lie with others she's worked with or for through the years and not the guy who knocked the latest Ringle out of office."

"I'd never thought of it that way."

"If you're trying to be a junior special agent, I'd advise you to think that way. Someone in that department is crooked and an off-duty cop or on-duty mafioso ran us off the road. Doesn't matter who, I'm betting they can be one and the same. Now if you feel alright, we need to call for a tow."

"And an Uber."

"Do you have any bars?" Rockfish said.

"Nope."

"We were lucky this was only a warning. We've got some walking ahead of us. They shouldn't be coming back."

I gotta reach out to Davenport, he thought. *The stakes have significantly increased.*

CHAPTER FIVE

The following morning, Rockfish found it near impossible to get out of bed. For a second, he had forgotten where he was and wondered what had happened to the inside of his trailer and then his body.

His eyes were sore from the airbags, his chest had a bruise that mirrored the seat belt, and his legs ached from walking more than he had in years. It took ten minutes for him to loosen up enough to hobble across the room and start the coffeemaker.

He'd live, but he wondered about Jawnie. Her mood deteriorated throughout the night. By the time the Uber dropped him off, he was pretty sure she wanted nothing to do with him, at least in the near future. She had been through a traumatizing experience, unlike any other she'd probably encountered in her entire life. But what she couldn't come to accept is that the crash was 99.9% about her. He had been in town only a few days and spoke with one old woman at a retirement home. At worst, he was guilty by association. Jawnie, her questions and something in those damn boxes that someone didn't want to come to light were the reasons behind it. Those were the ignition switch to yesterday's demolition derby.

Rockfish would give Jawnie her space, at least for the time being. He'd steer clear of her shop and let whoever drove that Jeep be comfortable enough to pass up their chain of command that the message was received, loud and clear.

Yeah, boss, that private detective isn't hanging around with her and she's not leaving her shop. Message received.

He, in the meantime, was going to make a call and find out exactly whose Jeep that was. A close second on the day's to-do-list was finding a ride to Westville to get Lana off Jawnie's street. That was a big factor of Operation Message Received. Plus, he needed to be back behind the wheel with his life in his own hands.

It'll be a cold damn day in hell before I let anyone talk me into riding shotgun again, he thought.

Once the coffee was flowing, Rockfish put in a quick call to his buddy, Lieutenant Dan Decker, back in Baltimore.

"...come on, Dan, these guys tried to run me off the road. I mean, they actually succeeded. Could have hung a big old Mission Accomplished banner from the wreck."

"Stevie, this isn't like calling down to the steno pool and asking one of the girls to run a Maryland plate. I don't know a goddamn soul where you are. And if I did, the first thing they'd ask is what the fuck are you doing up there and whose cage are you rattling. Well, whose are you?"

"You could honestly answer 'I do not know' to both questions," Rockfish said. "Danny, I try to keep you in the dark for a reason. Plausible deniability, it's a beautiful thing. How 'bout the Feds? You were at the big ribbon cutting ceremony for their new Baltimore field office. You don't get invited there without knowing someone. Come on, man, I'll owe you one."

"You mean another one, since you still owe me dinner at Jimmy's Famous Seafood. Let me make a call and see what I can do. I'll get back to you."

"I'm good for it, you—" Rockfish started to say but Decker had already hung up.

A half an hour after the room service breakfast tray found its way out to the hallway, Decker called back.

Bologna Construction, 328 Ewan Road, Ewan, NJ 08025

Rockfish plugged the address into his phone. His laptop was still locked away in Lana's trunk. Much to no one's surprise, Bologna had no web presence. Rockfish could find no website, reviews, or even a mention. Google Maps was his next app, and he put in the address Decker had given. He immediately switched to the satellite view and zoomed in. When the map would not let him get any closer, all he saw was an empty lot between two old houses. The only good thing was that Google said he could be there in thirteen minutes. Excluding the cab to Westville and then the drive back to Ewan. But in a perfect world, it would have been only thirteen minutes. He grabbed his notebook and headed down to the lobby. There he made use of their free masks for guests and called a cab.

Lana, I'm coming for you baby, he thought as the cab pulled away from the hotel.

An hour later, Rockfish was comfortably back in the driver's seat, staring at the empty lot. Ewan was the definition of a podunk town and the two-story houses on either side of the lot looked as if they'd come tumbling down if you so much as farted in their general direction. He looked around and took in the surroundings.

Hmmm, A Methodist Church across the street, he thought. *Looks like the only place here that might support intelligent life. It might be worth walking over and seeing if anyone there could answer a question.*

Rockfish turned off the car and got out. He hung his mask from one ear, in case someone surprised him and walked up asking questions about what he was doing there. He paced the lot in a grid pattern and stared at the ground, in case he ran across anything that he could use. His mind raced, trying to figure out what to do next. Rockfish didn't have to wait long. Next appeared in the shape of a torn envelope, half buried in a small heap of trash, and surrounded by broken glass. His eyes locked on the envelope's filthy, yet somewhat legible return address label.

Bologna Construction, PO Box 127, Ewan, NJ 08025

He had passed the single wide trailer that served as the US Post Office for zip code 08025 on his way into town. The Post Office was a little less than a quarter mile back up Ewan Road. The weather-worn, light blue building sat right next to the volunteer fire department. Rockfish assumed those two buildings made up the entire make-up of Ewan's downtown. He would need a story to walk in and start telling, so he drove past the Post Office and found an old boarded up pizza shop with a small parking lot. He pulled in and fired up his laptop and printer. Rockfish then emerged as Tom Taggert, United States Bureau of Contact Tracing, Field Supervisor.

Ms. Walker was the mid-40s, XXXL Postmaster who, despite it being a federal crime, took a long drag on her Pall Mall before looking down at the business card. Rockfish noticed immediately that she kept her mask dangling under her chin. That was the second law she openly flaunted. Ms. Walker was a rebel, at least in her own diabetic eyes. This might be a little harder than he thought to pull off. Not that she'd outsmart him, but was more likely to wear him down. She had carb energy for days.

"I'm not sure exactly how I can be any help, Mr. Taggert."

"It is quite simple, Ms. Walker, my agency in these trying pandemic times, has been discharged with contact tracing regarding those recently testing positive for COVID-19. Field Supervisors, like myself, and my team work to identify people who may have come into contact with an infected person. The head of the CDC mandated my crew to collect identifiable information about these contacts in order to better track this damn Chinese Virus. You may know it as the Kung Flu," Rockfish said with a suggestive wink. "All the information we collect will help with the CDC's predictive modeling. That's a fancy computer program that tells the bureaucrats in the swamp what areas to surge resources to in order to slow the eventual spread." *Wink*.

"Yeah, that's all a bullshit Democratic hoax. You're barking up the wrong tree, Taggert." Walker took another long drag of her cigarette before putting it out in the counter's built-in ashtray. She immediately reached for the open pack.

"I totally get it," Rockfish said. "I'm not exactly enamored with Fauci, myself."

"Goddamn socialist traitor."

"Some might say. But orders are orders. I got three youngins at home I gotta feed and a job is a job. I'm sure you understand. You know, one federal employee to another."

"Go on."

"Under the Geneva Convention I'm not at liberty to say more than that the Bolognas might be infected, but look, since this is all really bullshit, no harm in you knowing some of the inside baseball." Rockfish was playing a hunch. Her smoldering cigarette butt, the 'Git R Done' long sleeve t-shirt and the vibe he had gotten from the minute he walked through the door told him all he needed. If he had some rope, he could hang a clothesline over the counter, and she would be all over any gossip he could spill. That was his in.

"Like I said before, rules are rules, Dr. Fauci and such, took an oath you understand, but one of those illegals that Mr. Bologna hires on his job sites recently went to the hospital for kidney stones. He tested positive, and that triggers an all-hands-on deck for my office. And I'm not talking about him not having insurance and that triggering the damn Liberals to automatically raise our taxes to pay that bill," Rockfish said. He stopped for a breath to read his audience and liked what he saw.

"So, we start working our way backwards. Tracking Jose's steps to see where he's been, you know, who he's met with. You figure we're going to find a ton of other illegals, drinking, doing drugs and more or less killing time until the next caravan crosses the border, bringing reinforcements."

"Goddamn right."

"But, that's where you'd be wrong. Surprised me too when I learned what actually happened. You see, our investigation revealed this bad hombre was sneaking away from the job site and, I'll just put it out there, was banging Mrs. Bologna. She'd pick him up in her husband's car and drive Jose out behind the old, abandoned Kmart out on Route 45. Disgusting, I know, but that's why I need to locate where Mr. Bologna currently lives to give him a heads up if you know what I mean." Rockfish gave a wink and hoped she was buying it. "Between you and me, a lot of the people that work for me that came in under the last administration are worthless. All they gave me is an empty lot and this post office. Isn't there anything you can do? An honest man's been wronged here."

The twinkle in Ms. Walker's eye let Rockfish know he had succeeded without even having to slide some of his walk-around-money across the counter. Rockfish knew damn well Walker would be on that telephone, calling whoever she was responsible for calling on her version of the gossip phone tree, before Lana left the parking lot. He would give it until dinner before the fireworks hit the Bologna's domestic bliss. *Consider it a warning*, he thought. *I ain't the type to take one on the chin and then pick up my marbles and go home. There's a lot more work here to be done.*

A minute later, he had a photocopy of the Bologna's mail forwarding form and within fifteen; he parked down the street from Anthony and Pauline's new Mullica Hill McMansion. Rockfish sat in the car and surfed his data plan away waiting for, well he wasn't exactly sure but would know it when he saw it. And know it he did, as the road hog Jeep Grand Cherokee from the previous day emerged from the long driveway and exited through the development's gate. Rockfish waited and then slowly pulled out behind it, fully intending to show the Jeep's driver the correct method of tailing someone. He was a pro at this and had no concerns about being confronted, let alone being seen.

The Jeep made a handful of stops, each lasting only a couple of minutes before leaving town and hitting the highway. Rockfish hung back, out of sight until the Jeep exited and eventually stopped at a corner, directly in front of a cafe looking establishment. The sign above the door read Fortunata's. Rockfish continued on before hanging a U-turn at the next intersection and circled back. He could see the Jeep's driver exit and a teenage kid jump in and drive off.

Rockfish continued on past Fortunata's and parked a block up, where he could watch the front door in his rearview mirror.

He was compiling his notes from the morning's investigative activities when an incoming call flashed across his screen. The caller ID read 'Pitman Manor'.

****

Jawnie pulled the rental car into the Elk Township Municipal Complex and looked for the visitor parking. Her insurance company had delivered the loaner car that morning. The Scion was slated to be out of service for at least a week while some alignment issues were handled.

She had debated the trip over breakfast, flip-flopping over exactly what she wanted to do, until she chewed the last of the mini shredded wheat. After cleaning up, she fell back to the position where she was when she first awoke and picked up the phone. Jawnie called and made an appointment to see Chief Hasty, pushing everything Rockfish had said the previous evening out of her mind. Whether or not it was some sort of macho warning, she was terrified, and the choice was sitting at home with the shades drawn and or reaching out for help from those that were sworn to serve and protect. It had been a while since Jawnie lived in Elk Township, but she was big on the protection part right about now and didn't know where else to turn. The number of names she knew at the

Elk Township PD was one greater than the zero she knew in her new hometown of Westville.

She shut off the engine, reiterated to herself that she was doing the right thing, and walked through the front door into the Police Station. The entranceway opened into a large hallway with an alcove to her left where a secretary sat. The stench of cigarettes was overwhelming.

"He's ready for you now," said Betty Lou, the Chief's secretary. The woman wasn't wearing a mask and pointed at the Chief's door with a Milky Way bar. Jawnie then remembered what Rockfish had said about where the old woman's loyalties lie.

Jawnie got up from her chair and took a second to compose herself and adjust her mask before taking a wide berth around Betty Lou's desk. She hustled through the doorway into the Chief's office and made a point to close the door behind her.

"Jawnie, great to see you again. Thanks again for the help with that laptop. How goes the hunt through your great-grandfather's things? Somewhat of a cathartic experience, I should think."

She turned around after the door shut to see the Chief, masked up and standing behind his desk. She breathed a sigh of relief, and not only for his N95. If Betty Lou was playing both sides, Jawnie felt she was now with the one person in the department that would help her. That she could trust. She noticed he had hung his college diploma on the wall, behind his desk since her last visit. *How long had it been since anyone in this office got past the twelfth grade*? She thought.

"Forgive me if I can't walk around this desk and shake your hand," he added.

"No worries. We all do what we can to help flatten the curve," Jawnie said. "The laptop? Don't worry about it, that's what friends are for. And I'm still working on the boxes, thanks for asking." Jawnie gave a thumbs up as she couldn't smile through the mask. "I want to thank you again for making time in your schedule to meet with me on such brief notice, Chief Hasty. Are you aware your secretary isn't wearing a mask? Isn't it mandated by the state?"

"Please have a seat," Chief Hasty said and pointed towards the set of chairs pushed back from the front of his desk. "Betty's alone out in that office and over six feet from me, so we're adhering to the state's guidelines the best we can. Betty Lou's gonna Betty Lou. That was one of the first things I learned when I took over this job. But if it's any consolation, she wears it when she walks out for her smoke breaks."

"Thank you," Jawnie said and sat down. Hasty's answer didn't thrill her, and figured she might have to temper her expectations for what came out of this meeting. Or maybe it was his weird way to add some levity to the meeting. "I'm not here about the boxes, or at least I don't think I am. I wanted to speak to you about something that happened to me yesterday in the Pine Barrens, out past Basto Village."

"I'm sorry, Jawnie but that's far outside my jurisdiction, but If you'd like, I could put you in contact with someone from the Hammonton Police Department. Also, shouldn't you be reporting this to the Westville Police?"

"Someone shot out my back window. Shot out, I said. With a gun. Then they purposely ran us off the road into a ditch," Jawnie said, purposely ignoring his questions. She could feel her forehead turn red. Her eyes were wide open and hands gesticulated wildly.

"Ah yes, 'us'. I'm familiar with Mr. Rockfish. Anytime a private investigator starts snooping around a town, asking a lot of questions, it isn't long before someone gets their feathers all ruffled and calls the police. He ruffled at least one over at Pitman Manor and an orderly grabbed his license plate. Chief Wiggins let a few of us Chiefs in the surrounding localities know about it. My deputies saw that same plate over in Ewan the other day. You see, Jawnie, Rockfish's type tends to piss people off and eventually someone will try to scare him off the track."

"Ah yourself," Jawnie snapped back. "Look, does it really matter who was in my passenger seat? Don't I have rights? I'm still shook up. A bullet shattered my window. It could have hit me for Christ's sake." Her voice cracked, and she gripped the arms of the chair to stop her hands from flailing. Jawnie stopped and took a deep breath. *What is going on here,* she thought. *He was supposed to be my answer, save me from what's happening.*

"Can't you take a damn report and forward it to Hammonton? I can't drive down there after what happened. I've even got the receipt from the tow company and here are a couple of pictures I took before the wrecker arrived. If you call the body shop, you can probably dig a Goddamn slug out of the back seat, or god forbid, a headrest. But wait, you think they might have been after Steve?"

"Listen, Jawnie," Chief Hasty said, placing his hand on the desk and leaning out over it. "I can tell you're still pretty shook up over the whole incident. Think back. Are you sure you didn't accidentally cut someone off, or flip them the bird? Times are really tense with this election coming up, it doesn't take much to get someone to flip their lid. Heck, there are parts of Atlantic County that remind me an awful lot of deep, dark Mississippi. Like I said, it doesn't take much to set one of those good-old-boys off. They get angry, the car hits a rut, a finger slips, and a shotgun goes off. The gun was probably only loaded with buckshot."

"Chief Hasty, if I didn't know better, I would think that I was sitting here trying to reason with your predecessor. Is he behind that mask? We were driving. We weren't doing anything to anyone to warrant anything done to us. Whether it be a bullet, shotgun shell or rock salt." Jawnie threw up her hands in disgust and stood up. She stayed that way for a few seconds before settling back into the chair.

"Okay, I get your point, but you have to understand mine. While I'm not from South Jersey, I am familiar with the Pine Barrens. From the rumors of the Jersey Devil, to its being a mob body dumping ground, hunters shooting into the woods, other hunters shooting out of the woods, and finally not to mention a meth lab or moonshine still or seven. It's not a very stable environment for anyone at dusk or later to go driving on those back, dirt roads. Even if you are somewhat familiar with the area."

Jawnie silently wondered if she was wasting her time here, should she have listened to Rockfish? Was Hasty playing the devil's advocate for everything she said or told her to forget about it. Would her own PD have laughed at her too? *I only came here because I thought we clicked,* she thought. *Developed some sort of trust or relationship. I'm just not some crackpot citizen. Had I read too much into it?* As the thoughts raced around in her head, Jawnie nodded and Hasty continued to speak.

"I'll tell you what I can do," Chief Hasty said. He reached over and pressed the intercom on his desk. "Betty Lou, can you do me a favor and send in Patrolman Beckley and have him bring a blank incident form?"

After a few minutes of awkward silence in the Chief's office, there was a knock at the door and in walked Beckley, ready to take Jawnie's report. To her, the young officer looked absolutely thrilled to be dragged into this situation. She immediately noticed the man's uniform looked too new, not a wrinkle in sight. The coke-bottle glasses also screamed desk jockey to her. *Okay,* she thought. *Now they're just placating me.*

Beckley sat in the chair to her right but pulled it further back so there was a decent sized space between them. Beckley listened as Jawnie recounted every tiny detail she could remember about what had happened. She kept glancing down to the paper, as Beckley's pen moved from section to section. It looked like he was taking all of it down. Jawnie finished retelling her story by letting Beckley know that if he provided an email address, she would forward the reports from both her insurance and the tow companies. Additionally, she would attach a handful of pictures she had taken of the scene and the damage done.

"All of that would be great, really helpful," Beckley said. "I can attach them when I get this entered in the system. I've got one more important matter. Is there any chance you have the license plate of the Jeep?"

"I don't, my passenger wrote it down. I can reach out to him and get back with you later today if that's okay. I apologize, I should have thought of that before coming here today."

Jesus Christ, how big of an idiot am I, she thought. *My biggest piece of evidence and I totally spaced on bringing it. Fuck, the last thing I want to do is call him, ask him for it, let him know he was right all along about how helpful Hasty's been. Damnit! I may ask for the number, but I sure as hell won't tell him he was right.*

"That would be the infamous Steven Rockfish, who has the plate number," Chief Hasty interjected. "I think what would be better for all, would be if Mr. Rockfish swung by my office himself and dropped it off in person. I've heard a lot about this guy."

"When I speak to him again, I can certainly pass along the message," Jawnie said.

"Glad to hear it, because you know most of these gumshoe-types tend to stop into the local PD and give a professional courtesy. Just a 'hi, how you doing. I'll be driving around and asking questions.' We shake hands and they head off to do whatever they do and we're all good. While Officer Beckley took down your statement, I double checked my calendar because I don't remember Mr. Rockfish stopping by. And my calendar confirms it. I'm sorry, Beckley, you don't need to be here for this. I think we're good." Jawnie watched as Hasty lifted his chin towards the door.

Officer Beckley stood up and thanked Jawnie for coming in and let her know he would be in touch if anything came up. He stopped short of leaving the office and asked the Chief if he wanted the door open or shut.

"Shut, please," Jawnie replied. "I've got one more thing I'd like to talk to the Chief about."

"You heard the concerned citizen. Close it behind you."

Once the door shut, Jawnie went into the possible PPP loan fraud that she may or may not have stumbled across. She emphasized it was only somewhat vague information she found and started to look into. Hasty would need to assign someone to it and do a deeper dive.

"I'm going to stop you right there," Chief Hasty said, cutting off Jawnie before she could finish telling him exactly what he needed to do. "That's the Catholic Church that you're accusing of some serious crimes, federal charges at that. Nothing I can do from this seat about it. If you want to report it, you'll have to reach out to those agencies down at the Federal Building in Philly. If they want my help, they'll come ask. That's what professional courtesy is: Asking before you root around in someone else's backyard." He leaned back in his chair and then reached over to push the intercom button again.

"Betty Lou, can you dig up the phone numbers for the FBI and IRS and give them to Ms. McGee on her way out? Thank you."

The Chief stood up, walked over, and opened the door.

"I think we're done here, Ms. McGee. You be careful, and take care now. Please don't forget to get that message to Mr. Rockfish. I'd hate to send a car for him over at his hotel in order to start the conversation, but it's totally up to him."

Jawnie's shoulders dropped. She gathered her papers and walked out. The morning was a complete waste.

Should have listened to Rockfish, she thought. *Goddammit! What the hell do I do now?*

* * * * * * * * * * *

Gertie called to let him know that she had remembered something regarding Mary D'arnaud, but the call quickly deteriorated into the current conditions at Pitman Manor and Gertie's desperate need for a face-to-face conversation with someone who wasn't batshit crazy, hired to change adult diapers or looking for a handout. To hear Gertie tell it, over the course of the last two days, the great hoax had spread like wildfire across the facility. Due to the increase in positive COVID-19 cases, Pitman Manor was in complete lockdown with only employees allowed to come and go from the premises. She let him know his little skit wouldn't work again as all relatives and even lawyers such as Tom Ridgewell would no longer be allowed to enter the facility and have to opt for virtual visits.

Gertie circled back to the reason for the call and said she had napped and then slept on their previous meeting. She claimed to have remembered some additional information and suggested one of those computer video chats thingamabobs and had proactively reserved time on a computer in their Internet room, just before dinner.

Rockfish immediately thought 2:30 - 3:00pm and looked at the clock on Lana's dashboard. One fifteen stared back, and he had no desire to recreate this all over again in an hour, let alone wondering if Gertie would forget exactly what she remembered by then.

Might as well take the bullet now, he thought, and brought his attention back to the call.

"...I'm not sure what this MySharonavirus exactly is, but lots of people here are talking about it and new rules. It's practically martial law here." Gertie said.

"Gertie, you don't need to see my face to tell me what you remember," Rockfish said. "We're talking right now. You can tell me, and when the place opens back up, I'll be there with flowers and butterscotch candies. Come on, spill it."

"Okay, no need to get all testy with me. I woke up this morning and was eating breakfast in my room— can you believe they make us eat in our bedrooms now? I can't even leave the room for generic Cream of Wheat. The ladies are probably missing me at the table. I don't know what they expect—"

"Gertie, stick with me here. What did you remember about Mary D'arnaud?"

"Oh, that lady, yeah yeah. I remembered it was a long time, years, after that woman disappeared from the jail, that there was a knock on our door. I was visiting my parents' house. Mom, by that time, needed some help doing general chores around the house. I don't know why I couldn't remember this the other day, but when I did, I wanted to call you before some doctor shows up on CNN and claims this goddamn Italian Veronavirus is transmittable over the phone. And who the hell knows the price of a stamp anymore if that happens..."

"Gertie, Gertie, concentrate for me, honey," Rockfish said. "You remembered that a woman came to see your mom."

"Yes, of course. Actually, it was two ladies. Young and old, could have been mother and daughter, they looked so much alike. The younger lady asked for my mother. She mentioned her mother's name was Tisha Jack, or Jackson, or Jacksonville. I dunno. Something like that and she needed to speak to my mom. I can't remember everything about them standing on the porch, but when they came inside, my mom held up her hand. I wasn't allowed to follow them into the sewing room. Mom shut the door in my face. Heck, you know, mom never shut that door. That's how I knew it was important. Don't know why I couldn't remember the important thing the other day. Important things don't seem so important as time goes on here. And boy does time pass slowly here..."

Rockfish gave up trying to wrangle Gertie on point and instead let her ramble. He had faith that she would cover those important points, but he might have to sift through a lot of crazy to find them.

Gertie said that she wasn't able to hear through the sewing room door, but she could eavesdrop later that night when her mother repeated the conversation for her dad.

Tisha claimed to have been a friend of Mary's and having recently accepted Jesus Christ as her own personal savior, she wanted to get something off her chest and thought this sewing room conversation may provide some partial closure for our family.

Rockfish was all ears, enough so he had stopped paying attention to the cafe in the rearview mirror and was trying his damnest to listen and take notes at the same time. He noticed that Gertie had been silent for a couple of seconds and tried to prod her again.

"And?" Rockfish said.

"That's all I have," Gertie said. "My dad caught me standing in the hallway listening as they sat in the kitchen. My mom ran upstairs, and he yelled that none of this was my business. He pointed towards the door and I left. He made it absolutely clear that it wasn't anything they would ever share with me. But I thought you might find it interesting."

Rockfish thanked Gertie for remembering, reaching out and providing him with what she could. He spent another five minutes trying to get her off the phone.

After she hung up, he did a quick internet search on Tisha Jackson. He ignored the Jack and Jacksonville as misfires in Gertie's synapsis. The first page of search results were only links for the hottest new female rap sensation from Atlanta. Having learned since his arrival that 'The Lawns' was located outside the city of Aura, he added those two descriptors. He found what he was looking for on page three.

Tisha Jackson, of Stanger Avenue, Aura, New Jersey had passed away in 1996 and survived by her daughter Monique and only grandson, Rodney.

Next up on Rockfish's search parade was Monique Jackson. She, also of Stanger Avenue, died in a car accident in 2014. Rockfish hoped Rodney was still around and had a readily discoverable cell number.

CHAPTER SIX

By the time Rockfish found a working number for Rodney, the man had just gotten home from work. Turns out he still lived in the house he had shared with both his mother and grandmother. After an initial awkward phone conversation, Rodney agreed to meet, and Rockfish wasted no time in driving out. He found Rodney where he said he'd be, sitting on the Jackson family home front porch. The small rambler had seen better days and Rockfish didn't trust the DIY, wooden ramp leading up to the porch. Rodney looked as if he was killing time, much like Gertie, but in a better place with not quite as good a view.

Rockfish estimated Rodney to be in his mid-50s. He was putting a strain on the aluminum folding chair underneath him, but looked happy as hell to be in it and no longer at work. He was also putting a strain on a well-worn Parliament-Funkadelic t-shirt. As he moved closer, Rockfish squinted again at Rodney. The man didn't appear to be wearing a mask, so Rockfish took a chance and tossed his back over onto the passenger seat. He didn't want to roll up the ramp and spook him, especially if Rockfish needed the man relaxed and as talkative as Gertie, but way more focused.

Rockfish had made a couple of stops on the way to The Lawns. He picked up Chinese takeout and a twelve pack of Miller Lite to help speed the conversation and prevent some of the same awkwardness from their phone call.

"I hope you don't mind Chinese. I passed The Egg Roll Bowl on my way over. I got one kung pao combination and one shrimp and scallop with garlic sauce."

"Anything I ain't spending my own hard-earned money on is fine by me. I'll take the shrimp. The wife will hate me for the garlic later tonight, but that's her problem."

"Couldn't agree with that first part more," Rockfish said, and both men laughed. "And if you don't mind, I'm going to slide this chair over here, put some space between us."

"Do what you gotta do," Rodney answered.

The men ate and drank for a while without addressing anything Rockfish had come to hear. But to him, unlike Gertie's ramblings, Rodney's talk about the long history of African American's living in this section of town, was a learning experience.

Rodney wasn't sure why the white folks called it The Lawns but for as long as he could remember this is where they lived. His family for generations had lived on this straight stretch of road. The residents here called it the Northwest, short for Northwest Aura. They were poor, most finding seasonal work in the peach orchards and tomato farms that covered most of Elk Township and Gloucester County.

When Rodney waxed a little nostalgic about his time growing up, Rockfish decided he had heard enough of the local history to interrupt and not seem flippant to the struggle and oppression faced by the residents of The Lawns. He needed to steer Rodney back to the fact-finding mission that brought him here, dinner in hand.

"From what I've learned in my short time here," Rockfish said, "it didn't seem that Mary was hurting for cash at any point before she went missing. Did you ever hear anything about that? Types of stuff she was involved in? You know, good, bad, or ugly?"

Rodney nodded his head and took a long swig from his beer. The can was empty, and he grabbed another before continuing.

"Some of what I know, or heard, came from my grandma, but most from my mom. She was the one that had to take care of grandma later in life when she began regretting a lot of the choices she had made earlier in life. Those choices, no matter if forgiven through repentance or confession, ate at that poor woman right up until we lowered her casket into the earth." Rodney finished, shook his head and then stared down at the porch.

With those last words, Rockfish had a feeling this was going to be a lot deeper and more emotional than he expected. He too finished his beer and popped the top on the next. He placed the cold one on the deck alongside his left leg and settled in to take some copious notes.

"You see, my grandma Tisha wasn't the God-fearing woman she became later in life. Mom said she was the definition of a wild child in her younger years and got into a ton of trouble before she was even of legal age. Trouble and the law go hand in hand, and it wasn't too long after an arrest by Officer McGee that grandma essentially became that cop's eyes and ears in The Lawns." He stopped and took a long swig of beer before continuing. "While a cop could drive through here and not know what to look for or see, grandma knew. Wasn't something she was too proud of, especially as she got older. People out here just trying to make a living. But what really ate at her was how she kept silent all those years."

Rockfish's ears perked up at the mention of Edward's name. If Tisha was his confidential informant, it was her code name in his notes. It certainly explained all Edward's detailing the comings and goings of the Lawns.

"That McGee, he kept pumping my grandma for information. Mom said it was as if that guy wanted Tisha to drop a dime on everyone in here that did any damn thing against the law, no matter how small. It reminds me of when I worked at this plant nursery and instead of an hourly wage, you got a set rate for the number of plants you dug, potted, and transported back to the warehouse. Piecemeal, that's what they called it. It seemed like this guy McGee was getting paid per arrest, or something. But he wasn't returning the favor per nugget of information, if you understand."

"I do," Rockfish said. "Did a bit of nursery work as a teen, myself."

"Then, he started asking about Mary and the girls that came to stay with her. Other than Mary being a midwife to those in the neighborhood and in need and driving that damn Pontiac around like she owned the goddamn town, grandma didn't know much. But McGee asked her, or more like ordered her to get close to Mary. He gave her a long list of questions he wanted answers to and if he didn't get them, grandma would be back behind bars and he'd wash his hands of her at that point." Rodney paused and signaled for Rockfish to toss him another beer.

"More importantly, he wanted to know what became of the white women that came to stay with Mary, what happened, to the babies. Where did they go? Where was Mary getting her money from and who was paying her?" Rodney shrugged his shoulders. "Man didn't give a shit about any of the black babies, and grandma gave him everything he wanted. She was afraid of jail and in my mom's opinion, young Tisha learned to play the game. Once the cop saw that the info grandma was providing was spot on, he changed his tune towards paying for it. Maybe it was a little guilt that had him throw her a little something. She learned quickly to like the easy money. It was safer, at least in her eyes, than robbing folks or stealing what she could, and it paid damn near as well. Grandma wouldn't be driving no Pontiac, but she had decent clothes and some self-pride. You see, she believed she was helping rid the neighbor of a horrible influence, with all that she was learning. I kinda think this was where she turned her life around. That's my two cents from reading this book a handful of times since I found it." Rodney grabbed one of the takeout napkins, wiped his eyes and forehead before letting it fall to the floor.

The man had worked up a sweat and genuine tears, Rockfish thought. "A book? Your Grandmother kept a diary? Did she write down any specifics about what she was observing going on at the D'arnaud farm?"

"She did. Grandma got herself close to Mary by working on the farm. Mary needed help with outside chores on the farm and my grandma, like all us Jackson's, wasn't afraid of a little hard work. Technically, she was double dipping two salaries for what she did. Anyway, she eventually worked her way up to cleaning and cooking for Mary's family inside the main house, and that's where all the trouble started."

"Grandma learned Mary was caught up in a huge problem. One she wouldn't be getting out of unless the end of times came. Those white girls that dropped off with their babies ready to pop out? Their babies were sold to the highest bidders. White men would come in two cars. The babies would leave in one and the girls in the other. The other farm hands gossiped about the girls being killed even before they left the property and were dumped somewhere on the farm. Grandma didn't believe it for a second."

"You think she was a little naive?" Rockfish interjected.

"Maybe she was, I don't know. But she told that cop, and he didn't believe it either. He was more interested in the babies and where they went off to. One other thing she told him he didn't believe was that Mary was paying protection money to the Chief of Police. She believed the money came from somewhere else and Mary was the go-between. The Chief would send his wife over to collect. If she was late or didn't have it, he would threaten to arrest her and her entire family. He knew what was going on and chose to take a bribe and do nothing. I think one of the guineas were behind the whole thing. Mom used to say wops, but they all mean the same thing." Rodney turned his head and spit off the porch. "Hey you don't mind if I stop here, I gotta take a leak."

"Not at all, my man. It'll give me a minute to catch up on my notes. Take your time, I ain't going anywhere."

Rodney disappeared into the house and Rockfish wrote as fast as he could remember. *Goddamn, this is some good shit. Speculative at this point, but I can find some tangible shit to back it up, no doubt.*

When Rodney returned to his chair, he kicked back into his story. "Whether that cop ever thought the information was credible, he'd always thank her for what she came up with and give her an envelope with her 'pay'. Sometimes when something grandma gave him really panned out, he'd bring along a bottle, and they'd celebrate a little. The more they celebrated, the more she said his lips loosened up, and he'd talk about his findings. Grandma thought he found out too much, dug too deep, and then she never saw him again."

"Wait, wait. She never saw him again after this? Really?" Rockfish said. "He stopped coming around, or she stopped looking for him?"

"Probably a little of both," Rodney said. "He claimed to have followed one car with a baby all the way down to the Pine Barrens. Followed it all the way through the woods to some orphanage where he saw it handed over to a couple of priests that swapped it for a pretty well-padded envelope. Grandma said he thought rich white folks, who kicked back even more money to the church, adopted the babies. Those people were stupid, thinking their adoption was through the church and legit."

"Not long after, like I said, the cop turned up missing and Mary was arrested. Grandma tossed and turned about it for a week before she went to the Chief with what she knew. She cried and told him she felt horrible that what the officer was having her do might have played a part in getting him killed. She made a point not to mention what she knew about him and his wife, and it was two days later that Mary vanished from the jail and grandma began thinking she was responsible for two deaths and could be next."

"Grandma, already pregnant with my Mom, left town. She traveled down south to stay with some relatives until enough time had gone by that she could come back and not fear the Chief. On one drunken night she claimed to have heard that Mary and that cop had ended up dumped in an old well, same as those white girls, on the far side of Mary's farm. The well was soon capped and covered over with a ton or two of dirt after Mary 'escaped' from the jail."

"Years later, she said the police still didn't want to hear nothing about it, and it ate at her soul. Even after she found Jesus right down the road at the Aura United Methodist Church. Pastor there claimed Jesus wanted grandma to forget it all, that none of it happened and that would be the only way she could find peace."

"That's one hell of a detailed story, Rodney. Almost as if you were there, alongside her during all of this, just watching."

"I kinda was," Rodney said, and he reached underneath his chair and pulled out a well-worn cardboard box. His hands shook as he set it on his lap, and he reached for another napkin. "I told you she kept a diary. She started writing a few years before her death when she got too far into her own head and she couldn't turn to her church. Didn't want to turn to a bottle again."

Rockfish gave a low whistle and jumped a little for joy deep inside. *Did I say it couldn't get any better? Hot damn it just did,* he thought. This book was only more hearsay, and he could hear Jawnie repeating his own words back at him, but the circumstantial evidence was mounting. And it wasn't as if Davenport had to take any of this to court, he only had to lay it out in an entertaining fashion and let the viewers decide for themselves.

"As far as I'm concerned, I might have kept it all these years for this reason, maybe looking for the right person to pass it along to. Someone that could do some good with her story. Here, I don't think I need this anymore," Rodney said and pulled the book from the box and handed it to Rockfish. "It goes into a lot more detail, if you read it. I told you what I could only remember."

"Thank you, Rodney," Rockfish said, and he slipped the diary under his own notebook on his lap. The two men spoke for a little while longer, and Rockfish let Rodney know exactly what he would do with his grandmother's story. He'd pass Rodney's contact information on to Davenport and that someone from his production company would be in touch once this production got off the ground. And in Rockfish's limited Hollywood knowledge, this story needed to be told.

"Hey, your grandma did some brave shit for the times she was living in. Whether others called her a rat or turned the other way when walking down the street, she was good people. Sometimes doing the right thing isn't the easiest. She had a set of morals that a lot more of us should follow these days."

"Thank you, Steve. Those words mean a lot more than you'll ever realize." Rodney held out his hand and Rockfish didn't hesitate to shake it. *Sometimes, you just have to say fuck it,* he thought.

They said their goodbyes and Rockfish locked the diary in Lana's trunk for safe keeping. He was three beers in but thought nothing of it. They were Lite, after all and it was a short drive back to the Marriott in Glassboro. More importantly, it would be all back roads. As he put Lana in reverse and headed out of Rodney's driveway, Rockfish gave one last goodbye wave.

With what Rodney had told him and the diary, Rockfish couldn't help but think his time in South Jersey on this case would come to an end soon. If he could fill in some blanks with names regarding the historical Church's role in this whole scheme, he'd bring Davenport back one heck of a show the man could sell to a major network. Heck, he'd even suggest they get whatever permits were necessary to locate and to dig up that old well on Mary's farm. As long as they could locate it, even if it wasn't a dumping ground for bodies, the episode would pack in the viewers. Bad press is still good press, just ask Geraldo, Al Capone's vault, and that godawful Oak Island show.

* * * * * * * * * *

Rockfish backed Lana out of Rodney's driveway, straightened her out, and headed down Stanger Avenue. Lana's GPS quickly told him to make the next left onto Route 553, which would run him straight back to the hotel, but he ignored the instruction. From what Rodney said, Stanger Avenue cut through the center and ran the length of The Lawns. He wanted to get a better feel for the area. He wanted to drive past Mary's farm if only for the visual, even if it wasn't like that old well would be sticking up out of the ground. That reminded him, Davenport would have to hire a company that could run ground penetrating radar to locate its exact position. He wasn't sure if Hollywood-types knew about shit like that.

Rodney had told him to head back down Stanger for a half mile before making a right on West Boulevard. West would dead end at a cemetery, and what was left of Mary's property would be a five-minute walk beyond that.

Rockfish was two hundred feet from his turn when he was lit up from behind. The sirens chirped and then he saw the lights in his rearview.

Ah shit, he thought. *Only a matter of time in a small place like this.* He guided Lana onto the shoulder. While this wasn't his first time, it was his first time in rural South Jersey. He turned off the radio and then the engine before gripping the wheel with both hands and silently wished he had a mint.

"License, registration and insurance," came the instructions. The man was tall and broad. His chest took up the entire window frame.

Rockfish had all three documents easily accessible and ready to go. No need to cause a scene by rooting around in his glove compartment or center console. He handed all three out the window. He expected the cop to turn around, walk back to his cruiser and run the information, but that didn't happen.

"Umm, is there a problem Officer..." Rockfish leaned out the window and looked up to find a name tag. "...Sommers?"

"This is a mighty fancy sports car for this neighborhood, Mr. Rockfish." Officer Sommers said. "What's your business here? You're a long way from Maryland."

With all the help Rodney had provided, there was no way Rockfish was mentioning his name, not even if the cop had watched him walk down from the porch and pull out of the driveway which was exactly the vibe this clown was giving off.

"I'm just enjoying the scenery, officer. I'm on my way back to the Courtyard in Glassboro and thought I'd take some of these back roads, you know, open her up a little. I apologize if I was speeding, but sometimes a car like this has a mind of its own."

Sommers took a step towards the front of the car and stared at Rockfish though the windshield, before stepping back to the driver's window. "I'm going to tell you what I think, Rockfish. I think you're some rich bozo from out-of-town looking to score a little somethin' for some depravity tonight. I'm not a big fan of your types coming into my town and buying drugs. Is there anything in the car I should know about?"

"No sir, clean as a whistle. If you'd—"

"Rockfish, I didn't ask your opinion. Now listen to me and you listen good." Sommers leaned forward and gripped the car through the open window. "Imma gonna tell you what to do. Drop what you're doing here and drive this hotrod right back to where you came from. I don't want to see this car or hear that you're running around here asking any more questions. If you even so much as fart in my township over the next couple of days and I hear about it? I'll pull you over, run a dog around this car and in a million years you won't believe what you were dumb enough to leave in the back seat, right in plain sight. Consider this a friendly warning." Sommers smacked the roof of the car with his fist, turned and walked back to his cruiser.

Lucky me, Rockfish thought. *Second one in almost as many days.*

****

Anthony Bologna, aka Tony Boloney, stirred his cappuccino and observed the comings and goings of Fortunata's Social Inn from his large booth in the back. The restaurant was member's only, with most of his underlings milling around and conducting business outside. The inside was empty and smelled of the best Italian food you'll never have. Tony ran the crew and did his business from a spot barely visible from the front. That was how he liked it. He wasn't an office type of guy and liked to conduct business out in the open, as if he had nothing to hide. He heard the bell above the door and looked up to see one of his men, Salvatore Bertoni, aka Sally B walking in and he wasn't alone. Sally B was his right-hand man and dressed as if he was the boss. The suit was a nice touch, but a little too over the top for Tony's taste.

Tony did not recognize the stranger, and his haunches immediately went up. He whistled and motioned for his two bodyguards to draw closer. Sally B and the stranger walked across the cafe but stopped short of approaching the booth. They contrasted as the stranger wore a dumpy hoody and sweatpants as opposed to Sally's standard Armani. Tony waved them closer and then nodded to his bodyguards to pat the men down. It became apparent that under the hoody and sweats, the stranger had on a cop uniform. *You could never be too careful these days*, Tony thought. No matter how loyal Sally B claimed to be.

"They're clean."

"Gentlemen, please have a seat."

"Heya Boss, this guy here is our paisan over with Elk Township's finest," Sally B said. "I've mentioned him a few times to you before, prolly not by name though. He's solid and done more than earned his share in the past."

"Understood, but why couldn't you just tell me about it yet again, without dragging him in here while I'm thinking about eating?" It didn't thrill Tony to have a cop in his place, never mind the half-assed attempt to hide his uniform. If the Feds were watching, he bet they probably made this clown. *I gotta talk to Sally about losing this guy and soon,* he thought. *Fucking guy knows better than to bring him in here, disguised as if the Sisters of the Blind dressed him.*

"I want you to hear what he had to say, from the pig's mouth. No offense."

"None taken," the cop said.

"Okay, now that no one has any hurt feelings, speak," Tony ordered. He was losing patience, and it had been less than five minutes with these two.

The other man nodded.

"You can call me Louie, Mr. Bologna, it is a pleasure to finally make your acquaintance."

"I'd rather not know your name. And..."

"Yes, of course. I learned some additional information about the girl asking all the questions about that thing in the past. She came to see the Chief today to report that someone shot at her car and ran her off the road."

"I sincerely hope that whoever did that to this woman is swiftly brought to justice, and I know you'll do your best to make this happen. I too have a young daughter. But I do not see how this is any concern of mine," Tony said, holding out his hands and shrugging his shoulders. "The other thing she keeps asking about is of no concern to us. The old guard has too much invested in those that are long dead. I don't have time for that shit."

Tony watched as the man fidgeted and bounced from one foot to the other. He was clearly contemplating what to say next when Sally B lent him a helping hand.

"It's more than that. Tell him."

"You see, sir, my mom also works with me and she's in a position to hear things. Things she is more than happy to readily discuss at home on her lunch break whether or not she's had a cocktail."

"Madone, for Christ's sake, sometime today." Tony looked up at the ceiling and shook his head.

"She told me that when the girl met with the Chief, he told mom to look up the phone numbers for the FBI and IRS over in Philly and give them to the girl when she left."

"Louie, you have my full attention," Tony replied. "Please continue and in great detail."

"I asked mom what it was regarding and she said it had something to do with some initials the woman was droning on and on about. PPA, PPP or PPE. Something like that. You see, Mom couldn't hear too well though the door. She thought it might be a beef with the Philadelphia Parking Authority."

The mention of PPP made Tony's stomach drop, but you couldn't tell by his poker face.

"Your mother's retarded. No one calls the FBI or IRS for a fucking parking ticket."

"I know. I looked up the other two and concluded I should bring this to Sally B's attention."

Tony nodded, and Louie continued.

"One other thing, though. The Chief has us keeping tabs on this Rockfish clown. Making sure he doesn't step on his dick or fuck up any operations we've got going on. I heard on the radio that he was spotted over in The Lawns talking to some guy on his porch. I made a point of getting over there, pulling him over when he left, and making it very clear that he should pack his shit and go back to where he came from. There wouldn't be a third warning."

Tony smiled. The expression remained a cover for how freaked out he was about the mention of the Paycheck Protection Program Loan Program scam that was proving to be quite a fruitful income stream for the organization and its other associates.

"Okay, ya done good, Louie. Sally, you make sure there'll be a little something extra this week. You and your mom have our gratitude. God Bless." Tony motioned towards the door when he finished talking and watched the two men walk out the door. It was only then did he pick up his phone and send an encrypted text message to Don Provolone. They would need to meet, and she would not be happy with what he had found out. This line of inquiry would have to be squashed.

No dumb bitch or Baltimore private dick will throw a wrench in this thing of ours, he thought as he waited for her reply.

CHAPTER SEVEN

Annetta Provolone steered her G-Class SUV down Earlington Ave towards the newly rebuilt Holy Name of Jesus Church, the afternoon sun in her rearview. A hundred yards to the west was the much smaller Holy Name that she grew up attending. The church abandoned it once the larger and more modern version was completed. The growth Mullica Hill experienced over the past ten years necessitated a larger place due to the influx of Catholics, and Annetta had no qualms with a large donation to make the new building possible. Her family had a long history of big donations to the church. The older, smaller building still represented painful memories to her, ones that were buried deep down and it would take more than new stained glass to get past. But it was a start.

She drove herself to this meeting, not reliant on a driver to get her where she needed to be, or to provide protection. After all, how many A&E Mafia specials have aired showing the grotesque after pictures where both the Don and his driver were whacked at the same time? If someone wanted her dead, it would happen. Some meat-head behind the wheel was most likely not going to alter the future. But more important to her, as the head of the crime family that bore her name, Annetta wanted to project independence and reliance on no one.

She pulled into the narrow driveway which separated the two buildings with the same name and headed around the backside of the smaller. She preferred the all white, smaller church she grew up in, despite large amounts of cash she donated for the newer building. The updated building was too large and gaudy for her taste. The entrance to the cemetery was in the back, and so were the Provolone family plots.

She felt at ease amongst her family here, making decisions with the feeling they were watching and knowing those that came before her had her back. They understood what she faced each day and would be so friggin proud of her, especially her grandfather, Julius.

It had been almost five years since she wrested control of the family back from the Baccalieri's, without so much as spilling a single drop of blood. Annetta was the first female head of the family, her family, recognized and fully supported by the Rigatones of Philly, and the first to rule with brains and not trigger-happy testosterone. She was respected because of it, and that respect was a badge she wore with honor.

When she had received Tony's somewhat frantic message, she signaled back that she'd be at the usual spot within half an hour. She made it in twenty and waited the last ten standing outside. Tony eventually pulled up in an equally impressive Escalade, and Annetta motioned for him to leave his goons inside. She walked over to the gate and waited for him. She watched as he stepped out of the back of his car and held up a hand. He stopped dead in his tracks, set his Ray-Ban Aviators atop his head, and held up his hands.

"You know, where's your fucking mask?" she said. *He fucking knows better*, she thought, and for emphasis pointed to her own, in case he didn't hear so good. This wasn't their first face to face during the goddamn pandemic. Annetta wasn't taking any chances. If she were whacked by a rival, she was good with that scenario, but dying from COVID-19 was not fucking okay.

Tony turned back to the Escalade's rear driver's side window and knocked. When it rolled down, someone handed him one of the blue generic disposable masks.

At least they had one, she thought. *Probably ripped it from that truckload highjacked on the Parkway last week.*

Annetta entered the code to the gate, another upgrade thanks to her generosity, and the two of them stepped inside the cemetery.

"Thank you for meeting me on such short notice," Tony said as the gate shut behind them. "I also have this for you."

Tony removed a white envelope, held together with scotch tape to prevent it from bursting at the seams, from his pants back pocket and handed it to Annetta.

Weight's about right, she thought. She opened her pocketbook and dropped the envelope in and asked, "What else you got for me?"

"Should we wait for G?" Tony said.

"He won't be joining us. I've got him up north meeting with our purple hatted friend." G was Tony's god-awful shorthand for Annetta's consigliere, Giovanni Bianchi. Tony had watched too many movies. Not everyone in the family had to have a gimmicky nickname. She mentally circled back to his question. The urgency of Tony's text had Annetta debating on whether to divert Giovanni from his meeting in Camden, but she knew that was an issue that needed to be resolved yesterday. Tony's problem, who knew? *I'm the Goddamn boss here, what's this guy's fucking problem,* she thought.

"Got it, but this actually involves them too," Tony replied.

"Let's walk," Annetta said. She turned her head in the direction she wanted to proceed, hiding the anguish that clearly showed beneath her mask. As of that morning, there was only one thing they were involved in with the Church, but that one was big. Gravy train big.

She led him down a row of small tombstones laid long before they built the original church. The old stones were dirty and in need of a good cleaning. They moved further down the pathway, towards the more recent burials. Large family plots and expensive marble dominated the back rows. During these meetings, Annetta would stop and conduct business at a different set of memorials each time. She assumed that if the Feds could bug hubcaps and lamp posts outside Gotti's social club, they sure as hell had mic'd her family's mausoleum and stones. It didn't take a surveillance specialist to realize that she spent a lot of time here with her underboss, consigliere, and capos. But in budget-tight times like this and cries for smaller government, the FBI could never find it financially beneficial to wire up every last monument in the cemetery. The odds were in her favor, and she'd take them along with the calmness this place brought her.

Tony recounted the scene from earlier at Fortunata's for Annetta. Nine out of ten times in this situation, Annetta would listen attentively, not interrupting, but instead wanting to understand all the facts before deciding the route best taken. But today was different. When Tony got to the part where Chief Hasty recommended the McGee girl reach out to the

Feds, she blew a gasket. So much for the cemetery's calming effect and serenity now.

"God fucking dammit, this would have never happened if that piece of shit giamoke Scott Ringle had listened to a goddamn mother fucking word I told him!" Annetta brought her fist down on the headstone before her and immediately crossed herself. "We wouldn't be having this conversation. Our chief, the one we bought and paid for, would have known how to handle it. Instead, we got this outsider in there, not willing to play ball."

"We really haven't approached him yet, I mean the election was last month. He had recently taken over the office a little less than two weeks ago," Tony said. She could see he was trying to calm the waters, but Annetta would have none of it.

Annetta had been playing the 'coulda woulda shoulda' game in her head since the election results for the Chief were called. She had paid for enough voter fraud and stuffed ballot boxes for six elections.

The odds favored Ringle to cruise to an easy third term. He was an Elk Township original, a third generation Police Chief, one that knew all the members of law enforcement across the tri-county area and had long associations with most other Chiefs going back years. He knew how to work them and grease whatever palm, road or project Annetta told him to. Because of these reasons, the Provolones had invested a lot of money and effort to secure the election in his favor. All that was needed in return was for Ringle to run a competent campaign. Instead, he failed miserably.

Despite many sit downs and warnings, Ringle failed to realize that the demographics had been changing over the past decade. Elk Township was no longer your father's agricultural center. Young families flocked to the suburbs. Farmers sold their land for high prices and housing developments soon replaced the soybeans, gladiolus, and tomato fields. This younger generation didn't mind adding an hour to their commute, if it meant quality life outside the office. These new voters were also not the same rubes that fell for colored hats and snappy racist slogans back in 2016.

Annetta had invested in the hope of continuing business as usual, but instead she got an unknown and an empty seat at the Triumvirate.

Her grandfather originally came up with the idea of The Triumvirate. Based on the old Roman idea of three men holding power, in particular the unofficial coalition of Julius Caesar, Pompey, and Crassus in 60 BC. Annetta's grandfather's updated version consisted of himself, the Elk Township chief of police at the time Chuck Ringle, and Bishop Johnathon McMichael from the Church's Camden Archdiocese. Each chair had their own things going on but would drop everything to work together when it was financially advantageous to all parties.

Upon taking the reins of power for the Provolone Family, one of Annetta's first goals was to recreate this alliance and its money-making abilities. Triumvirate 2.0, got off to a rocky start for her when the current Bishop wanted absolutely nothing to do with her or her overtures. She waited him out and was rewarded when he soon went down in flames over a sex scandal that sent him packing all the way back to the Vatican. Annetta had much better luck with his replacement Bishop Clinton O'Hanlan, who now donned the purple hat.

It didn't take much to persuade O'Hanlan to pull up a chair at the table. He saw the long-term investment strategy and profitability the opportunity represented. The 'joint ventures' Annetta had in mind would literally print money for all involved and did for a short period until now. With Ringle fucking up the election, her Triumvirate was now missing a wheel and Annetta wasn't sure how long or how much it would take to get the new guy over to the dark side. From initial indications and some research, it would not go well at all.

"So, we're still in a good spot. McGee hasn't done anything yet," Tony said. "As soon as that pig left my place, I reached out to our friend at the phone company. Now her number ain't with his carrier, but like us, he knows a guy."

"It's always good to know a guy," Annetta said.

"I mean, it's no freakin' wiretap, but we'll get word if she calls either of those Federal numbers. That guy went back and pulled up her call logs back to when she left the Chief's office and nada so far. We're good for now. That wreck might not have put the fear of God into her, but I think we still have time to get there."

"And this Rockfish?"

"The cop is sure that he got the message and should be on his way out of town. We can put a guy at the hotel and escort him across the bridge if he hasn't left already."

"No, don't waste our resources on it," Annetta said. "Let that cop handle it. If you know that Rockfish hasn't left town in a timely manner, or is poking around where he shouldn't, then drop the dime on him. Let that cop muddy up the waters and do his thing. The girl is our problem, right now. I don't need to deal with two unless it becomes absolutely necessary."

"We can grab her," Tony said. "Consider it done."

"No violence, for right now. Let the phone guy do his thing and monitor the situation. If it evolves into something, then I will readdress it. Look, she's not a cop. She's not going to run her own investigation into whatever allegations she's making. Plus, even if she did, safeguards are in place, O'Hanlan assures me. I got this, we got other pressing business to go over. Now tell me about the shipment of Sony 8K televisions that's scheduled to come into the port of Wilmington."

****

Rockfish laughed to himself when he saw Jawnie get out of her rental and walk towards the restaurant.

They always come around, he thought.

She joined him at an outside table, and before even looking at the menu; she began apologizing.

"Steve, I'm so sorry. I should have listened to you, but when you're raised a certain way and you think you know what the right thing to do is... but then you find out you couldn't be any more wrong if you tried."

"Umm, can you fill me in as to what you're actually talking about? Last we talked, you were going home to soak your bruises."

"Yes, I'll have an unsweet tea, please," Jawnie said to the waitress. Rockfish asked for a refill on his rum and coke before Jawnie continued.

"I went to see Chief Hasty. I know what you told me, but he's the only friggin' Chief of Police that I actually kinda know. Good guy, white hat, the whole nine yards here. That's what I was thinking."

"And?" Rockfish had a good idea where this story was going. Women tended to not listen to his advice until after the second time they crash and burned.

"He was absolutely no help. I told him what happened to us, the window being shot out, the car hitting us and pushing mine into the ditch. I don't think he believed a word I said. He probably believed it, but maybe it was more like he just humored me."

"He is the Chief," Rockfish said. He shifted his chair to the left so that the awning would block the sun that was beginning to fry his eyes. Of course, his sunglasses were back in the car. "He's an experienced law enforcement officer, I would think. It's his job to listen and decide a course of action. Tell me, did he at least make a patrolman take a report to make you happy? That's the bare minimum he should have done."

"He called in some officer and had me go over the entire story for a second time, and then I signed a form. The cop will enter it in the computer, and then forward the information to the Hammonton PD, since that is where the 'crime' allegedly happened."

"I mean, that's what you wanted, right? The reason you drove out to see him? It's not like he's going to assign a shit ton of officers to a special deputized task force to look into it." He watched her frown and glance down into her ice tea. He assumed she was second guessing meeting this morning. "Look, I'm not trying to pee on your parade, but I've got a lot more experience with cops and how they operate. Good and bad."

"Would you like to hear some more?"

"Not particularly," Rockfish replied. *I'm not sure what she's going for,* he thought. Maybe she just needs a little sympathy? *I could pat her on the head, pull out a cherry lifesaver and say everything was going to be okay.*

"You never gave me the license plate of the Jeep," Jawnie said. "Not really much an investigator can do without that, and I kind of looked like a fool when they asked if I had it."

"I can give it to you now. Back when we were walking down the road to get a cell signal, I didn't think there was really a need." Rockfish thought it best not to let on that he already had the plate run and knew that it was most likely one of Anthony Bologna's lackeys at the wheel.

"I don't want it, Hasty does. He asked if you could swing by his office when you can and give him the number so he can add it to the official report. I think he also wants to talk to you about what, and I quote, 'What you are doing running around his township, bothering his citizens, all without giving his office the professional courtesy of a heads up.'"

"And what did you tell him I was doing?"

"I played the dumb girl role, the one time I took your advice during the time we talked. I told him I never asked, and you didn't tell me. You came into my shop with a laptop problem, we got to talking, yada yada yada, you offered to help go through those boxes with me."

"Anything else I should know about?" Rockfish said. He hated to think it, but Hasty was right. In any other circumstance, Rockfish would have paid the chief a visit and somewhat filled him in on what he was hired for. He didn't extend the courtesy this time as researching a crime that may or may not have happened a very long time ago didn't rise to that level. Rockfish didn't need to chat with the Chief, considering he hadn't originally planned on staying that long. He had planned on spending a few days sitting in the library or talking to a few people and then be back home.

Jawnie kept talking, and Rockfish listened. He stopped counting the times in his head that he would have advised her differently as her exchange with Hasty wrapped up. But it wasn't until she mentioned the orphanage and the possible PPP fraud loans that he actively jumped back in the conversation.

"...Hasty had his secretary look up the numbers for the FBI and IRS over the bridge in Philly. He said everything to do with the Coronavirus and stimulus funds is out of his jurisdiction. Federal money, federal investigations he said."

A light bulb went on above Rockfish's head and he did a spit-take. "Wait, his secretary, what was her name again? Didn't you say she had been there a long time?"

"Betty Lou Sommers. She's had the job for most of my lifetime. And do you need another napkin?"

"I'm good, but just what I thought," Rockfish exclaimed. "One of Hasty's boys, a real clown, pulled me over yesterday in that area of town called The Lawns. His name tag read 'Sommers'. Fucktard threatened me and said there would be severe consequences if I didn't leave town. Makes a lot more sense now. Remember what I said before about her knowing everything that goes in and out of Hasty's office? She could pass any interesting tidbits on to her son, nephew, cousin, whatever, and God only knows who he's leaking to."

"Wait, he told you to leave town? Like in the movies?"

"Yeah. But I'm not doing anything illegal," Rockfish said. "Guy thinks he can scare me, but I'm here to do a job and the law is on my side. I'm going to need to be more careful, that's all."

"I'm sorry, Steve, but that's a lot to digest there."

"There always is, but look, based on what you told me, I don't think Hasty is some mastermind out trying to stop you from finding the truth about what happened to your great grandfather. He's not behind that Jeep that ran us down. But I will bet you dollars to donuts that this clown, Sommers, and probably others still working in that building might be. As for 1-800-CALL-FBI, he's probably right. And even if he's not, being newly elected of an inbred back-assward department, he's got more pressing local shit on his plate than he can handle at the moment."

Jawnie sat there and picked at her salad. Rockfish was less and less sure he was actually getting through to her than he was fifteen minutes ago. But when she did finally speak up again, he could tell she had been listening. And thinking. Kudos to both the teacher and student.

"What were you doing out in The Lawns? A little surveillance of your own on Mary's old farm? Not much to see, I would guess. Most of it could be a housing development the way things are growing here."

"Actually, that was next on the to-do-list, when Sommers pulled me over. I was following a lead from our notes. You remember the constant mention of Hickory in the journals?"

"Yeah, you thought it might be some sort of code name for an informant."

"Bingo. Old Hickory was President Andrew Jackson's nickname. Tisha Jackson was Edward's source into all the bad things going on in The Lawns. I found her grandson, and we shot the shit over some equally shitty Chinese food."

Rockfish gave Jawnie a condensed version of his meeting with Rodney and his gifting to the cause, Tisha's own diary.

"Now, we've got Tisha's written words, and I know I told you the other day that those other journals would be considered hearsay and wouldn't do us a bit of good trying to prove whatever hypothesis we came up with."

"But this is a second source. It collaborates some of what we already have," Jawnie said.

"Yes, it does. You've had to have watched Law & Order, right?"

"I've binged a time or two on a rainy weekend, yes."

"McCoy always said, that if you get enough circumstantial evidence, without forensic evidence or even a body, you can sway a jury into a guilty verdict. Now we're not headed to court, but I think in clearing up exactly what happened to Edward, Mary, and those pregnant women, we're on more solid ground now. For both you and my client."

Jawnie smiled. Rockfish assumed she was more at ease than when she first sat down. He neglected to tell her about the long ago well and its probable role in Edward's resting place. There would be a time, but from Rockfish's limited interactions with Jawnie, sometimes she didn't seem very good at holding it all together and he didn't want this to weigh heavily on her. There would be a better time, and he'd explain it.

Rockfish felt a little calmer too, keeping this detail to himself. He told her that as soon as they finished eating; she needed to take the diary and lock it up in a safe place. The journals too. He didn't trust the hotel room and his car was most times parked out of the line of sight from his room.

"Dad had an old gun safe in the basement that I never found a use for in the past," Jawnie said.

"Great. I want you to know that, based on my interactions with Sommers, I don't plan on going anywhere. If Hasty wants me to come for a fireside chat, I don't see the harm in stopping by and getting a better read on him and this Betty Lou. With any luck, I can pass Sommers in the hall and let him casually know I called his bluff. Which I absolutely will when I chat with his boss."

"And I wanted to let you know, I don't plan on calling the FBI or the IRS with absolutely no proof of any kind of federal loan scam," Jawnie said. "They'd laugh me out of the building worse than Hasty did. I'll go back to the shop, hunker down, and see what else I can uncover. If I can put something together that is actionable, then I'll reach out to them."

"Sounds like a plan," Rockfish said. "You keep working the present and me the past. I would bet that it's only a matter of time before we run smack dab into each other. Same teams, most of the players' last names are still the same and the money is just as dirty."

Davenport's gonna give me an executive producer credit. Oh yeah, he thought to himself. Hollywood money would get him out of his trailer and into a place closer to the water.

"I'll call you or stop by the shop, depending on how my meeting with Hasty goes. I have another angle I'd like to try. We've not looked at the Church angle heavily yet. I pulled up the Camden Archdiocese website and under 'Staff' they have a historian listed. I'd like to talk to that guy, see what he has regarding the makeup of the Archdiocese during the war, the orphanage and the group of nuns that ran it." Rockfish stopped and ran his hand through his hair.

"You seem almost as concerned as I do," Jawnie said. "That means you're pretty damned concerned!"

"It'll be okay, you just have to trust me," Rockfish said. "Now, whatever you dig up, no matter how damning on the loan fraud front, keep it under wraps until I talk to this guy. If you go to the Feds, no matter what they say to you, that will leak back here faster than shit through a goose and no one is going to want to talk to me. That affects my wallet."

"I promise, this time."

They ended the meal on a good note, and Rockfish kept Lana in the parking lot as Jawnie's rental turned left onto Delsea Drive and disappeared into the distance. He wanted to make sure he didn't spot a tail on her, and when he was satisfied she was traveling back to Westville alone; he pulled over and searched his GPS for the Elk Township Police Department.

****

Rockfish pulled into the municipal building's parking lot, shortly after 4pm. He didn't call ahead and now second guessed himself. Calling would have ruined the element of surprise and an advantage in the first minute of the conversation, but then again, if Hasty was out on a call and not in his office, this was a wasted trip. He turned off the engine and hoped for the best.

The police shared the building with all the other township services, but the door to the front of the building had a big sign over it that said 'POLICE' with an arrow to the left. *French doors, wood,* he thought. *I've seen nicer sets on those new doublewides they've installed at the park.*

He chirped the key fob and followed the sidewalk around the left side of the building where he found the door. Rockfish put on his mask and reached for the doorknob.

When he walked into the foyer, nothing emphasized small town policing than a small entranceway with a solitary desk off to his left. There was no front desk where a cop sat behind bulletproof glass ready to assist or answer questions from John Q. Public.

The large women sat to his left and look annoyed to say the least.

"Can I help you?"

Betty Lou Sommers, in the flesh, he presumed. The cigarette in her hand and the forty-four-ounce Big Gulp on the desk blotter were also dead giveaways. Rockfish noticed the confederate bandana, most likely Betty Lou's attempt at protecting the public from COVID-19, lay on the far side of her desk, most likely out of reach.

That thing ain't protecting no one, he thought, and took a step back to maximize the distance between them.

"Afternoon Betty Lou," Rockfish said, despite there not being a nameplate anywhere on the desk. "I heard through the grapevine that Chief Hasty wanted to talk to me and figured I'd turn myself in, before, you know, he sends that boy of yours again out to harass me."

Rockfish chuckled when he saw the grimace on Betty Lou's face. Her breathing intensified, and she took a long drag on the cigarette before putting it out.

"Excuse me, Sir, but you can't walk in here and demand to see the Chief. He is a busy man. I would recommend calling ahead next time. He's in a very important meeting down the hall in our conference room. He is with the Mayor and specifically told me he was not to be disturbed."

"Thank you, ma'am, I will remember to do that." Rockfish said. "You mind if I wait?"

"Ain't no law against it. You can sit over there for all I care." Betty Lou pointed to a couple of folding chairs along the wall on the other side of the room.

"That's mighty hospitable of you," he said and pulled up a seat. He'd give it half an hour max if the Chief didn't come out of his meeting before Rockfish would head back to the hotel. With the late hour, he hoped that Betty Lou would head home sooner rather than later, and Rockfish didn't have to worry about her snooping on his conversation.

It wasn't ten minutes later Chief Hasty stuck his head out of the door from behind Betty Lou.

"Hey Betty, can you find out—"

"Chief Hasty," Rockfish said as he jumped up from the chair and interrupted the man's line of thought. "Steve Rockfish. I heard you wanted to see me, not to mention I've got some information for you." The first thing Rockfish noticed was Hasty's lack of height and build. *Damn, he could pass for an older Tobey Maguire,* Rockfish thought. *I guess with large capacity clips and technology, you don't have to be built like The Rock.*

Chief Hasty looked stunned, and he looked back and forth from Betty Lou, to Rockfish, and back.

"Yes, yes, I do, Mr. Rockfish. If, ah, you'll follow me into my office, I can move a few things on my calendar and make some time for you now."

"Thank you very much, Chief Hasty," Rockfish said. "Now I don't want to get all up in your personnel business, but you might want to give some thought to sending Betty Lou here home to rest up for tomorrow. Apparently, she thought you were down the hall in some sort of important conference room type meeting with the Mayor."

Confusion filled Hasty's face, and he glanced again, back and forth, between Rockfish and Betty Lou. Rockfish didn't wait for the Chief to say anything further and instead walked around Betty Lou's desk straight through the doorway. He made sure to stop, turn around and give Betty Lou a wink before closing the door behind him. *Love you too, boo,* he thought.

"Well, Mr. Rockfish, take a seat and let's handle some official police business before we cover other ground. Ms. McGee mentioned you had the license plate number of the car that ran her off the road the other day in Hammonton?"

"Don't forget the back window getting shot out too, Chief. I've got the number right here. Jersey plates, 613-WIH." The office was smaller than he thought it would be. The walls were bare, excluding the Rutgers University diploma hung just above Hasty's head. *No personal pictures either,* he thought. Guy's either the slowest unpacker ever or doesn't want everyone knowing his business.

"Good, good, good. I'll get this information to Patrolman Beckley right after we finish here, and he can close out his report from our end. The ball will be in Hammonton's court, if they want to pursue it further."

"Of course," Rockfish said. "Hammonton, the hometown of Kellyanne Conway. They must be so proud."

Hasty laughed aloud at the comment, and Rockfish knew he had found some common ground, no matter how small. "Anyway, I can save you and the other department some time. I found out the plate is registered to Bologna Construction." He dropped the bomb with the anticipation that he would spot some sort of recognition in Hasty's face, but the man never even blinked.

"I don't know no Conway or Bologna, unless you're talking Tim and Oscar Mayer." Hasty said. "But I'll also pass that bit of information along to the proper authorities." He stood up and leaned over the desk before continuing. "Now I'd like you to tell me exactly what you're doing in my township, nosing around asking questions that appear to have led to you and Jawnie McGee being shot at and run off the road. I mean, I've got a pretty good clue, my own set of informants and conclusions I've drawn, but I'd like to see how closely your story matches up with mine. After all, you're sitting in my office."

Rockfish gave Hasty the Davenport party line, without mentioning his client by name.

"So, I'm trying to dig up as much information as I can for this guy, so he can make the best damn television podcast thingy he can. It was dumb luck that one folk I spoke with referred me to Jawnie and I could set aside some time, off the client's clock of course, to help her go through those boxes you were damned sure nice enough to return to the McGee family. Put a professional eye on the contents, so to speak, and kind of help her determine exactly what her next course of action could be. I don't think she really has a plan, it's more of just some closure for her family because the official report really doesn't sit well with any of them. And I gotta say..." Rockfish leaned forward himself and picked up a pencil off Hasty's desk. "... I read through all of it and it doesn't make this department look good at all." Rockfish put the pencil behind his ear and he could see the veins stand out on the back of Hasty's hands.

They stared at each other for a minute before Hasty retreated to his chair. *Guess he's content with that,* Rockfish thought.

"That was three generations ago. Those folks are long gone. This is my department now and that's the sole reason I returned those boxes. Doesn't do a bit of good for this department to rehash any of that. I've got limited resources and drugs are ravaging this township. Seems like a simple choice on where to allocate those very limited resources. Speaking of, that's a taxpayer funded pencil. I'd appreciate it if you returned it."

Rockfish busted out laughing and pulled the pencil from his ear. "Wouldn't dream of stealing from your constituents. And, Chief, you shouldn't have a thing to worry about with her research or mine. I think that pretty much wraps us up here..." He stood up to emphasize the point and held out his hand, knowing full well he had hand sanitizer in the car.

"One last thing, Mr. Rockfish," Chief Hasty said. "Are you aware of the advice I gave Jawnie regarding her to run her other issue past the FBI, IRS, or the US Attorney's office?"

Rockfish had expected this one and mentally adjusted the dunce cap he wore to the party for this occasion.

"Chief Hasty, I don't know what you're talking about. Hand to God. The last time I spoke to Jawnie she mentioned you needed the plate number and wanted to speak to me. So here I am."

"Really?"

"Absolutely. But if you have another minute, I have one other item to discuss and this one shouldn't involve the Feds at all," Rockfish said and sat back down in his chair.

He rehashed the encounter and subsequent veiled threat to plant evidence by Officer Sommers. By the time Rockfish finished the story, the look on Hasty's face said he wasn't at all surprised.

"I'll pull his log records and verify the traffic stop happened."

"And I'm sure you'll find no record of it, but if I'm suddenly in your jail on remand because thirty-seven kilos of coke were found strapped to the roof of my car, do me a favor and please remember this conversation. I believe that Officer Sommer is working for a higher power, so to speak."

Chief Hasty said nothing and only nodded his head. Rockfish took it as his cue to leave and noticed on the way out that Betty Lou's desk was vacant. Perhaps she had run straight home to heat up some Dinty Moore for her boy and fill him in about the Chief's last appointment of the day.

What Rockfish could do is reach out to Davenport. It had been a few days since he checked in with his client, and he was damn sure Angel would be happy with what had been uncovered.

****

Rockfish received a text from Jawnie that evening. He couldn't tell if she wanted to see if he survived the meeting with Hasty, or was she fishing to find out exactly how it went. Either way, he let her know all was well and that he would stop by the shop in the morning and fill her in.

The following day, Rockfish swung by a spot down the street from Jawnie's shop to pick up some breakfast. For him, it was an extra-large coffee, black, and the Shoehorn Diner's own version of a McGriddle. He ordered two and asked about their vegan breakfast options. The woman behind the counter looked at him as if he was from Mars. He settled on three Boston cream donuts. It was the thought that counted.

The sign on the door said 'open' so he didn't knock. The bell above the door signaled his arrival, but Jawnie never looked up from the laptop she was hunched over. Rockfish couldn't help but notice that the whiteboard behind her desk resembled the chalkboard from the movie *A Beautiful Mind*. There was a ton of text, some circles inside squares, other shapes just hanging out on their own. Arrows connected some of the shapes, others ended in question marks. She had been busy, and Rockfish's only thought was to hand her the coffee. Jawnie probably needed it more than he did. His cup was probably a lot fresher than whatever gourmet mess was in the pot.

"Here, I picked this up in case you were out or too busy to have gotten up to a fresh pot. I'm going to go with the busy answer. It looks like you might have fallen down an information rabbit hole?"

"Have you ever seen the movie Tremors?" Jawnie asked. "More like the holes dug by those creatures."

Rockfish had no idea what she was talking about, but went with it, anyway. "That big, huh? Pick your head up and let me go first. I guarantee that what I have to say is a lot shorter."

He covered his meeting with Hasty and expressed his thoughts on whether Betty Lou had run to tell her son that Rockfish was meeting the Chief, or if she was outside blowing off the aggravation he had brought, in the form of a king-sized Milky Way. Either way, Rockfish expected to run into Officer Sommers in the not too distant future, but he hoped his talk with Hasty would prevent the world's biggest set-up from happening.

When it was Jawnie's turn, Rockfish pulled up a chair and started eating. He had a feeling he would need a lot of energy and brain power to keep up with her as she explained her findings.

Jawnie started off with a history lesson on the Coronavirus Aid, Relief, and Economic Security (CARES) Act and how as part of the Paycheck Protection Program (PPP), the federal government provided over half a trillion dollars in financial support to various large financial institutions. These banks would then make low-interest loans to companies and nonprofit organizations in response to the economic devastation caused by the coronavirus pandemic.

"Okay, I'm following so far," Rockfish said. Inside, he wondered why the hell he hadn't heard of this before and applied himself. Rockfish Investigations was hard hit because of COVID-19 just like the next mom and pop shop. "And I'm guessing with any Federal Government hand out, the bad guys were right alongside the good with their hands out."

"Exactly, a wave of fraudulent activity followed as the loans were distributed as quickly as possible and with a lot less scrutiny than other traditional business loans. You can thank our fearless leader for that one. Most crooks lied about having legitimate businesses or claimed that they needed PPP money for things like making payroll or expenditures. A simple Internet search shows how prevalent and far-reaching this crime is."

"And you're able to find out, online, about those people or companies that applied for the funds?" Rockfish said.

"Yes. There are publicly accessible databases set up for all companies that received between $150,000 - $10 million. The information is all there. Unlike the CDC and other health related-sites that no longer track and publicly provide guidance and solid numbers on COVID-19 infections and death. It appears, to me at least that this administration is more interested in hiding the number of infections and death from the public than who got what amount from this program. It's all out there for anyone to look up." Jawnie stopped, picked up her coffee, and sipped before continuing.

"I really don't think they were smart enough to think anyone would care where the money went. But no one bothered to tell the investigative journalists, fake news or not, who uncovered PPP loans to the President's family, friends and shady business associates. All I had to do was read what these reporters wrote and follow their playbook."

"Is it too late for me to get some of this free government cheese? Lord knows I'm hurting."

"Sorry, but submissions closed a few months ago," Jawnie informed him.

"Story of my life," Rockfish answered. "What about our players?"

"Like I said, the bad guys lined up alongside the truly affected. Any organized crime group with half a brain should have been salivating over this. And for our purposes, I'm including the Catholic Church in that group. I'm good with the Stereotyping. Okay, so stay with me here. Here's how the Church and Provolones abused the system."

"Explain it to me like I'm five, please," Rockfish said, knowing damn well Jawnie was about to go full Rainman on him.

"If these yahoos could figure out how to abuse the system, you'll understand just fine." Jawnie said and painted a picture of how legitimate PPP loans mixed with the fraudulent.

"The first thing I found when you searched these databases is that you can search the applications by organization, lender, zip code and business type. I started with the orphanage, because we know for a fact they boarded it up, and it no longer serves any purpose. That one's straight up fraud. The information that came back for New Hope Catholic

Charities Orphanage showed a loan approval for $350,000 - $1 million, the database shows ranges not exact amounts, and the number of people employed by the orphanage that would benefit is forty-three."

"Forty-three people to do what, finish the demolition on the building?"

"Exactly, but here's where it gets interesting. The financial institution that loaned the money was Farmer's National Bank. They handled three of the Archdiocese's applications. The church submitted another four and those were processed by a completely different bank, Chemical Bank, out of New York."

Jawnie further explained how she was able to find that all the Archdiocese's subsidiaries that received PPP loans through Chemical Bank had actual websites, informational news stories written about them, and for all intents and purposes were straight up legitimate. The three that received loans through Farmer's National? There was not much listed for those companies, and any records she could come across were at least fifty years old.

"Now, here's where it gets really interesting," Jawnie said. "I've got three potentially fraudulent loans with this one bank. I went back in and searched the database by lender this time. I found an additional four PPP loans processed and distributed through Farmer's National for companies that exist on paper, but not anywhere else."

"Oh, teacher, pick me," Rockfish said and raised his hand. "Provolone front companies?"

"Bingo," she said, and smacked the table. "Like I said before, with the pandemic beginning to rage and the cry for government assistance growing louder every day, the Federal Government did what they do best and just threw money at the problem. Add in no real oversight and a mandate in order to get these funds distributed ASAP, and criminals were licking their chops, and not only here but all across the country."

"So, Provolone and the Archdiocese must have been like, 'we're getting the band back together'," Rockfish said.

"Or maybe they never split up. That alliance has always been there, and it's easy to flip the switch when a financial opportunity presents itself."

"Like COVID-19. Good Catholics, staying home on Sundays, practicing social distancing, and that means those collection plates aren't being filled like they had in the past," Rockfish said. "You can either mope about it, pressure your flock to attend in person and risk death or reach out to an old buddy who you've had a good working relationship with through the years. They fill you in on the current grift they're working, and all your cash flow problems go away." Jawnie rubbed her hands together, mimicking a good washing.

"And then some. Times one thousand," Rockfish said. "Have you been able to come up with the total take from Farmer's National?" Rockfish asked.

"All I have are ranges, but it looks like the Archdiocese took in anywhere from $450,000 to $1.05 million. The Provolones, experts in gaming the system so to speak, were more daring. Their take ranges from $1 million to as high as $2.7 million. Here's the kicker, though. Loan recipients can apply for loan forgiveness, again through the bank that provided the loan, if they meet certain criteria. Rigging these numbers on a loan forgiveness application shouldn't be too hard, especially if the bank working with you is on the scam."

"Sounds like you're ready to include this bank as a willing participant. Do you think the Provolones have someone on the inside at Farmer's National?" Rockfish said.

"I'm betting more than one and at least one in management. Loan officers, underwriters and probably someone in the C-Suite to keep everything tucked away from any regulators," Jawnie said. "I think this is too big to be slipping a teller an envelope each week and hoping for the best. Especially if they are running the forgiveness angle and never legally obligated to pay back one red cent. Not to mention paying taxes on any of it."

"Not like they were planning on it anyway," Rockfish said with a shake of his head. If Jawnie was even partially right, she had done one hell of a job in practically no time.

"Yeah, but this way, it's all legitimate and no one is the wiser to go back and check. Christ, from what I read, the IRS is asking citizens to report any fraud they are aware of. It doesn't appear that they are actively looking for it on their own."

"I gotta tell ya, Jawnie, this is amazing work. Just absolutely amazing. If you don't mind, I'm going to take some pictures of your white board here in case it gets erased. Mr. Murphy tends to follow me around from time to time. And please save your work to that cloud, a thumb drive and half a dozen floppies so we can always get to a copy."

Jawnie busted up laughing. "I'm a nerd, remember, grandpa? It's on my network here and saved to a physical device. I secured all the files with a password. Guess wrong twice and a worm launches. Copy the file and try to open it on your home PC, you're fucked. In a nutshell, I don't tell you how to PI, you don't tell me how to geek."

Rockfish could only imagine the giant Cheshire Cat grin under her mask. "Two wrong guesses? Are you an expert typer and rememberer of passwords?"

"I'm very careful," Jawnie said.

"Okay, we'll each revel in our own expertise, I'll leave the digital realm to you," Rockfish replied. He had no idea what she meant by worm, but he wouldn't ask another stupid question. He would look it up later.

"What's our next step," Jawnie asked.

"Tell you what, I'm still working for Davenport and I had planned to drive up to Camden to interview this Archdiocese Historian priest guy. I need background, names, and anything else I can get out of him. Try to find a nugget and research the hell out of it like you did here. I want to ask him about the orphanage, but maybe throw out the names of those two other scam subsidiaries you found and see if he squirms. But, I want to do this before you call the Feds and bring this entire house of cards tumbling down. Gimme a day or two more."

"Kirkoff Holdings and Farnsworth Equities, Inc. But we'll need an in, this historian won't reserve time for us if we just knock on the door," Jawnie said and raised her eyebrows.

"You're in, huh?" Rockfish said. "Let's start with you pretending to be my secretary and make us an appointment. When we show up, I can be Angel Davenport, big time Hollywood producer and you my head writer. This way, if the guy Googles the name, we're covered."

"Unless he clicks on the image tab," Jawnie said.

"Always with the negative waves, McGee. Our story can be that we're doing a documentary on how the Catholic Church assisted communities hard hit during World War II. You know, dealing with death, rations, and some other shit. You're smart. Come up with an elevator pitch that will get us on his calendar and from there we'll come up with a script by the time we're traipsing through the door."

CHAPTER EIGHT

Rockfish drove past the Camden Archdiocese building before looking for street parking. Being it was a weekday afternoon; free spots were going to be scarce. What wasn't hard to come by, he noticed, was money. The Archdiocese's campus sprawled across an entire city block, each building covered in marble, and a large topiary garden with walking paths filled the inner shell.

Guessing they need this latest scam to keep up appearances, he thought.

The city of Camden, on the other hand, was a shithole. Open-air drug markets on each corner flaunted the law, abandoned buildings outnumbered occupied ones, and after choosing your finest vial of crack, one could have their pick of Pepper Jack's finest hoes to share it with.

A tiny Taj Mahal, smack dab in the middle of Sodom and Gomorrah, was how Jawnie put it. Rockfish could tell by how she slouched down in her seat as Lana passed each corner that it had been a while since Jawnie had visited the big city, or the projects.

"I'm going to take another lap around to see if I can find a spot closer," Rockfish said. He was looking for the false sense of security a parking garage would provide, but would end up settling for a space on the street. "I want to be able to hear the alarm from inside if it goes off."

For today's adventure, Rockfish would play the part of Angel Davenport and Jawnie went with Constance McGee, up-and-coming writer recently brought on board to helm the production company's new project. And surprise, she had a matching business card. The ink may or may not have dried.

The first thing Rockfish noticed as the door shut behind them was the long hallway covered with photographs. The hallway itself was grandiose with a high, chapel like ceiling and marble floors. Their shoes click-clacked on the floor and announced their arrival before they reached the small receptionist's desk.

"Good morning, Mr. Davenport and Ms. McGee to see Father Renfield," Jawnie said as she confidently approached the receptionist.

"That would be me, Abe Renfield," the man behind the desk said.

Rockfish noticed that the man wasn't in the best of moods as he struggled to grab a mask from the desk drawer. *Man, with that giant bald spot, put a robe on this guy with a rope drawstring and he could pass for Friar Tuck,* he thought.

"I'm sorry about that, I was working on this spreadsheet and didn't hear you enter. No offense, I know it's the law, but sometimes God understands."

"None taken, Father," Rockfish said.

"With this darn pandemic I've got too many people out indefinitely, some working from home, and I'm covering the desk while I also try to get my actual job done."

"It's like that everywhere," Jawnie said. "You should see our studio out in LA, it's like a ghost town. Empty lots, stages half built and abandoned, but I'm guessing that most of your employees are high risk due to Sunday services?"

The State of New Jersey had recently lost a lawsuit brought by a religious organization allowing worship services be excluded from the governor's shut down order. Rockfish couldn't see how going to Church and having super spreaders sit on either side of you made any sense. Unless it was all about the grift. News flash, it was all about the grift.

"No, no, no," Renfield said. "No one is catching the virus during sermon. God is protecting all, if anything, that space is considered a safe zone by all in attendance."

Rockfish and Jawnie looked at each other and their raised eyebrows. While the sign above the door read 'Camden Archdiocese' it might as well read 'Fantasy Island'.

Renfield coughed and got both their attention back. "If you'll follow me, there is a small conference room on the other side of this wall we can use. Just let me put a sign on the door and activate the video doorbell. If anyone rings to come in, I'll have to jump out and handle it. I hope you don't mind."

"Of course not," Jawnie replied.

The three of them walked down a short hallway and Renfield ushered them into the first door on the left. A large picture of the current Pope hung on the far wall, and those prior to him lined either side. Renfield sat at the head of the small rectangle table, with Rockfish and Jawnie on either side. Renfield put his cell phone down on the table and folded his hands. Rockfish's first impression was that the man had now entered listening mode. It might be tougher than he thought to pull the information needed.

Jawnie went into the pitch for the fake show that the two of them had drummed up on the drive over. It impressed Rockfish that she could tap dance and improvise when necessary and she had an informative, well thought out answer for Renfield's few questions. Jawnie wrapped up with how successful a potential network thought the show would be and how this particular episode would cast the Archdiocese in a very positive light. One, that despite the current climate the country found itself in, people would feel the need to reach deep into their pockets and possibly give.

"We could, of course, put your website, phone number, Venmo, whatever, on the screen at the end, prior to the credits rolling," Jawnie said.

Renfield sat there, a blank expression on his face, when she finished. Rockfish thought she had left it open-ended enough that the priest would have jumped in with additional questions, but apparently, he needed some more coaxing. That or direct interaction.

"Can you tell us about New Hope Catholic Charities Orphanage and the group of nuns that ran it," Rockfish asked. "From our research it was very successful despite it being off the beaten path in the woods. Like Ms. McGee said, if everything works out, we'd like to focus a twenty-minute segment on that endeavor, for one of our early episodes in the series."

Renfield let out a sigh and shook his head. "What I can tell you, Mr. Davenport is that the church chose the location not because of the remoteness, but due to its closeness to the Sisters of the Holy Name convent in Egg Harbor City," Renfield said. "The area was convenient to the staff in their comings and goings and that was very important to the Bishop at the time, Johnathon McMichael."

"A short commute. Who wouldn't love that," Jawnie said, playing up the part a bit too much for Rockfish's liking. "OMG, you should see the 405 in LA during rush hour. An absolute parking lot for hours at a time. Sometimes in the morning, I literally eat a bowl of cereal while I drive."

"Yes, indeed," Renfield said, brushing aside the comment. "The entire endeavor was Bishop McMichael's idea. He found a very wealthy benefactor that donated the land, in addition to the cost of building materials to the Archdiocese. The project was something coming out of the Great Depression, that the church wouldn't have been able to do on its own, but with this gift could do God's work for the community and those needy children."

"Wow," Rockfish exclaimed. "I could use Bishop McMichael's fundraising skills on this project. That benefactor, is he still around, that would be a great interview. Maybe Bishop McMichael could be there as well."

"I'm afraid that is quite impossible," Renfield said. "Bishop McMichael passed away on the grounds of the Orphanage, in late 1945, not long after the opening. The exact date escapes me at the moment. He passed on to the Lord's house, helping those in need, doing what he loved most in life. A few of the Sisters found his body in a patch of uncleared land that was going to be developed into a larger medical wing for the Orphanage. The Bishop was walking the grounds for a reason only he knew when it happened. The doctor said it was a heart attack, but that didn't stop the people outside the church from spreading rumors."

"What kind of rumors?" Jawnie asked. "Why would people make up something about such a great man?"

"I couldn't agree more. It appears that those people in the area, still suffered economically, whether it was from the Great Depression or the severe rationing that came with the war. The Church's flourishing was the object of much jealousy and scorn. In order to hurt the Church, they spun tails of a supernatural battle between the ludicrous Jersey Devil and the Bishop." The volume of his voice increased as he went on. "This fight was over the Orphanage being built on the Devil's land and by losing, the

Bishop lost his soul-and those of the children inside-to the Devil. Utter nonsense, but to this date, I am told the counselors at the YMCA boys camp in Basto still tell this story to scare campers on their first night. It is a place that should be honored, but its memory has been lost with time and replaced with one of a land possessed and devil worship." The room grew eerily quiet when he finished.

"Horrible, absolutely horrible," Rockfish said. He needed to get the conversation rolling again, but in all honesty didn't think the folklore was probably too far from the truth. Replace the Jersey Devil with a pissed-off Godfather, who, over the killing of a cop might have been as simple as tying up a loose end and covering his own ass. The Bishop simply knew too much, should the walls crumble down.

"If you don't mind, Father, back to this donor," Jawnie said. "I mean, if it wasn't for him or her, the amazing work the nuns did to care for and find homes for these children wouldn't have happened."

To Rockfish, her voice even sounded sincere. *Way to go girl,* he thought.

"Not a chance in hell, excuse my French," Renfield replied.

"You're excused, Father," Rockfish said. "But if you could provide us with the name of this generous benefactor, no doubt he has passed on by this time, we would at least like to honor him and maybe secure an interview with any of his surviving relatives."

"I'm sorry, but that will be impossible." Renfield stiffened his back against the chair. "Our policy is not to release the names of donors, no matter the amount of tithing. It's something that just cannot be done."

Rockfish looked at Jawnie and did a small shrug of his shoulders. Neither one would give up so easily, and he pressed on.

"I understand, but this was a rather large sum of money, I gathered from what you said. This was in the middle of the Great Depression, and the local population couldn't afford to eat and were barely surviving. There couldn't have been that many parishioners that well off. I would think it would become obvious who the donor was with a little research, and we've got a large group dedicated to such tasks. Do you see where I'm going, Father?"

Renfield sat stone-faced.

"At this point, I'll come out and ask you," Rockfish said. "Father, do you think the donation could have come from ill-gotten gains? Less than honest work? The result of criminal activity?"

"I'm not sure what you mean," Renfield said, stone firmly still in place.

"Less than honest occupations. Bootleggers, gambling, extortion? La Cosa Nostra?"

"Mr. Davenport, I resent those allegations, and I am not sure how much more time I can give you today." Renfield picked his papers up off the desk. "I cannot make it clear enough that the land and building materials were donated and the Church did what it could to verify the sources. When Bishop McMichael said the money came from answered prayers, there was no reason not to believe him. God provides for those who worship him. Those funds resulted from the excellent work done by this Archdiocese. I cannot state more firmly that there is no truth to any of the salacious things you said, and I think we should begin to wrap this meeting up."

Renfield rose from his chair and Rockfish needed him to sit back down, at least for a few more questions.

"I'm sorry, Father, I truly am," Rockfish said. "If you can see my point of view, it would make sense. I need to vet that question with you, because there's a good chance a viewer of the show, someone sitting out there in middle America, but realistically it would be more like a couple hundred thousand viewers, could easily draw that same conclusion. Materials were scarce at that time. I don't know, I'm not a historian. That's your job and exactly why I asked, so we could answer the question and leave no doubt in the viewer's mind. Today, when people have questions that aren't answered in the show, they tend to migrate to social media and spread their own interpretation of the tale. We are trying to stop the spreading of salacious rumors, as you mentioned before."

"Apology accepted, Mr. Davenport," Renfield said. "But I do really have to be going. If there isn't anything else you need—"

"Father Renfield, what can you tell us about the Archdiocese's current relationship to Kirkoff Holdings LLC and Farnsworth Stratagem, Inc?"

Renfield's usual post-question stone face returned, but this time, it took on the color of dark crimson. Rockfish knew the tea kettle was about to blow and their time was over. While the man would not answer the question, they got a non-answer they could work with.

"I think that's all the time I have. I appreciate meeting you both, and I wish you all the best with this television production of yours. God bless, and let yourselves out." And with that, Renfield disappeared through a separate doorway, leaving Rockfish and Jawnie to stare at each other before exiting the room.

"Smooth move, Ex-lax," Rockfish whispered under his breath once they closed the conference room door. Jawnie didn't reply, but stared daggers back in his direction.

"As for the mafia connection," Rockfish said. "He didn't deny it. Side stepped the fuck out of it, but never denied accepting money from the mob. We could have dug a little further, but you tried that hail Mary and it backfired. Spectacularly, if I must say."

Jawnie stayed silent on the matter and lengthened her stride. She remained ahead of him until about twenty feet from the door when she paused in front of a bank of framed pictures. Rockfish caught up and looked over her shoulder to see what snagged her attention. She pointed at two pictures.

"He's gonna cast a spell on us if we don't get moving. Let's go."

"Hold on. Look at this," Jawnie said. She pointed to a picture of the Orphanage's cornerstone being laid to mark the beginning of construction.

"I got nothing," Rockfish said. He watched as Jawnie's finger traced the outline of the cornerstone. "Well, fuck me," he whispered. It was subtle but damn prominent once you spotted it. The initials 'JP' engraved on all four corners.

Julius Provolone

"And on this one, too," Jawnie said. Her finger moved to the picture above it, which was a shot of the building from what appeared to be the ribbon cutting ceremony. "Here, in the stained glass under the front arch."

"I'll be damned," Rockfish said. "JP again. Ego wins out every time."

Jawnie held up her phone and snapped off a series of pictures and with that, they both hustled out the door and back to the car.

"You got some eagle eyes on you, girl," Rockfish said and started the car. Jawnie didn't respond, as she had her nose buried in the pictures she had just taken. Rockfish said nothing else and let her revel in her find. He also didn't say a word when she pulled down the visor and flipped the mirror open as Lana pulled onto the street. *That's my girl,* he thought. She was learning alright.

****

The wind whipped along the Ocean City boardwalk and despite the late summer temperature, Annetta debated whether she should walk back to her home and get a shawl. The clouds firmly blocked the afternoon sun. She looked at her watch and decided there wouldn't be enough time. She prided herself on punctuality, despite being the Boss, and damn well nothing could get started without her.

She was on her way to meet Bishop Clinton O'Hanlan at the Ocean City Veterans Memorial Park. The park lay between the expensive houses that lined the boardwalk and West Avenue. The trees and small benches gave older visitors a place to keep out of the sun as the kids played in the water. The Bishop called the impromptu meeting and the message Annetta received was that the man was worried to death over recent events. She would settle him down, as she had in the past, and business would go on.

Annetta walked under the park's entranceway from the east and realized that the trees were not adequately blocking the wind as she hoped. *That shawl would have been a lifesaver*, she thought, and second guessed her decision not to go back. Instead, Annetta popped the collar on her polo and spotted the Bishop, sans flowing robes and purple hat, sitting on a bench, twenty yards ahead of her. His eyes said he had spotted her.

"Annetta, so happy we could meet today," the Bishop said as he stood to greet her. "Forgive me, if I don't hug you."

"Keep your distance, Padre. I'm happy you didn't 'forget' your mask this time. He was dressed in a three-piece suit and even without the sun she could see the sweat forming on his brow. *Sticks out like a sore thumb,* she thought.

The masks added an extra layer of security. If the Feds were peeping from any of the bushes, they'd have a hard time reading lips. They both kept their voices low and, as she expected, O'Hanlan immediately got down to business.

"Annetta, understand my predicament. There are people asking questions about our business dealings, both past and present. From what little I can gather, this could negatively affect our current arrangement. That is unacceptable to my side of the house, especially in these dire economic times." He spun his head and looked directly at her. "I cannot help when you hide things from me. We are partners after all."

Annetta turned her head and nodded in his direction. She understood where he was coming from, but it didn't mean she bought any of it.

"Look, Clint, I understand your fear, but we've got a long history, not to mention a financially successful one. I'm assuming you drove here in that Tesla Model X, the one that's registered in your mistress's name?" Annetta wanted to let him know who the fuck was running this show, let alone this conversation. She wanted there to be no doubts about that when he drove back north later. She continued on after he failed to answer her simple question.

"Based on our mutual history, it pains me you've come here throwing around accusations that I don't have my shit together or you think that unless you are meticulously involved, shit's gonna go sideways. I'm Annetta Provolone, Goddamnit," and she punched the back of the bench. "Daughter of Angelo and granddaughter of Julius. Just because I'm the first woman that your side has had to work with, do not think I'm a fuckup or easy to walk over. I run the southern half of this state for a reason." Annetta paused for dramatic effect before continuing.

"You feel out of the loop? I do what I do, so that the Church can have some sort of plausible deniability. Me and mine? We're in the paper's every goddamn day with some wild accusations. You want to stay below the waves, don't you, Bishop? Enjoy the calmness and float along while I fight the white caps? I can see on your face. You don't do well in choppy water."

"I'm not questioning your abilities to complete the task at hand, but what I am asking for is a little insight into how the sausage is made," O'Hanlan retorted. "I can picture it when you've finished, sitting there in the deli case all packaged and looking good. I need a little behind-the-scenes tour so my agita can be ratcheted down a little. Or a lot."

"Anxiety, really? Take a fucking pill like the rest of the pansies. Now, I've got shit in motion to solve all our problems. Even your case of the worries." Annetta paused. "Look at me. I want to see your eyes. That you understand."

O'Hanlan turned his head and Annetta continued. "But if you like, I can grind it all to a stop and let you take the wheel. It's really one way or the other, Clint. But I don't see you making the hard calls when the time comes."

"You'd be surprised, Annetta. But for this one time, I will defer to your lead. As a partner, I ask that you nip this trouble in the bud as quickly as possible. No matter who wins this coming election, there will be a firm push for a second stimulus bill. If Trump wins, we're good because that mechanism is already in place. If Biden pulls an upset, then we might be in a better place because socialism will always throw more money towards the flunkies." He shuffled closer to her on the bench. "I need reassurances that we are to be positioned to scoop up as much as possible. And that which we can't grab for ourselves, I need to make sure those same flunkies are dumping it in the goddamn collection plate, week after week."

"Clint, put your hands away, you're going to hurt someone with all that flailing. We've known each other for a little while and I would very much like to tell you to take your cut and shut the fuck up, but I won't. I also won't resort to the heavy-handed measures I'm getting from your tone of voice."

"They were in my house, Annetta. Asking questions. Do you understand how serious this is?"

"I do, that's why I'm here trying to get your panties out of a bunch. Nobody will care about Joe Hardy and Nancy Drew uncovering shit from centuries ago; but for your sake, you have my word this podcast, documentary, whatever the fuck Rockfish is planning won't happen. Neither will some grand expose on our stimulus loans. Look, I have got it under control. Just because blood is not being spilled doesn't mean I'm not working. I do things differently than the others. You know that." She turned and faced forward again, her point made.

O'Hanlan's nodded, somewhat in agreement.

"The last thing any of us need is for two individuals to disappear and bring down even more heat," Annetta said. "Fuck, with our luck, a freaking swarm of true crime media wannabes would descend on South Jersey trying to figure out what happened to the people trying to find out what happened. Each one thinking they could create the next big '*Making A Murderer*.' Or even worse, '*Who Killed GamGam: Serial Killers, Mafioso and the Quest for Docudrama Dollars.*' You see that one? That was a real stinker. If crap like that happened, then we'd be back in the same sinking boat, but with half a dozen more leaks."

"Okay, Annetta, I believe you. But when they were at the Archdiocese, Father Renfield ended up in quite a tizzy by the time they left."

"In that case, give him one of your chill pills. Look, I can't say it enough. I got a plan for Rockfish. One that will send him back to Baltimore with his tail between his legs. Then I'll let Angelo's men down there handle him." Annetta wiped her hands in the air for emphasis. "Capice?" she asked, not waiting for a reply.

"And as for the girl, she's a local, so it's more of a delicate matter. If she calls the cops, we're prepared. If she goes to the Feds with a wild story, I've got a plan. We have a contingency plan in place for whichever way she turns. And a few that would push her in a direction beneficial to both of us."

"Annetta, I get it. But any mention of the Feds really scares the shit out of me."

She noticed the change in his voice, and the sweat now ran down his forehead.

"Afraid they'll repossess your prized Tesla? The condo in Seaside Heights? Clinton, look at me. If I gotta spell it out for you so I can get back to my beach house, I friggin will. Those clowns at the bank, they know nothing about you or me for a reason. Fall guys, pure and simple. And if anyone tries to track down a living, breathing human from any of our applications, it won't get them anywhere other than the cemetery where we pulled the names from. And if this McGee bitch goes local with her complaint, that's going to die on the vine. I had dinner with our Mayor the other evening and he's beginning to see things our way. It's funny what a costly divorce and skyrocketing child support payments can do to improve one's vision and views towards certain electoral situations."

Annetta could tell O'Hanlan wasn't in any better shape than when he arrived at the park, but she couldn't keep spinning her wheels so his tum-tum would stop hurting. She had real shit to do, and with an 'we'll agree to disagree', Annetta sent him on his way.

She waited until O'Hanlan had left the park before waving Tony over from his vantage point in the gazebo.

"We're good. For now. Can't say he won't be a problem in the future, though. Go drop the dime on Rockfish to the new chief. It's nice to have him back in our pocket. Then go pick up the broad. Woman to woman, I can make her come around and see things differently.

Southern New Jersey Times

Elk Township Police Chief Ned Hasty Suspended by Mayor
Allegations of Misconduct in Recent Election

By Ken Garland (email the author)
SNJT.com - Online Edition
September 1, 2020 @ 3:45pm

Aura NJ - On September 1st, Elk Township Mayor Sam Lobosco announced he was suspending newly sworn Police Chief Ned Hasty pending an investigation into allegations of voter fraud and intimidation in the most recent election for Elk Township's Chief of Police.

Mayor Lobosco stated that a whistleblower from the Hasty campaign contacted his office immediately following the election, but only recently offered evidence of the serious allegations against Chief Hasty. Effective immediately, the Mayor has placed Hasty on administrative leave and has asked former Chief Scott Ringle to serve in an acting capacity for the time being.

The Mayor's press secretary has announced Mayor Lobosco will hold a press conference at the Township's Municipal Building on Wednesday morning. This reporter has learned that at that time the Mayor will announce the formation of a special investigative task force to look further into the allegations.

CHAPTER NINE

The morning after the uninformative meeting with Father Renfield, Rockfish decided to take it easy for a change. While the meeting sucked, the pictures Jawnie noticed on the wall had not and it was a win in his book. He cancelled his wake-up call and slept in. A small celebration was in order. He had looked forward to this first day in a week or longer with absolutely nothing pressing to do. The previous evening Davenport had video conferenced in and Rockfish got him up to speed. To say the man was a happy client was an understatement, and it had been a while since Rockfish had one of those.

Davenport showed a ton of interest in Jawnie's research and wanted Rockfish to make an introduction hoping to getting dibs on that story too. He felt so strongly about it, that Davenport mentioned putting the entire missing girls/child trafficking/dead cop story on the back burner until this fraud storyline could be addressed. Now that was a feeling Rockfish was more used to, watching people jump the line in front of him. But he gave credit where credit was due. She had put some of his fact-finding skills to shame in uncovering the fraudulent PPP loan scam.

During a call with Jawnie the previous evening, Rockfish told her to hang tight and keep a low profile until she heard from him. She was sitting on a time bomb and he felt responsible for her safety should anything leak out prior to or after she talked to the Feds. He wanted a day to think things out, how best to proceed on this, especially for her safety. If Hasty had any contacts over at the Federal Building, the Chief wouldn't have tasked Betty Lou with looking up phone numbers. He thought of Decker, back in Maryland. The man had contacts with the FBI in

Baltimore. Could he leverage that into a point-of-contact in Philly for them to meet with? A meeting with the Feds was the best way to proceed on the matter, and he made a mental note to make that call.

Rockfish walked over to the room's small desk, grabbed the bottle of whiskey, and poured one over ice. He had stopped and picked up the bottle on the way back from the Archdiocese. Before leaving Camden, he had pulled into a liquor store parking lot. It was a defensive move, he told Jawnie; in an attempt to see if anyone was following them. He watched, but none of the cars that passed by turned off and waited for Lana to leave the parking lot. A minute later, Jawnie returned from the store with his order in hand. They pulled out of the parking lot and it didn't appear anyone was on their tail.

The whiskey burned down this throat and again in the pit of his stomach. But to him, it was the good kind of burn. No breakfast to mess with it, just eighty proof goodness. He could picture that in a day or so, he'd be back on I-95 South and then happily sitting in his trailer. There he'd type up a final report, including expenses for Davenport and attach his bill. Until the next client came along, his biggest dilemma of the day would be if his dad had again raided his refrigerator and eaten the steak Rockfish was de-thawing for his own dinner. He would have to change the code on the new lock when he got home.

It only took a few large sips, daydreaming of the good life, and the paper cup was empty.

That was fast, he thought. *I must have lost track of time there for a second. Oh well onward*, he thought. Rockfish stood back up and headed over to the desk. He refilled the cup with ice, all the while contemplating on pouring a double or single when a loud knock at the door interrupted his thought process.

POLICE SEARCH WARRANT OPEN THE DOOR!

"Make it a double," Rockfish said to no one and poured. He set the cup down and walked over to the door. Rockfish opened the door but left the top swing bar lock engaged.

"What's up, guys? Busy day?" Rockfish said through the two-inch opening. Laser sites met his cheeriness and camaraderie, blinding his eyes to what he imagined were barrels pointing straight at him.

"Okay, okay. Everyone relax," he said. "Unarmed old white guy."

OPEN THE DOOR NOW. GLASSBORO POLICE. SEARCH WARRANT. OPEN NOW!

"I've got to shut it again to disengage the top lock. Please don't take it as a hostile move and shoot through the door. I'm unarmed unless you count the whiskey." Rockfish shut the door and for a microsecond in his brain, he pictured himself diving out the second story window and running across the parking lot, but this wasn't television, or the movies, and he knew his only choice was to face the trumped-up music.

They were dressed in riot gear and poured into the room's narrow foyer. One handcuffed Rockfish and led him back out into the hallway where he was unceremoniously dumped on the floor. Things happened too fast, and he wasn't able to recognize any faces with the riot helmets and N95s on. He remained on the hallway floor for the next thirty minutes with two cops standing guard outside his room.

"Can anyone tell me what this is about?" He had asked that half a dozen times, but each was met with silence. "Maybe loosen these cuffs up a bit? Can I see my copy of the warrant? Perhaps one of you can get it and hold it so I can read? Is there anyone here in charge, that has command of the English language?" Each question received the same answer, but he would not give either of these two the satisfaction of just sitting in the hallway, until they decided it was time to talk.

"Any chance one of you fine officers could go inside and retrieve my drink for me? Jameson on the rocks. I set it down on the desk when you fellas came knocking. Feel free to take a little for yourself, if you're parched."

His results were the same, and all he got were stupid stares.

A few minutes later, the hotel room door opened and from his vantage point Rockfish could see a pair of legs walk out of the room and step toward him. His eyes followed the legs up and up and without the helmet and mask, he wasn't at all surprised.

"Officer Sommers, I must say this isn't a total shock." Rockfish grinned up at Sommers. "Aren't you a tad out of your jurisdiction?"

"Glad to hear that you're capable of at least understanding some things, Rockfish," Sommers said and grinned just as wide. "Perhaps you should revisit our last conversation, as I drive you back to the station, and figure out where you went wrong. Get this piece of shit out of here. Extradition order from Elk Township. I'm taking him back to the Chief."

****

Rockfish didn't take Sommers' advice as he bounced around in the back of the squad car, still handcuffed behind his back. Rockfish couldn't stay still and could not concentrate. He sat mostly silent in the back of the car, hoping that he didn't break his neck as the car bounced across rough roads back to Elk Township.

Rockfish asked again what the charges were when the cruiser turned into the PD's parking lot. Sommers nor the other officer answered, but got out of the car and pulled Rockfish from the backseat. Here, the other officer pushed him up a ramp and through a side door.

I'm guessing they'll fingerprint me and take a booking photo before I can make my damn phone call, he thought. *Shit, you know what they say about assuming.* He was right and instead walked through a heavy metal door, down a halfway and unceremoniously dumped into a holding cell.

Rockfish sat down on the cement bed and dumped his head in his hands. It went so wrong, so fast. An hour ago, it went from celebratory drinks to pooping on cold metal out in the open. *Shit went south, literally, real fucking quick,* he thought. As he sat there, his one hope was that at some point someone had to tell him something. This wasn't Ceaușescu's Romania after all. Rockfish was due some sort of South Jersey version of due process.

As he waited, Rockfish consciously chose not to rehash the events of the past two hours in his head. It wouldn't get him any explanation, nor would it get this cell door opened any sooner. He had to play it patient and act as if this was no big thing. At some point he would learn whatever information he needed to start making smart, sound decisions, but there was no reason to get wound around the axle over something he currently had no control over.

Rockfish closed his eyes and breathed deep. After a couple of minutes, he found himself crabbing off his favorite pier along the Chesapeake Bay with cold beer and a good cigar. His dad, Mack, would wait back at the trailer to steam the keepers in cheap beer and Old Bay seasoning. It would be Rockfish's job to fill the cooler with beer and ice before dragging it out to the old picnic table that faced the trailer park's small pond. Father and son would tune in an Orioles game on the radio, and both would agree there was no better summer night. Damned if he couldn't almost smell that seasoning and taste the beer.

Rockfish's mind came back to the present with the sound of something metal dragging across the concrete floor, coming down the hallway. He opened his eyes and watched as a cop stopped in front of Rockfish's cell and unfolded a metal chair. This man was one of the few Elk Township police Rockfish had not had the pleasure of meeting, because if he had, he would have remembered, definitely remembered. The man's uniform shirt had enough ribbons and garland on it to resemble a Macy's Christmas tree display, and the fabric itself was stretched far beyond its safety limits. Rockfish didn't think any of the buttons could reach him if they suddenly popped, but he shuffled a little more towards the head of the bed. *No need to risk losing an eye,* he thought.

"Rockfish, I'm Chief Ringle," the cop said as he sat down.

"What happened to Hasty?"

"Don't you worry about that. You got a heap of shit on your own plate."

"No, I met with him. He was the Chief not more than forty-eight hours ago. Did I sleep through the coup d'état? Is that why I'm in here?"

"Sommers said you were a smartass. Now from this point on, I'm going to do all the talking and you're just going to sit there and take it all in. I cannot make myself any clearer." Ringle leaned forward and ran a steel baton across the bars.

"Copy that..." Rockfish said. *There was a new sheriff in town,* he thought. *This complicates things a little.* Dealing with a corrupt officer is one thing, but the guy who suddenly runs the department most likely has ties to organized crime based on his lineage, and could probably manufacture evidence out of the air, was a whole 'nother pain in the ass altogether. "...but can I get a phone call? Says so in the Geneva Convention."

"You can listen like I asked, or I can have Officer Sommers come in and teach you some of the MMA moves he learned from the Joe Rogan

Podcast. This is *my* township and the only rights you have are the ones I feel like giving to you. I'm not booking you for committing any crime. I'm not charging you with anything. Crime? There was no crime, at least on your part." Ringle holstered his baton, leaned back in his chair and laughed. "Now we've learned of some fraudulent activity being committed in the area and believe you have additional information which might corroborate our current intelligence. You're being held as a material witness in an ongoing investigation. I can hold you here till the cows come home, if I so desire. And I desire."

Imma desire you to choke tonight on those seven Cheddar Ranch Blasted, Big & Bold Hot Pockets you'll inhale for a post dinner snack, you fat fuck, Rockfish thought, thus obeying the order to stay quiet.

"Oh, and as for Hasty, he's got some issues, kind of along the same lines as you, but he's out of a job, and not lucky enough to be rockin' three hots and a cot like you. At least not yet."

****

It had been a couple of days since Jawnie was around the house long enough to settle down and do some chores. Aside from the dust and dishes in the sink, she thought of the mail piling up on the dining room table. Not to mention the three or four newspapers out at the end of the driveway that she had forgotten to gather up each morning. She opened the front door and walked down the steps to toss them.

I'll just dump them in the bin and maybe check out today's headlines, she thought. But it was the one headline atop yesterday's Southern New Jersey Times that caught her attention as it landed on a pile of water bottles and broken-down Amazon boxes:

Elk Township Police Chief Ned Hasty Suspended by Mayor - Allegations of Misconduct in Recent Election

Jawnie couldn't believe what she thought she had read. She pulled the paper from the bin and re-scanned it. She hadn't misread the headline the first time, and ran inside to look over the rest of the article. Back in the living room, she walked over to her favorite chair, but anxiety kept her standing.

Jawnie wasn't quite finished with a third read-through, comprehending little more than the first time, when there was a sharp rap on the shop door and then another quickly followed on the house's front door. Jawnie wasn't expecting anyone at either location. She stood frozen in her living room.

Rockfish? She thought. *Not if he's banging on two doors at once.*

The voice cursing outside the window to her left was definitely not Steve Rockfish. Jawnie backed away from the knocking, trying not to make a sound. She grabbed her phone from the dining room table and headed for her hidey hole. From there she could check the camera without the chance of being seen.

The spot under the stairs was a favorite place to get away from her parents and read ever since the day her father suggested it and then spent another couple of days working on the space to her liking. The dead space was perfect for a reading light, beanbag chair, and a small dog bed for Meatwig. He had cut the small door from the existing wood and as a nod to the spy novels Jawnie was such a fan of, one would need to know which corner to press on to have the door swing open. On this day she pressed it and fell into the beanbag, fiddling with her phone as she collapsed. Once the door was firmly shut, she opened the video doorbell app on her phone. Both the front and shop doors had cameras installed into the frame.

Each video feed showed a different man standing and alternating between banging and waiting. They could wait 'till the cows came home, but Jawnie knew that a response on her part wasn't coming. She was scared. Frozen beneath the stairs, too scared to call for help. Unable to do anything other than stare at the video feed.

Both men were casually dressed, and the one at the front door wore a black Adidas tracksuit. She was never a fan of the Sopranos, didn't know who Paulie, Christopher and the Russian were when Rockfish brought them up, and sure as hell wasn't a private eye, but she knew a shady character when she saw one. They were straight up gangsters. The lack of any type of laptop, desktop or tablet in their hands showed they weren't even pretending to be potential customers.

Jawnie stayed safe under the stairs but feared the telltale sound of a window breaking. At that point, all bets were off, and they would either give up after a quick search or stay until they found her. She continued to watch the men via the app. They were cursing louder now, their body language showed growing agitation. Tracksuit finally pulled out his own phone, held it to his ear and began pacing back and forth across the driveway. The conversation appeared animated, but it wasn't long before he shoved the phone back into his pocket and yelled to the other one. They dashed out of frame to what Jawnie presumed was a car. The camera mic had picked up the sound of an engine turning over. A second later it drove past the front of the house.

Jesus Christ, Jawnie whispered to herself. A Jeep Cherokee. What color was the other one? Her mind raced and came up blank. Synapses fired off in all directions and concentration needed for an answer was out of her reach. Jawnie felt as if her heart was in her throat. Spots danced in front of her eyes.

Goddamnit! Breath. Deep. In and out. Relax, they left. Or did they? I don't fucking know!

It was half an hour before she left her newly designated panic room, and another after she garnered enough courage to peek out a window. The Jeep wasn't anywhere she could see. She ran across both floors, making sure all the blinds were pulled. Then out to the shop for those windows and door. Once they all were down, she breathed a small sigh of relief and hoped it would be impossible for anyone to see inside now.

She called Rockfish, and it went straight to voicemail. *Where the hell are you when I need you most,* she thought.

Her stomach growled in response and she realized she had panicked her way straight through breakfast. She grabbed a banana and two vegan granola bars from the pantry and hoped they would tide her over. She sat in her recliner and inhaled the food. All the while she began thinking of the future, the immediate future. What if they came back? What if they thought she wasn't home and were waiting somewhere down the street for her to return? Even if they had driven off, it would only be a matter of time before they came back. Neither looked smart, but they could do the basic math. She would have to return home at some point.

Knock

Knock

This second set of knocks surprised Jawnie as equally as the first, despite knowing that it was most likely coming. *Had they returned that damn fast,* she thought? She took a deep breath to steady her finger and put in her passcode. With the shades drawn, she felt safe but still found that her legs and mind had her headed back to the panic room.

Safe and somewhat secure, Jawnie watched two police officers, situated out front as the goons were a couple of hours previously. Their patrol car was in the driveway, but something made little sense. Or did it? The cop at the house door had an Elk Township Police Department patch on the left shoulder of his uniform. The shop camera didn't have a good angle to see where the second one was from.

Elk Township cops, she thought. *But why the hell are they in Westville?* It didn't pass the smell test. She tried Rockfish again and got his voicemail. *I'll wait them out. Same as before,* she thought.

The second set of men spent less time standing in front of the house than the other two before leaving, but Jawnie still hung tight and didn't leave the panic room. Instead, she tried to calm down and piece her thoughts together. The first thought that came to her head was regarding how fucked she'd be if any of those men came back and thought about trying to force their way in through the back door. There were no cameras there to give her any kind of warning. Her mother's voice filled her head.

Run, Jawnie run. Get your ass as far away as you can from all this; don't think twice and only worry about what to do once you're safely far away.

She burst from under the stairs and grabbed an old lacrosse duffle bag. She threw a couple days' worth of clothes in it and moved to the kitchen. In went some fruit, more granola bars, bottles of water, three masks and a phone charger. Jawnie zipped the bag closed and stopped in the front hallway.

Think, girl, think.

The Scion was still in the shop, and the rental sat smack dab in the driveway. If either group was monitoring the house, they'd see her leave and she probably wouldn't make it as far as the diner before someone swooped in. Maybe, like in medieval times, the gangsters and cops could fight over her, but Jawnie knew in this situation both factions were probably working together.

The backdoor, across the Gardner's yard and out onto Walnut Street, she thought. She could worry about real transportation after putting a couple of blocks between her and the house.

Jawnie reached for the doorknob and stepped out into her backyard.

A hand grabbed her left bicep, and she screamed.

"Whoa, Jawnie, quiet, quiet, it's me Ned Hasty. You're gonna be alright."

Jawnie shook her head to make sure she wasn't seeing things. The tight grip on her arm let her know he was real. Hasty was in tactical pants and a t-shirt. She hadn't seen him out of uniform before. He stood tall in her eyes and his voice strong. He was the rock she needed. "Ned, you scared the living shit out of me," Jawnie said "Are you with those other two cops that came here earlier?" She tried to get control of her breathing. Her heart continued to race despite having what she hoped was one of the good guys alongside her.

"No, you might have read, I'm not the Chief anymore."

"Matter of fact, I did, but then a couple of mafia goons followed by two cops banged on my door earlier. Your headline got lost in the shuffle. They didn't break in, but I thought there was a good chance that either of the groups would soon return with reinforcements. I thought you were one of them hiding in the backyard. What are you doing here in my backyard?"

"I took an oath to serve and protect, that's what I'm doing," Hasty said. "I don't have the authority any longer to call Westville PD and have someone come out to check on you. I've lost all credibility with any other department. But I still have ears on the force and heard things. But first, turn off your phone. If they were real cops, they'll be able to locate you with that phone bouncing off every cell tower you pass. If necessary, we can pick up a burner phone once you're situated and safe."

Jawnie kicked herself for not thinking of this first. While it wasn't Tech 101, it sure as hell wasn't the advanced graduate class either. She pulled the phone from her back pocket and powered it down. Next, she instinctively looked back to Hasty for her next move. *Shit... this is new,* she thought. *Better learn to swim, girl. You might drown.*

"Enough chatter. We need to get going," he said.

Jawnie had a million questions about the paper's headline, who his source was, but there would be time for clarification later. She followed him across the backyard, and they slipped through the neighbor's gate and into their yard. The gate shut behind her, but Jawnie stopped and turned around.

"I have to go back. I forgot some shit, gimme five."

"You have three minutes or else I'm coming in expecting that you ran into uninvited visitors."

Jawnie turned her phone on and ran back into the house. Once it powered up, she put it on airplane mode and headed for the door that led to the shop. There, she grabbed the thumb drive which had all her research on it, did her best Rockfish imitation, and took a handful of pictures of the whiteboard. Jawnie turned off the phone again and tried to clean the board the best she could in seventeen seconds. When she finished, Jawnie took a step back. Her erase job wasn't great and some of the wording was still legible, but it would have to do. She raced back out of the shop and through the connecting door to the house. The bedroom closet was her next stop and she reached up on the top shelf, pulling down Edward's notebooks and Tisha's diary. She had never quite gotten around to putting them in the basement gun safe and thanked the lucky stars for her laziness. Into the gym bag they went and she headed back out the door and across the yard to meet Hasty, who was still standing in the neighbor's backyard, patiently waiting the best he could.

CHAPTER TEN

Hasty looked back at his passenger. Jawnie and her gear were lying across the back seat of the car. He couldn't take a chance anyone would spot her while sitting up front pretending as if nothing was going on. Who knew where either set of men from earlier were? His investigative instincts told him they weren't far, if they weren't already parked on a side street waiting for the first sign of life in the house. Or further orders, whichever came first. When Hasty told Jawnie to get down in the back and toss her bag on the floor, he got only one argument.

"Ned, I know I'm a few feet from you, and you're facing the windshield, but where's your mask?"

"All Liberal bullshit, Jawnie." He had waited for her to say something, after emerging from her house the second time, wearing one.

Hasty heard an unzipping and a second later, a mask decorated with ones and zeros landed on the center console.

"Look. I don't give a fuck what MAGA God you worship, but I've got the freakin' mob and dirty cops looking for me. Neither wants to pin a medal on my chest and I'm not going to be infected and die from the 'Rona while all this shit plays out."

Hasty picked up the mask from where it landed atop the gear shifter and put it on. If he was here to serve and protect her, as he so heroically quoted just fifteen minutes earlier, if that meant wearing a mask to help keep her mind at ease, he was all for it. It wouldn't change his view on the so-called pandemic, but that wasn't the conversation for this moment.

"Are we headed to Rockfish's hotel and picking him up too?" Jawnie said. "Someone's gotta let him know everything is turning to shit. I tried calling him earlier, but it went straight to voicemail. I figured maybe someone tapped my phone after seeing the cops outside."

"Yeah, about that. Rockfish is in jail, and the new Chief is the same as the old Chief. You read the article, so you know what I'm talking about. Ringle got Glassboro PD along with some of his own deputies, my former lackeys, to raid Rockfish's hotel room yesterday under some bullshit scenario and then took him down to the Municipal Building. He's in a holding cell, not in danger, at least not at the moment. Their plan is to scare him back to Maryland, as the previous times hadn't worked as expected."

"How do you know? Did you see him?" Jawnie said.

"Temporarily, I may not have my badge or gun, and they changed the locks, but I still have a set of loyal eyes and ears there, filling me in as needed. I got a call letting me know what Ringle's plan was. What my man didn't say, but I put together, now that Rockfish is on ice, it was only a matter of time before they came after you."

"Oh, they did. Two different sets. Can I ask what's your plan and where are we headed?"

"I'm taking you back to my house. I doubt anyone would look for you there. As far as any of them are concerned, I'm not involved in any of this. I'm only a disgruntled former employee." Hasty knew it was more than that, but didn't want to go into it. He was considered a roadblock. Someone that was in the way of what the real bosses, not the mayor or township committee, wanted to get accomplished. But that was a later battle for him, somewhere down the road.

"The Provolones are behind Ringle, aren't they?"

"At the very least," Hasty said. "Those are the people calling the shots that Ringle is taking. Ringle is all spun up over you two and some perceived threat to Annetta and her minions." *Jawnie was a smart one*, Hasty thought. She was picking up on the parts he wasn't laying down. There was no reason for him not to be fully honest with her anymore. "I'm sorry for what's happening to you, none of us have any control over it. I'm just trying to help."

"We're good, okay? No need for apologies."

"Understood," Hasty said.

"And it's just not Annetta and Ringle. Don't sleep on those fuckers from the Catholic Church," Jawnie said. "It's all about the PPP fraud I tried to tell you about. I've got a ton more evidence now. Way more than when you suggested I to go to the Feds. But you were right, and I didn't listen and now look where that got me. We do that now. Not to your house, take me over the bridge."

Hasty could hear the anxiousness in Jawnie's voice. He couldn't blame her. She was looking for the quickest way out of danger. The fastest method to end this madness and let her life return to a semblance of normalcy. To her, that meant turning over her evidence to the Feds. But what Jawnie wasn't thinking about was how slow and meticulous the Feds investigate. Her immediate danger wouldn't evaporate. She couldn't hand over a binder of documents and expect ten minutes later a cavalcade of black SUVs would be cresting the Walt Whitman Bridge into New Jersey armed with thirty arrest warrants and a ton of forfeiture orders. And as for Rockfish, well, that man would be fucked six ways to Sunday if any of the bad guys learned the Feds were on the way. Rockfish would end up more like Jeffrey Epstein than Mary D'arnaud in that jail cell. Hasty tried explaining his line of reasoning to Jawnie, but he wasn't sure she was buying any of it and sounded nowhere near onboard.

"Look, you go to the Feds. Life doesn't return to normal until they are locked up. You'll constantly be looking over your shoulder, just like you are now. Maybe even after a trial it would continue to haunt you. Whoever the Feds take down, there are people waiting to fill those voids and some might be loyal to those you helped take down." He looked back at her through the rearview and raised his eyebrows. Jawnie was calmer, but not where he needed her, yet. "And that doesn't even take Rockfish into account. Whatever bullshit they are holding him on, looks very real on paper. Ringle could make up additional charges or allegations out of thin air just as easy. He might never get out." Hasty left it at that. He didn't want the image of Rockfish hanging from a bedsheet to be anywhere near Jawnie's mind at the moment.

"I think I follow," Jawnie said. "At least better than before. But why can't we go to the Feds and then once the FBI knows, they can work to get Rockfish out."

"Mary D'arnaud, that's why. If they don't hurt him outright, then poof, he's gone." *Gee, I'm sorry Mr. FBI Guy. He was here a second ago, not sure how he might have escaped,* Hasty thought. *Sorry about that. Our bad. Won't happen again. Or at least for another seventy-five years.*

"If you're worried at all about him, we'll come up with a plan to get him out and to safety before the Federal tsunami comes down on these clowns. And by the way, you're itching to go see them, I'm guessing you really have the evidence to start the storm?"

"Right here," Jawnie said, and Hasty could see her pat the duffle bag in the mirror.

The rest of the drive was mostly silent. Hasty could tell Jawnie was trying to process it all and slowly grew frustrated. She remained prone across the backseat until Hasty's automatic garage door closed. She could get out of the car, but he recommended remaining in the garage until he could double check and make sure all the curtains and blinds were closed in the house.

When Hasty finally gave her the all clear, Jawnie came in and tossed her bag on the kitchen floor. She stretched and then pulled up a chair.

"At the very worst the neighbors think I'm drinking my problems away, in the dark," Hasty said as he walked back into the kitchen. "A few have stopped by to offer their condolences and feign anger at how I am getting the shaft. Make yourself scarce if there's ever a knock at the door."

"That, I'm well-versed in."

Hasty put on a pot of coffee and started scrambling some eggs. "This shit always makes me hungry. While you're my guest, please don't ask. Grab anything you need from the fridge or panty."

"I could handle some eggs right about now, thanks."

They made small talk over brunch and then after sticking the dishes in the sink, Hasty gave Jawnie a more detailed overview of the situation than he did on the drive over.

"As long as you're here, you're safe. If you're safe, then we can assume that they won't do anything to Rockfish."

"Thank you, Ned. I know it's not much, but I'm breathing normal and I do feel safer."

"At some point they may realize they need to use him to get to you. If they have you, so to speak, then all bets are off on his safety and its basically game over. They don't have you, and that is our one advantage right now."

Hasty looked her in the eyes from across the table as Jawnie nodded. But he wasn't a hundred percent she was following along. She had been through a whole hell of a lot the past few hours. The trauma was serious, a sudden, unexpected shitstorm that the average person would never have an idea on how to deal with. He trudged on with what he thought she needed to know.

"We could run into a problem if you try to go on the offensive. I don't necessarily mean going to the Feds. It could be something as simple as instead of sitting here in the dark like a mushroom, you went outside. Or used your phone. Now I know Ringle doesn't have the smarts or tech to put any kind of an illegal tap on your phone, but I can't speak for the Provolones." He paused and made sure they had eye contact. "Bad guys these days have the cash to keep up with technology and can buy the services of whatever they need. That's the complete opposite of small township governments where they are constantly looking to cut spending year after year. What I fear is that if they find out you're here, or somehow grab you, then Rockfish becomes cannon fodder— either literal or figurative."

"Cannon fodder?"

"He becomes expendable."

"Jesus Christ," Jawnie said and shook her head.

"Now my guy back on the force is keeping me pretty well up to date on what is going on at the PD, but there are two other arms on this octopus that we don't have eyes or ears on. That's gonna be a problem, always gonna be a problem. Ain't no two ways about it. But it's best if we only dwell on what we can control. That means no worrying or playing the coulda, woulda, shoulda game."

"Okay, I'll have to work on the worrying part, but you don't have to worry about me diving in feet first into the sidecar to play Robin."

"I'm glad I won't," Hasty said. "My guy and I are working on a plan. It's not something that will happen in the next five minutes or five hours. It's going to depend on timing. I'm going to head out later this afternoon and meet with him for an update and to do a little strategizing. I'll fill you in when I get back. When the timing is right, we'll move forward. Don't jump the gun while I'm gone."

"No chance I can ride in the back again?" Jawnie said. "It's not a sidecar."

"Correct. No chance. I've got a small handgun, a Glock 26, and I'll leave it with you. It's small, compact and should rest in your hand easily. Ever shoot?"

"I shot skeet growing up, but no handguns."

"I've got some time before heading out. Might as well start that classroom instruction now."

****

Chief Ringle reached over to switch on the lights and sirens to get around some slow-ass driving motherfuckers when he realized he was in his personally owned vehicle. He would have to make do with traffic like the rest of the world, but it didn't mean he would like it. After all, he had his badge back, was hot shit and the proles better get used to it. Ringle had some time to make up for. *Fucking rush hour starts earlier and earlier each goddamn day,* he thought.

He had been out of the office on his lunch break when the message came through. He was ordered to get his ass to Jawnie McGee's house. The order came down from the top and Ringle knew he couldn't show up there in his uniform and squad car. He radioed Betty Lou and let her know that Del Boca Vista's tacos had run clear through him and that he was headed home for a little while and would be available by cell if needed. He didn't care if she bought the ruse or not, he wanted something official down on paper saying he was unavailable for the time being.

Ringle had long waited for this meeting with Annetta Provolone, now that he was back in the fold. Ever since Bologna filled him in on her plan to get him back behind the Chief's desk, a little late in the process he thought, Ringle wanted the opportunity to help steer this ship where it needed going. He could help make things right, he wasn't the dumb muscle side of the equation. In the past Annetta wouldn't give his suggestions much weight, but given this second chance, Ringle was going to make the most of it. He would speak up without fear, no longer be the voice mumbling in the background.

He parked the car around the corner from Jawnie's house and walked down the sidewalk and up the driveway. A couple of mooks were standing outside the shop door, and he figured he'd at least check in before barging inside to meet with the boss lady.

"Hey fellas, she in the house or repair shop?"

"You da cop?" The first guy said. Wearing polo and slacks, he was overdressed for look-out duty.

"Perhaps," Ringle replied. "Why don't you let me know where she's at and save us all the trouble of you playing tough guy."

The guy swirled the toothpick around in his mouth. "They said you'd have an attitude. Boss wants to see you inside," and the guy pointed towards the front door to the house.

Ringle followed the second look-out, dressed almost identical to the first, into the house before he turned around and put a hand against Ringle's chest.

"Wait here."

Ringle stood in the foyer while the man walked down the hallway and disappeared. In the rooms to his left and right, more Provolone soldiers were going through the place and apparently had no desire to put anything back where they found it. The guy reappeared and motioned with his hand to follow. Ringle walked down the hallway and hung a left into the kitchen. The room was straight out of the fifties, with lime green cabinets and a small rectangular Formica table. *I guess the kid never got around to updating after the parents left,* he thought.

Much to his surprise, it was Tony Bologna holding court at the table and not Annetta Provolone. *Passed down to deal with an underling, yet again,* he thought. *Mother fuckers.*

"When your guy here said the boss wanted to see me, I figured you'd be here, but sitting in one of the side chairs," Ringle said. "Whoa, shots fired," He laughed aloud.

"What's so fucking funny?" Bologna questioned angerly. Condescending was this clown's specialty, and Ringle smirked. Bologna lived up to expectations.

"I've got that same Instapot thing, that's all. Wife swears by it, but I can't taste the difference in the sauce."

"I didn't bring you here to talk fucking appliances."

"I didn't come here to talk to an underling, but we all don't get what we want. It's that kind of world in 2020."

Bologna shook his head. Ringle wondered if the man thought better and swallowed his comeback.

"So why am I here?" Ringle asked. "I could be back directing my men across the tri-county area to find this dyke."

"You're admitting that you and your men don't know where she's at?"

"It wasn't my guys who missed her first this morning," Ringle said. "Just trying to help you clean up another mess, that's all."

"Okay, lets both put our dicks back in our pants," Bologna said. "This ain't about you or me. We need to solve this tiny problem before O'Hanlan and my boss become involved. That, my friend, is the last thing either of us wants."

Ringle could see Bologna was trying to play nice, but the condescending fuck still managed to come through. Time and time again.

"We? Us?" Ringle exclaimed. Tony Boloney had forgotten that Ringle had a seat at the big table. *This fucking guy thinks this is an important meeting?* He thought. *Shit, he's at the kids' table. I'm the one alongside O'Hanlan and Provolone. I don't work for him. I give orders.*

"Yeah, we. Use your contacts. Put out a friggin' APB or some cop thing. From the Shore to Delaware." Bologna pulled the unlit cigar from his mouth and waved it around.

"Newsflash, I don't take orders from you, Boloney. I work with your boss and direct what you do. Now I can stand here for an hour or two and toss around ideas with you, but in the end I'll do what I want and you'll do what I tell you to. You might as well be sitting here talking to your boss." *I'll fucking stand here for another hour 'till the dumb wop got it through his thick skull,* he thought.

"Yeah. Sure. Whatever, dude. You got a set of fucking balls on you," Bologna said. "Look, you think you're some sort of big shot here? You wanna hook your highchair to the table with the boss and the purple hat, you gotta earn it back. This ain't some high school football game. Here, if you lose your position to injury, you gotta earn it back on the practice field. You don't waltz back into the starting lineup because you fucked up something as simple as a hillbilly election and then need us to come in and bail you out yet again."

"Fuck you, dago wop," Ringle said. "I don't have time nor the patience to deal with the likes of you right now. You want this broad? I've got the bait sitting in my jail. You decide to grow the fuck up, let me know and I'll cast out the line and reel her in for you."

"Okay, I'll humor you, fucking jamoke. What does your prisoner say? Is he talking? Or should my boys come over and show you how you get someone to spill their guts?"

Fucking guy, Ringle thought. *I'm getting nowhere fast, time to tuck my dick back in and zip up.* He had made his point and now it was time for him to sell this clown on what needed to be done. Not ransacking a house, not driving around to every gay bar in town hoping you luck across her.

"He's not said a word. He's sticking to his story. Claims he's got no idea where she could be. The man claims not to be her keeper. Tell you what, I believe him. They aren't long-lost friends, just a couple of idjits that met up and started working on a joint project that got a lot bigger and dangerous than either expected. But I will tell you what I also believe and that is I can sense his concern for her safety and that is what we prey on."

"I can agree to that. My guys need to finish here first," Bologna said. "You never know what you might find. People hide shit all the time. I doubt we'll find anything that will give us a GPS location on her, but that's where my other guys come in. I've got one at the phone company seeing what location data he can pull, and my nephew works at the Best Buy, one of those Geek Squad fanooks. He's going to go through the computers in the shop and see what we can get. If she left something behind, that's where it would be."

Hmm... sounds like a legitimate good idea, he thought. *No way in hell I'll give him the pleasure of saying it, though.*

"Annetta's got one other question. What about this jamoke that beat you in the election, the Chief—"

"Former Chief," Ringle blurted out. "And he ain't got a damn thing to do with it. Hell, the girl brought him some of the evidence and all he did was point her towards the Feds. Good goddamn thing she didn't listen, but any relationship they got stopped there."

"You sure?"

"I'd stake my old and new badge on it. All he's been doing since he cleaned out his desk is mope around the house. Probably drinking, thinking that crawling inside a bottle will magically make things all better. Been there, done that. It doesn't work. And in any case, I've got a guy monitoring him." Now that was the biggest lie he'd told since crossing the foyer. He didn't feel Hasty was a concern, and there was no way he was going to waste resources on a sore loser. But that was the answer Ringle thought Bologna wanted to hear.

"I know you probably don't believe me, that he's not involved, but I've met the guy and not only at the debate. I'm a damn excellent judge of character and right now he's sitting in his worn old Lazy Boy, crying in his beer, and standing by the phone waiting for that call that will clear him of all the charges. Little does he know." Ringle rocked back on his heels with a wide grin.

"Okay then," Bologna said, rubbing his temples and then a hand through his hair. "Let's get back to the girl. Her car ain't here, but a rental is in the driveway. I can't find one person who laid eyes on her since she and that private dick came back from their meeting with the kid touchers up in Camden. If she ran for the hills then, that's one hell of a head start. But I don't think it was that early. She had no reason to, didn't know jack about your men arresting Rockfish. I'm betting it was minutes before or after both of us sent our guys to pick her up. And that is why we need to coordinate better. Stupid shit like that. Che schifo!"

"Then where do we start?" Ringle said.

"Right where we're at. I'm just waiting on my nerd to point us in a direction."

"And when that fails?" Ringle said, not waiting for an answer. He provided one himself. "You have my number. I can have Rockfish reach out to her and set some sorta meeting. We can lie and say he'll be there, and we'll do an old fashion exchange: this prick for whatever she hid that your guys still wouldn't have found by then."

Ringle turned and walked out of the house without saying another word or waiting for an answer. He knew it wouldn't be long before Bologna called. They always do.

****

Ringle drove home—not back to the station— in order to cool off. He grabbed a drink and listened to some Merle Haggard until his blood pressure returned to normal. He felt good about how he handled himself back at the house in Westville, and even better each time he replayed the episode in his head. Hell, he felt better than good; he felt great. Large and in charge, as his wife says. He liked that feeling; and if it weren't for Mrs. Ringle having left for Bingo, he might have been even later getting back to the office.

That dumb Italian didn't know what hit him, he thought. When his little hacker kid comes up with diddly, Ringle would play his cards, and he could imagine the look on Provolone's face when he walked both Rockfish and Jawnie into Annetta's place. *A bigger piece of the pie*, he thought. *Don't mind if I do.*

He pulled into the parking lot and noticed only one car left. Betty Lou was long gone, and the second shift was out on patrol. That only left him, Rockfish, and the one patrolman working the overnight desk. Ringle closed the door to his office and sat down. In the bottom desk drawer was a fifth of Old Paw Paw Bourbon, the first thing he put in his office when he was back on the job. He pulled it out, cracked the seal and drank straight from the bottle. He couldn't be bothered with getting up to find a glass. It had been a long day, one that tried his patience, but he'd not let it be that kind of night.

Annetta, Boloney, none of those wannabe gangsters could hold his jock. After all, he was a third generation Chief of Police in this township. He ran shit and shit ran through him. It had been that way since Chuck Ringle and Julius Provolone agreed to work together before the war and it would quickly get back to that way, if any of them knew what was good for them. When he was growing up, Ringle's dad and grandfather were never hurting for money, but since this damn broad took over, Ringle's quality of life was on a downward trajectory and rock bottom came with the election loss. Annetta was the one that told him not to worry about his re-election campaign. Things were under control and he'd have another landslide victory under his belt. Ringle knew how that story ended, with him leaving his office, disgraced and losing face with his men. Yeah, Annetta got his job back, but only because she realized she needed him. She couldn't handle matters on her own and needed to bring back the heavy hitter in order to get shit done. Despite that, she obviously still didn't understand his role, the final straw being the nerve to call him to a meeting and send her goddamn lackey instead.

Ringle took another long swig of bourbon and drunkenly contemplated radioing out to one of the men on patrol and ordering them to pick up Tony Boloney. Stick his ass in the same cell as Rockfish. See how tough that clown really thinks he is. Elk Township Fight Club, Season One Episode One. It would make for great content. Ringle chuckled aloud and put that idea in the Ideas That Rock column. By the time he finished griping to himself about his current business arrangement, the bottle was close to a third gone.

He looked at the clock on the wall, realized it was too early to head home to an empty house. The wife wouldn't be home for another two hours and he didn't feel like watching television. Instead, Ringle got up from the desk with bottle in hand, and walked his kingdom. Officer Willoughby was on the overnight desk this week, but he was one of Hasty's new hires. Ringle knew little about the guy and was in no mood tonight for one of those 'Hi I'm the Chief, nice to meet you.' introductory conversations. He'd rather go shit talk to Rockfish. Maybe a little drinky-poo would loosen Rockfish's tongue.

Ringle grabbed the same chair he used in his previous sit down, and drug it down to Rockfish's cell. "Go back to command and watch us on the monitors," he told Willoughby. "I'll yell if I need your help, which won't happen because I run this jail. Just because I didn't hire you, don't you ever forget it."

Rockfish was sitting up on the concrete slab that served as both the cell's bed and sole place to sit.

"Heard you coming down the hall, Chief. Sorry I didn't have time to tidy up the place," Rockfish said. "I'm still working on the decorations, but your guys don't give me much to work with."

Ringle put his chair down and stumbled a step before grabbing the back of the chair and righting himself. He took another swig and then plopped down. The man on the other side of the bars didn't look so tough. Or smart. *Can't be that smart, if he's in my jail,* he thought. Ringle reached out with his keys and unlocked the cell door. He pulled it open and offered Rockfish the bottle. "It ain't gonna fit through the bars. Rockfish, I do believe we got off on the wrong damn foot."

"That's mighty nice of you, Chief, but there's a goddamn pandemic going on outside these walls. Not that I don't trust you with masks and social distancing, but I ain't gonna get the coronavirus and die in this cell. I had more grandiose plans for that occasion."

"Drink. Or else we could start talking about those plans tonight," Ringle said while continuing to hold the bottle out. Rockfish eventually relented and took it from the Chief.

"That's what I'm talking about. You see, Rockfish, you and me, we ain't that much different. We're both for hire, but ain't all men?"

"I'll drink to that," Rockfish said and lifted the bottle to his lips and then held it back out.

"No games when I take this back, Rockfish. Got it? Or else there's some pain coming your way."

"Wouldn't dream of it, Chief and give up all this?" Rockfish looked around his home for the past day.

"Good," Ringle said. "Imma give you a sneak peek into the future, because you're a stand-up guy. I could use a guy like you working for me, but that's a whole different world at the moment. But tell you what Imma do. I need you to do me a solid and I'll return the favor, just need you to have a little trust in me and what I say."

"You're the boss and I'll play my part," Rockfish replied.

"Exactly. I knew for some strange reason I liked you. Sometime here in the next day or two Imma need you to call that dyke for me. Gonna have some faith that at some point she's going to turn on that phone. She'll either pick it up or get a voice mail from you. Right now, I'd settle for either."

Ringle brought the bottle back to his lips and again, offered the bottle to Rockfish. The prisoner declined, and Ringle didn't push it this time.

"You're going to pass along a message to set up a meeting that she needs to attend if she knows what's good for her. And you, of course. Now, Imma let you in on a little secret. Those wops want her to think that if she cooperates and turns over whatever she has, I'll release you. But that's all bullshit on their end. But guess what? It ain't on my end and Imma gonna run this show. I'm in a fucking mood and I'll fuck those other two six ways to Sunday and leave the door open for you to walk out. You skedaddle, my men will turn a blind eye, assuring that you don't show your mug around this area ever again. Get your ass back to Baltimore. I'm good like that. You've recently dropped a few notches on my fuck-with list. Congratulations." Ringle concluded the mini rant with another long swig of the bourbon.

"You're the one in charge here, boss. I do what you say. You don't know how much I want to get back to my trailer and get as far away as possible from those here in your township."

"Good. Go back to taking pictures of fat fucks cheating on their wives, or vice versa. Stop playing wannabe cop," Ringle said and tried passing the bottle through the cell doorway again. "I can't give you no sounder advice."

"I'll pass again. But yes, sir, I seriously don't want to fuck with you or anyone in Jersey anymore," Rockfish said. "I'll tell you something... I feel sorry for the church dude and the broad. It's only a matter of time before you're running circles around both of them."

"Drink!" Ringle said. "And not because that's a damn agreeable thing to say to me, but because I'm a nice guy and letting you leave town. It's a celebration swig."

"I'll drink to goddamn that," Rockfish said and took the bottle from Ringle.

The rant continued and Ringle gave up caring if Rockfish wanted to hear it or not. He was a captive audience, and Ringle even ignored the occasional eye roll that was done in his general direction.

"I have no desire to keep playing their fixed game. It's not like Imma gettin' a fair share of this government cashola. My guys have done all the heavy lifting, strong armed the weenies at the bank and our take is far less than a third. 'Partners' my ass." Ringle took another swig from the bottle.

"But you, buddy, you're my golden goose, my ticket back to the table. You help me out and Imma gonna show them what I'm capable of, and it's only a matter of time before I regulate that bitch to the back seat like she was in high school." He lifted the bottle to his lips again.

"Yeah, I was a few years ahead of her, but I heard the stories. Probably fucked her way to the top now, too. Don't get me started on who that kid toucher probably fucked. I got it on direct authority, he's playing the pedo shuffle game both around this state and in others." Again, he took a swig. "Just the goddamn shell game with these types. Guys like me go after them and always pick the wrong cup. The ball is never, ever under the one we think it is. Meanwhile, the cup with the ball is long goddamn gone. I'm going to put an end to that shit after I get done with the whore. Ain't gonna be no triumvirate. I'm going to be calling the shots around here for a long time. Dick-tator-ship."

Ringle took one last swig, and the bottle slipped from his fingers. It bounced on the concrete and rolled in front of the next cell before coming to a stop. What was left spilled out across the concrete. Ringle looked at the dead soldier and tried to think back to what he was talking about. He drew a blank but didn't sweat it. In the morning, he wouldn't remember a goddamn thing. *Speaking of which, it's about time I get my ass home,* he thought. *Or the old lady's gonna have it in a sling.*

"Night-night. Keep ya' butthole tight!" Ringle said as he stood up and kicked the bottle further down the hall. At that moment, it didn't occur to him that Rockfish was the only prisoner. Ringle closed the cell door and had some trouble getting the key into the lock, but with some direction from Rockfish, the cylinders finally clicked. Ringle took a couple of steps down the hall and then turned around. He looked back and left the chair.

"Fuck it," he said and kept stumbling back up the hall. "Maybe I should let you go now," Ringle said as he got to the end of the hallway. "I've seen how they want this movie to end. They try to make me the fall guy. Me and mine end up bending over and taking one for the team. Maybe I'll eat one of those ghost peppers before they try and fuck me. Painful for me? Painful for you, Boloney mother fucker."

CHAPTER ELEVEN

Rockfish thought he could hear Ringle puking before the hallway door closed, but he wasn't sure. He was just happy it was the chief that was doing all the talking about getting fucked. Jail wasn't his scene, despite being the only one held captive at the moment.

"What a fucking shit show," he said. Rockfish had no idea why the guy felt he needed to unload his soul tonight and to him, of all people. He kicked his feet up and laid back down on the concrete slab he called home the past couple of nights.

Rockfish was too tired to make any sense of it tonight. Odds were he'd most likely be the only one that remembered it come morning. No matter how sore a subject with the Chief, Rockfish made a promise to himself to bring it up in great detail the next time the two men spoke. He hoped it would be soon when the Chief promised to leave the door open for him. Rockfish could picture Lana in the parking lot, started and ready to go. But there was that one thing that kept nagging at the back of his brain.

Jawnie. What would become of her if he waltzed out of here and returned to Maryland like nothing ever happened? Where was she now? The bad guys obviously didn't have a clue or else Drunky McFuckstick wouldn't have spilled the beans on how they wanted his help in locating her. He had a lot to worry and think about, but for the time being, he needed some sleep so that future strategizing could be done with all his faculties.

Rockfish did not know how long he had slept when a rapping on the bars caused his eyes to snap open. *The Chief, back for more*, was his first thought. But he thought wrong.

"Morning, sunshine," the voice said. Rockfish blinked, got his eyes to finally focus and was shocked to see Hasty sitting on the edge of his bed. In an evening full of surprises, this one was definitely up there.

"Hey, Chief—"

"Former Chief."

"Yeah, I heard something about that. You missed the new guy. He was lonely and wanted someone to drink with. If you run, you can still catch him. I fake sipped the best I could, but he was a fucking wreck by the time he stumbled out of here."

"That's an understatement," Hasty said. "I hung back 'till he serpentined out of the parking lot and down the street. Ringle is on his way home, to a whorehouse or DUI'd into a ditch somewhere, but either way, we're safe for the time being. The only other guy here is still on my payroll. You can trust him."

"Willoughby? That guy's been the only one of these clowns that hasn't been a power tripping dick to me. But let me tell you what you missed."

Rockfish recounted to Hasty, Ringle's largely one-sided conversation. By the end of the story, Rockfish himself was still trying to wrap his head around every word of it. He wasn't sure what Hasty had concluded.

"Like I said, he was wasted. Not sure if he was looking for someone to unload on, like therapeutically. He may have been tired of drinking alone and saying all this shit to himself night after night. I guess I was his Dr. Drew for the time being. Or he was straight up fucking with me. Still not sure which." Rockfish shrugged his shoulders.

"But during his ramblings, were you able to determine why they want this meeting with Jawnie? Is it to use you as bait and then hold you both hostage?"

"They think she has something they need. Ringle thinks they will swap me for it, or at least make her believe that's what they'll do. But we shouldn't let it get to that point. Do you know where she's at? Is she safe?"

"She's good," Hasty replied. "Don't you worry about her. I got her away from her house before they started closing in."

Praise sweet baby Jesus, he thought. *That kid's a survivor.* "Great. Let me apologize up front for trying to convince her not to trust you. My bad."

Hasty shook his head. "Plenty of time for that later."

"Whatever, dude. What I need you to do is keep her safe and out of their hands. That's job number one and you seem to be off to a good start," Rockfish said. "My take on what he said is that they feel that she's young and impressionable. They can throw money at the problem or scare her straight. Ringle doesn't feel that violence is their endgame here, but I don't believe he's thinking straight. Not for a minute. He's talking about letting me go just to fuck with them. As long as you keep her safe, we're buying time and I'll figure out a way to get out of here on my own."

"That doesn't bode well for the long game," Hasty added. He filled Rockfish in on the evidence that Jawnie had copied onto a removable drive. "I don't think for a second if she turns over the USB that you'll be let go, with everyone living life as normal. But I'm not in those high-level discussions. You said Ringle believes that there's a chance if Jawnie hands over what she's got, they'll let her go?"

"Yeah. He spun a half decent argument of Provolone wanting to scare her straight and then leave me here to rot. Not the best bow, but one they would be happy to tie after all of this. You know, Ringle has his own grudge and is willing to set me free and look at them and go 'whoops'."

Hasty shook his head again. "He'll never have a chance."

"Ah, I hope he does. I am getting real tired of the shitty chow served in this joint. Unless you wanna bust me out right now?"

"I can't now. See these cameras? It's the first thing they'll watch after I walk you outta here."

"Fuck me, dude," Rockfish said. "I just wanna get out."

"Don't you worry. Willoughby and I will get you out, preferably at the same time that they call this meeting for. If all goes well, she will give them what they want, and we'll have you out of here at the same time. This way Ringle has to go back with egg on his face and in a perfect world, these dumb fucks eat their own and forget about us."

"It's always good not to be the center of attention," Rockfish said with a laugh.

"Now back to the setup for this meeting. Ringle said he'd give you your cell back to make the call?

"Yeah, said he wanted the caller ID to match the contact saved in her phone. This way she would pick up and not send it straight to voicemail. Even if she doesn't pick up, she'll recognize the number and listen to the voicemail. Hopefully sooner rather than later."

"Maybe he's smarter than we think," Hasty said with a laugh. "Is she saved in your phone?"

"Yeah, why?"

"I'm going to have Willoughby go in and change the number saved under her contact. Jawnie's phone is off and I don't want it powered on and find out it was the sole reason they located her. Pay no mind to the man behind the curtain. Dial the number under the contact and we'll be good, trust me."

"I'm in no position to call shots or ask extremely detailed questions, so I'll follow your lead."

"Great. Now you hang tight. I'll make sure she's safe until we hear about this meeting. Be ready. Willoughby says we'll have about ten minutes to get you out and off the grounds when the wheels start turning."

COVID-19 be damned, the men shook hands, and both silently prayed the other knew what they were talking about.

****

Jawnie awoke and immediately thought of Hasty. He left yesterday afternoon and by the time she finally fell asleep; he hadn't returned. She tried not to worry but failed miserably. She attempted to stay up and at least confirm to her anxiety that he had made it home safe, but failed at that too. The couch was too damn comfortable. But combined with a day unlike any other that had taken her far past her limits, she literally passed out after turning on the television. Awake now, she got her bearings, stood up and took a deep breath. The smell of coffee filled her head.

I've seen this movie, she thought. A walk into the kitchen would end one of two ways. Hasty would be there, all in one piece, and there would be a slight bit of normalcy returned to her upside-down world. The anxiety in her head bet on the polar opposite and her heartbeat joined in on the fun. A bad guy—there were so many—pick one, would wait patiently for her to have woken. With a gun shoved in her ribs and a burlap sack over her head, Jawnie would be pushed into the trunk of a car and driven off.

With her heart ready to burst from her chest, Jawnie grabbed the gun from the coffee table and tiptoed down the hallway. She dipped her head into the kitchen doorframe.

Hasty was sitting at the kitchen table, coffee mug in hand.

Jawnie's eyes quickly scanned the rest of the room to make sure it wasn't a setup. Again, the movie would have some bad guy inside the doorway that would grab her as soon as her guard was down. And then the big reveal was that Hasty was one of them all along.

"Morning, sunshine. Yeah, I didn't bother to wake you. I told you that couch was dangerous."

Crisis averted, she walked the rest of the way into the room and pulled up a chair.

"So, we're kind of a team here," She said and Hasty nodded in agreement. "You left here late afternoon to meet 'a guy' and the last time I remember looking at a clock, it was after 1am. There needs to be some better communication on your part for me not to have a mental breakdown." She put the pistol on the table for emphasis.

"My mistake. Can't guarantee that it won't happen again, but I can try. Let me take that now," Hasty said, and he moved the gun to the counter behind him.

Jawnie accepted the half-assed apology and listened as Hasty recounted his earlier meeting with Willoughby and then how he slipped into Rockfish's jail cell after the Chief had drunk himself silly and gone home.

"The big cheese literally and figuratively, wants to talk to me?"

"She does but remember these are the drunk ramblings of a redneck cop who apparently has an axe to grind with his business partners."

"Do you think this meeting thing is safe," Jawnie asked. "I mean, I had plenty of time to think yesterday and came up with my own plan that I went over and then tweaked while you were out gallivanting."

Hasty waved her off with his hand. "It'll be safe. I gave Willoughby the Google Voice number to put in Rockfish's phone under your contact. No worries about having to power up your actual cell. You can answer the call on the computer and to those sitting around watching Rockfish make the call, it all looks legit. As for the meeting, we'll insist on a public place for the safety of all involved. If they are as desperate as I think to acquire what you have, then they'll capitulate to us picking the spot. No matter if they renege on a promise to let you go or not, I'll be watching and bring holy hell down upon them. But again, according to Ringle, you'll walk away. Annetta's adamant about no violence. A kinder, gentler white-collar mob."

"You've got this all planned out, so I assume you have the perfect spot picked out?" Jawnie said.

"Not yet. Still thinking about it. I want someplace with a large group of people, milling around. Difficult to find during a pandemic, but there are a lot of deniers out there. This way, you can walk and talk, with a ton of places for me to watch from."

"How about a local carnival? Westville is running one this entire week, and it's not too far from my house. They hold it in the field behind the volunteer fire department. Based on previous years, its packed with rednecks every night. I don't see it changing this year, not with how MAGA most of the residents there are. A million witnesses and you could probably hide in plain sight."

"I think that could work. But how the hell did someone get permission to hold a super spreader event with funnel cakes, broken down rides, and registered sex offenders around every corner?"

"My thought exactly. If I recall correctly, I thought you were on Team Hoax." Jawnie said.

"No, the shit is real. I don't think wearing a mask is the end-all that they claim. Yes, I totally get old people are catching this and dying. Younger, stronger immune systems are carrying it. Just because I'm anti-mask doesn't mean I'm pro 'Lets shove a thousand people in a small tight area and roll the dice'. Remember, protect and serve."

"Masks work, but as to the carnival, I saw the add on Facebook and it included a link to a CDC document. I clicked it and it said that if visitors wear masks, social distancing practiced, and if the riders are able to seat themselves without the help of the carnies, it's all good," Jawnie said and sipped her coffee. "Shocked the shit out of me too. There is no way in hell I agree with it, but Trump is relaxing every statute he can to make people believe things are back to normal."

"Okay, then you go and meet. Give them what they want and walk out of there. If that doesn't happen, I'll be by your side as soon as I see the jig's up. But again, Rockfish, and more importantly Ringle, think they'll be happy taking what you give them and scaring the shit out of you. I'm not so sure, but willing to go along with it for the time being. As soon as the meeting is over, we'll meet at a prearranged spot. You gotta trust me with this. I'll try to have some backup with me."

"Okay. Say I have this complete trust, what if they don't let Rockfish go?"

Hasty grinned, and Jawnie could almost see the canary's feathers sticking out from between his lips.

"By that time, the decision will have been taken out of their hands, whether or not Ringle planned to free him," Hasty replied. "Because he'll already be gone by the time this meet-and-greet is over. And well on his way to a rendezvous spot where we'll pick him up."

"I'm guessing your man on the inside will handle this insignificant detail?"

"And others. I was getting to that. While I'm watching you, my guy, name's not important, will throw the circuit breakers and out go the lights. With the security cameras on the fritz, he'll get Rockfish out of the cell and off the grounds. The cover story will be that he was escorting Rockfish to the showers when the lights went off and despite being handcuffed, Rockfish overpowered him and headed for the hills," Hasty said as he ran his hand through his hair. "I mean, it won't look good for him, but he's got plausible deniability, and it's only his word. Good kid, stellar record. And if they railroad him, it wasn't like he planned to spend his entire career working for this podunk department, anyway. He understands it's for the greater good of the order."

"Got it, a slight bit of collateral damage. But what about the cameras? Won't they show Rockfish in the cell when the lights go and not being walked down a hall, when someone eventually reviews them."

"Good point. I didn't think of that," Hasty replied. "But my guy says he's got it all under control."

"Even if he does, I think I can help there and give him some additional plausible deniability, but I'll need access to a computer. This scenario reminds me of something I dealt with when I was working with the local middle school while trying to recover some of their corrupted CCTV files."

"Excellent! We'll take any help we can get. At that point, Rockfish will get his phone back and my guy on the inside will show him where to go so that we can pick him up. You both stay low in the car until we're safely back at the house. And from that point on we'll have to put our heads together and come up with our next move, or where we're running to. But for now, the plan is to get them off our case and everybody's safe. After that's accomplished, we'll move on from that spot when we have to."

"Sounds good. I'm gonna pray it proceeds and goes exactly how you plan."

"In this line of work, you realize they seldom do, but you need to trust that I know what I'm doing. I know I keep saying the trust thing, but it's true."

"Do you?" Jawnie said.

"Yes." Hasty reached across the table and held her hand. Jawnie's first reaction was to pull back. *No idea where that hand's been,* she thought. But it helped calm her, so she left it there but made a mental note to get to her stash of hand sanitizer.

"Good, now we can get working on my plan."

Jawnie had plenty of time the previous evening to think about everything she had collected and exactly what good it was doing in her old lacrosse bag, far from any prying eyes, but also far from doing any real good. If something happened to her, the thought of it being lost and never exploited worried the shit out of her.

"Last night, I found that Canon DSLR camera next to your computer in the office. Arrest me, I like to snoop, but I spent last night photographing Edward's notebooks and Tisha's diary, cover to cover," Jawnie said, and she could see right away that Hasty didn't know what she was talking about.

"Right, you don't know about the diary. It gives a first-hand account of the shenanigans the Ringles and Provolones were involved with around the time of my great grandfather's death. It's more Rockfish's side of this total mess, but its important evidence or history. Edward had a CI who later in life, felt the need to unburden herself on paper. It tells a great story. Now stay with me, I'm going to need access to your computer through your password or create a guest account, I don't care which. You look clueless, but if you login, I can show you."

"First stop is Amazon. I need to order a bunch of 1TB flash drives, along with some padded mailing envelopes. The faster the shipping, the better. If you don't have Prime, I can Venmo and reimburse you somewhere down the line once I can turn my phone on again. This way you open the door and pick up the package from the front step. No chance someone sees you out at the Staples buying all this shit. My plan is to make six copies of everything I have, pictures, notes, and screenshots. I'm going to mail one copy, along with an anonymous letter to the FBI, IRS, and the US Attorney's office in Philly, as well as the one in Camden. I'll leave one copy here for safekeeping with all the originals and the other I can take to this 'meeting' whenever it happens."

"Anonymous letter?" Hasty said. She could see the disgust in his face, or maybe it was him not seeing what she wanted from her point of view.

"I'm not putting my name on it. I don't want this to follow me to where I spend the rest of my life looking over my shoulder. I want this over sooner, rather than later."

"You really think that if this anonymous letter launches a Federal investigation, the Provolones won't think it was you? The mob isn't a Federal Court; they don't need to prove your guilt in this matter beyond a reasonable doubt. They throw a dart in the dark and move on it."

"It's what I want to do. Please don't mock me. Someone recently said it was all about trust." Jawnie waited for Hasty to counter, but he moved back to the mailing conversation.

"You want me to drop them off at the post office? Pay for the postage too?"

"No. Like I said, I thought long and hard on this last night. If I'm hiding out here, shades drawn and such, I don't want to take the chance someone is watching you, for whatever reason. You drive to the post office and mail a stack of manila envelopes, someone's gonna question that, just like if you went to Staples and bought stuff." Jawnie's eyes were wide, and she hoped Hasty was taking in the importance of her plan. "What I need you to do is wait till it's dark and walk all this shit out to your mailbox and put the flag up. I'll rubber band the envelopes together and stick a twenty under the band. This is rural America. Your mailman will get us the right postage, send them on their way, and the next day your change will be in the box with your daily mail. You'd be surprised how helpful the civil servants are out here, despite all the anti-government rhetoric and billboards."

"I find that hard to believe," Hasty said, and the look on his face matched the doubt in his words.

"Hasty, I know you haven't lived out here in the country as long as I have, so you'll have to trust me on this one. Public servants out here go take pride in their jobs, believe it or not."

"Okay, so that's all you need from me? Access to my computer, my mailbox and Amazon account?"

"I need one more favor, now that I think about this whole Google Voice deal. That burner phone you promised. Can you run to Target, Walmart or your convenience store of choice and pick it up for me, the sooner the better? Convenience store is probably better. People would think you're getting gas and a Hoagie. Cheapest one you can get, with a data plan. Should run you like thirty bucks. I'm good for it. Like I said sometime down the road. Activate it in the parking lot."

Jawnie could see confusion had never left Hasty's face from when they started the conversation. While he probably did not agree with her regarding her grand anonymous mailing scheme, he also wasn't standing up and telling her it was the dumbest idea he's ever heard. She'd take the frowny face as a win.

"He calls this Google Voice number and we let it go to voicemail. No way I'm talking to him over your PC. Google will automatically transcribe that message and email it to the Gmail account tied to the number. I'll have the burner phone signed into that account, and then I'll text him back and block the new number. Can't get safer than that. As you like to say, trust me. Any who, Amazon will deliver same day as long as order before 10am, so how about you get me settled on that Dell of yours before you head out to the store? If you go to Wawa, pick me up their vegan buffalo chicken Hoagie, banana peppers, no onions. Trust me, it's a thing."

****

The wait for the call from Rockfish flowed into the next day and the day after. While it only increased Jawnie's anxiety—waiting was never a strong point of hers—she felt safe because it also meant that Ringle, Provolone, or both hadn't a clue where she was. They would grow tired of looking; it was only a matter of time. That made her have a little more faith in Hasty, and likewise his plan. With each passing minute, the odds that Rockfish would call to kick start Ringle's grand plan for criminal organization domination increased exponentially. Or at least it did in Jawnie's and Hasty's minds.

Sunday afternoon soon came, and the Eagles were dominating the Cowboys at home. The teams headed into the locker room at halftime with the Birds up 21 - 3, when the burner phone's notification chime drowned out the Fox halftime show. Jawnie leapt off the couch, opened Gmail, and read the transcription.

Hey Jawnie, it's Rockfish. This is kinda important, so I really wish you had picked up. I've run into some people who would like to meet with you. Might benefit both of us if you can make this happen. Please call me back as soon as you can. They don't look like the kind that will wait around long and might just take it out on me.

Jawnie closed the app and opened Frownies Private Texting SMS and put in Rockfish's number. The app was an added layer of security and would hide her TracFone number from being seen by whoever was now holding Rockfish's cell.

Monday 8pm Westville Shriners Carnival. Gravitron ride entrance.

Jawnie hit send and placed the phone down on the seat next to her and waited. Would the clowns on the other end balk at not hearing her voice or knowing the number from which the text originated? Would they or Rockfish even text back? The questions mounted as they waited for some sort of confirmation.

Hasty had already agreed that they would show up at the fair whether or not there was a reply to the message. He had given Jawnie a quick lesson on the criminal mind and ego and took this into account when he decided. With them attempting to dictate the meeting location and time, the other side might not be thrilled, might feel that Jawnie was overstepping her bounds, but in the end, they were getting what they wanted and would relent. Or at least Hasty thought they would. Hoped they would.

"With that line of thought, I can turn this off and go back to watching the second half?" she said.

"No. We still want confirmation they agreed, if they bother with a reply. Might make each of us relax a bit. Right now, a couple of meatheads are debating who's on the other end of this anonymous text. If their guard is up, it'll be Rockfish who will convince them to let him at the very least call again. Bet on it."

They waited. The Eagles game ended in a blowout victory for the good guys, and they waited. The 4:25 games started, and they continued to wait. Midway through the Giants and Raiders game the phone chirped again.

Jawnie looked at her screen and opened the anonymizer app. "It's Rockfish, via text." She said and read the one-word answer out loud. "Agreed."

Jawnie left Rockfish on read. Somehow, she didn't think it was his first time.

****

"Okay, let's go over this one more time for good measure," Hasty said, hoping repetition would help with Jawnie's nerves.

Sunday had quickly turned to Monday, and the witching hour that day had come faster than either had expected. And as the clock ticked closer, the knot in her stomach only got worse. Jawnie kept that secret to herself.

"You're going to 'yes' them to death. Whatever they want, they got it. Offer them the thumb drive without being prompted. Put them on their heels a little and let them know you are all business. You're a woman of your word and expect no less on their part. I'll be watching. As soon as I see Ringle there, I'll call Willoughby and he'll let Rockfish go."

"How do you know Ringle is gonna be there?" Jawnie said.

"Because he's got an ego on him the size of buffalo balls. He's the one who is setting this whole thing up, feels like he's being slighted by the other two, and maybe even pushed to the side. If I read him correctly, and I did, he'll be there, because above all, he thinks he's in charge."

CHAPTER TWELVE

The moon shone brightly down upon the carnival's midway and with the strip lit up like a Tijuana whore house on half-price Thursday, Hasty had no problems getting a clear and focused view of the playing field. The warmer than normal fall weather continued this evening, and the patrons crowded the midway for a Monday night in the middle of a pandemic. People milled around with some unsure of exactly how far six feet was, others playing fixed games and a handful hoping for a big insurance payout once a ride malfunctioned. In the end, attendance was much less than it would have been over a typical weekend.

Hasty took up position behind a funnel cake stand. *Oh my God, the smell,* he thought. *How long had it been since he had dough bathed in powdered sugar? Too long. Probably since I last screamed on a ride like these kids.*

Jethro was making the doughy powdered sugar bombs and couldn't care less if a jealous husband set up shop behind him to catch his cheating whore wife in the act. Jethro sounded as if he had first-hand knowledge of a situation like this, but it was probably more likely the forty dollars Hasty over-tipped for a funnel cake that sealed the deal.

From this viewpoint, Hasty could see The Gravitron ticket booth and Jawnie milling around. He also had a decent line of sight, should anyone approach the booth from a good thirty yards in any direction. For how nervous Jawnie was on the drive over, from thirty yards away, she looked at ease, bent at the knees, and making small talk with a mother and toddler. He wondered if Jawnie knew them. She lived in Westville, so the odds were in her favor. Hasty tried to will the two people away, and much to his surprise, a second later Jawnie stood back up and the mother and child were on their way.

Prior to arriving on site, Hasty had Willoughby text him pictures of Annetta Provolone and her top Capos, so that he'd at least be familiar with their facial features and able to spot them. Well, as familiar as he could be with them, likely wearing N95 masks. Hasty taped a piece of paper napkin across their faces, much like a flap he could lift up or down to better identify them as soon as possible and not by the time they approached Jawnie.

Hasty spotted Ringle's enormous frame coming down the Midway from the Hall of Mirrors Fun House, a few minutes before eight. He was alone but kept glancing at his watch and walking in small circles like he was waiting on someone. Hasty wondered if the hotdog in his right hand was some sort of prop in order to blend in, but Ringle inhaled it in two bites and Hasty chalked it up to the man trying to calm his own case of nerves.

Hasty's eyes perked up a few minutes later when he clearly saw Annetta Provolone and Anthony Bologna approaching from the opposite direction. Jawnie was now in the middle as the two sides casually and slowly narrowed the distance between them. If he didn't have the pictures to go off of, Hasty would have thought they were any other couple out for some COVID-19 cotton candy and fixed carnival games. From where Hasty stood, the picture on his phone didn't do Annetta justice. She was pushing fifty-five but looked forty and dressed closer to twenty-nine. The large hoop earrings, bare midriff and platform flip-flops screamed 'Little Italy'. Hasty wasn't one to stereotype, but if he was...

When they were within twenty yards of Jawnie, Annetta and Bologna stopped while Ringle continued on, making a wide berth around Jawnie to meet up with them. Hasty hoped that Jawnie spotted Ringle as he walked by, but by her body language, he wasn't sure. Ringle stopped when he reached the others. The three had a brief discussion before making their final approach. Hasty scanned the crowd, hoping to spot any of her goons that he knew would be on site, sitting back, perhaps just out of view like he was.

When his eyes returned to the three, they hadn't moved. The conversation was progressing and it wasn't long before Ringle's hands gesticulated wildly, telegraphing to all that he was already not happy with something. But Annetta put a quick end to that. Hasty didn't know what she said, but her actions spoke loud enough as her index finger tapped his chest twice, in rapid succession. Ringle's hands dropped to his side. With what appeared to be a one-sided agreement on the way forward, the trio walked towards Jawnie. Annetta was in the middle, flanked by both men.

At this point, Hasty reached for his phone and hit send on a previously typed, ready to be sent text message. *he's here, all clear*

Game on, Hasty thought, and said a brief prayer for his partner.

****

Rockfish stared at the clock hung high in the jail hallway.

7:45pm

Shit's about to get real, he thought. He also thought about his dad and Davenport, to a much lesser degree. *I sure miss those breakfasts with the old man. Gotta stop taking that time for granted. I owe Davenport a catch-up call. But only after I hug dad and relax for a day or two.*

Rockfish paced in his cell. He was familiar with bits and pieces of both side's plans, but had no firm grasp on what the entire thing looked like, and that worried him. *I'm not a big fan of sitting back and relying on others to get my ass out of jams,* he thought. *Not comfortable with it at all.* He liked to be in control, or at least be the brains of the operation, knowing all the intricacies of a plan.

The clock's big hand had clicked to five after eight when the lights went out.

Showtime, Rockfish thought, and stood up. He walked in the direction of the cell door, his hands out in front of him. It would be his luck to run into the bars face first and get knocked out on the night of the big prison break. He waited, and that was his other pet peeve. Waiting for someone else to do something before he could react or do his part. But the wait wasn't long, and about two minutes later the door at the end of the hallway opened. Footsteps. He assumed they were Officer Willoughby's, echoing towards him.

"Let's go, man," Willoughby said, and with a key jingle and turn of the cylinders, the door opened. Rockfish hustled his way out into the hall and headed towards the light from the open door, Willoughby on his heels.

"Hold on," Willoughby ordered and put a hand on Rockfish's shoulder. Rockfish stopped in the doorway and turned around.

"Couple of quick things. Here's your phone and a small tactical flashlight."

"What about the cameras?" Rockfish said. "They didn't get a shot of you on tape flipping that breaker?"

"Taken care of. Your friend sent me a corrupted file to copy over in place of the video recording file. I have to use the same naming convention and if anyone tries to open the file, the computer will crash. I hope she's as tech savvy as Hasty says. But we don't have time for this. Seriously, no time. Just listen."

Rockfish put his curiosity aside and shut his mouth. It pained him to be in the dark, literally, and figuratively.

"Here's your phone. On the maps, the pin drop is where Hasty will pick you up. It's a billboard out on the highway, a fair amount of underbrush you can hide out in until he shows. About three miles due east of here."

Rockfish nodded, although in the poorly lit hallway, he wasn't sure if Willoughby had seen.

"Sit tight and out of sight. If the sun comes up and you're still waiting, then text the number under the contact *Spanky*. I'll come pick you up and we'll figure what's up from there. Although if you are texting me, it's probably not good." Willoughby walked around Rockfish and through the doorway.

"Thanks, buddy. I owe you a crab feast next time you're down by the Chesapeake."

Willoughby didn't reply but kept walking as Rockfish headed towards the rear door he had been brought in through. *Safe travels, my friend,* he thought as he and Willoughby parted ways.

Rockfish hit the steps two at a time and jogged across the asphalt. The minute his foot hit the grass, he was relieved and scared at the same time. Light suddenly flooded the parking lot and municipal building. It was as if someone had flipped a switch which of course someone had. He sped up, crossed the street, and came to a stop after slipping behind Nicholson's Feed Store. He pulled out his phone and looked at the directions. His ETA was fifty minutes, but apparently Siri didn't know exactly how out of shape he was.

****

The hand on her shoulder caused Jawnie to whip around, fists clenched and ready for a fight, despite knowing who it most likely was. She was a tad jumpy, and that was putting it mildly.

"Ms. McGee. Let's walk, shall we? You want Rita's?" The woman now standing in front of Jawnie said. She had a second to take in the three people. In addition to the woman, a man flanked her on either side. She thought wooder ice sounded good at the moment. *My throat's dry, and after all, Hasty said to yes her to death,* she thought.

"Yes, ma'am. That would be fine," Jawnie said. *Can she sense I'm scared shitless?*

The younger man to Jawnie's right stepped aside, giving her enough room to slide into position. His sunglasses, at night, gave Jawnie the sense he was trying to hide out in the open. They walked back up the midway, four across. The older man was Chief Ringle. The gut was a dead giveaway.

The Rita's Italian Ice stand was not that far away. Jawnie could squint and see the sign, but it was just off the midway, more towards where the Tilt-A-Whirl was set up. Jawnie hoped Hasty could hang far enough back to follow them as they made their way through the crowd.

The group hadn't taken more than a couple of steps when Jawnie felt something brush against her left hand. She looked down and realized that she was now holding hands with Annetta. The first thing Jawnie thought of was the massive mid-life crisis this woman had to have been undergoing, and the second was that her heart had slowed and for the first time tonight, calm was closing the gap on anxiety. Annetta had calmed her down. *She actually knows what she's doing,* Jawnie thought.

"Ummm, I'm supposed to give this to you," Jawnie said, following Hasty's orders to the letter. She had pulled the USB drive from her right front pants pocket and held it out across her chest. She watched

Annetta's eyes take in the device and then looked forward towards the wooder ice stand.

"Why don't you hold on to that for now, honey," Annetta said. "We can handle business after we have our ice."

Jawnie ordered cherry and Annetta, vanilla. The men didn't partake but stood guard a few feet away as if they were keeping groupies away. Jawnie offered to pay, but Annetta had none of that. They stood off to the side of the stand, away from the crowd, and ate their ice in silence. Annetta ordered Chief Ringle to take their empty cups over to the garbage can, and Jawnie noticed a slight change in Annetta's tone. Must be business time, she thought. *Sooner we start, the sooner I can get the hell out of here.* It was the only thing on her mind. Walking out of this place alone and waiting for Hasty to pick her up.

"Let's walk back towards the midway," Annetta suggested. "The noise from some of these rides is driving me nuts. I'm sure we can find a nice little spot to handle what we need to."

She led Jawnie to a small roped off area, slightly off the main drag, where half a dozen plastic picnic tables were spaced apart. Most of the tables were empty as people tended to carry their food and ate as they walked. They all sat down, Annetta and Jawnie on the same side. Jawnie thought back to the original advertisement she had seen with the link to the CDC document. Sitting four at a table had to be breaking one of the rules.

"I'll take that from you now."

Jawnie pulled the USB drive back out from her pocket, and as she dropped it into Annetta's outstretched hand, Annetta then took her left hand and sandwiched the drive and Jawnie's hand between hers. The woman's eyes were piercing as she spoke.

"This is your only copy, correct? And I mean only because anything, and I do mean everything, you had on your network back in your shop is toast. It's the damnedest thing, but all your network storage devices—as the kids say these days—were reformatted via sledgehammer. And don't even think about those copies you saved to the cloud; my nerd got those too."

My business. Every cent I have was tied up in the shop, she thought. *It's all gone. Was there anything left salvageable?* Jawnie tried to hide these thoughts that ran through her head.

"I'm going to ask one more time, to make sure you've had a second to think about it. This is the last of the copies you've made?" The pressure applied to her right hand increased to the point of it being painful, and the woman still looked straight through her with those eyes.

"Yes," Jawnie said as smoothly as if it were true. She wondered if Annetta had included the physical backups Jawnie stored in the crawlspace under her house. The term network storage devices was open to interpretation, but Jawnie didn't want to go there at this moment.

"Thank you, my dear. You have no idea how pleasant it is to do business with someone like yourself. We agreed to meet, like civilized people, and you gave me what I needed. In return, you have my word." Annetta winked. "But, my dear, this ends here and now." Annetta released her hands and poked Jawnie in the collarbone with her index finger to emphasize the point. "I don't give a shit about you, your half-assed 'My husband has porn on this. Can you erase it' business, or that private dick and his History Channel project. I'm going to go my way and you go yours, but first, it's not that I don't trust you, but you can never be too sure these days."

Annetta handed the drive to the man still hiding behind his shades, who walked it over to a young kid with a laptop sitting at the next table.

Where the hell did he come from, she thought? *How did I miss him walking up and sitting down and with a laptop, for Christ's sake? Were those eyes that mesmerizing?*

"Chenzo here is going to take a peek at what you brought. I hope you don't mind, but the last thing I want to do is get home and find out you gave me a drive full of your mother's old recipes or pictures from your trip to Key West the August before last."

The words were meant to catch Jawnie off guard, and they did. She felt her heart beat a tattoo in her chest.

"Now don't get your panties in a bunch hon, it's just my job to do my homework before these types of meetings. I can't afford to have buyer's remorse."

They all turned to Chenzo, with the other man watching over his shoulder, as he plugged the device into the laptop and did his thing. *Whatever that was*, Jawnie thought. She paid attention to his eyes as they darted back and forth across the screen while his fingers mashed at the keyboard.

"All clear. Nothing malicious," Chenzo said without his eyes or fingers stopping. "I'm going in."

Jawnie swallowed hard when Chenzo began pointing at different parts of the screen. The man behind him leaned closer. They spoke softly and seemed to confer before coming to some sort of agreement. Hard as she tried, Jawnie couldn't hear any of what was being said. Finally, after what felt like an eternity, Chenzo yanked the drive from the laptop and closed the lid.

"It matches what we found in the shop," Chenzo said. At the same time, Jawnie exhaled deeply and spilled a sigh of relief, despite coming into the meeting, knowing exactly what was on the drive. She had made a point of not including the photos of Edward's notebooks or Tisha's diary.

Annetta nodded as Chenzo handed the drive back to 'sunglasses', who pocketed it. He followed Chenzo as he walked away. They stopped short of the midway where they shook hands and the man returned to the picnic table alone.

"You were a woman of your word, Ms. McGee," Annetta said. "I am very happy that you didn't try to fuck me over in this deal. In my business, being a female, people think they can get one over on me easier. It happens more than you can imagine, but being a female business owner, I'm sure you encounter it as well."

"Yeah, sure." The answer came from Jawnie's mouth before she could clear it with her brain. The answer showed her true feeling. Jawnie was nowhere like this criminal, not on any gender playing field. While she didn't break Hasty's yes her to death rule, the sarcasm that hung from that two-word reply was potent. The expression on Annetta's face let Jawnie know that the meaning behind those words was not lost on her.

"I'm sorry. Have I perturbed you?"

"I apologize, ma'am, I'm very nervous, tired, anxious. Maybe a huge mixture of the three. I did not mean any disrespect."

"Now see, Jawnie, that's where we differ."

Jawnie thought the use of her first name should emphasize the difference between the mood of the conversation only five minutes ago and now. She received the message loud and clear. She swallowed hard, trying to keep all those emotions and the anger that was beginning to build deep inside her. Annetta leaned closer to Jawnie and again took her hand in hers.

"There is a sizeable difference in my book between giving respect to someone and humoring them. It appears you aren't as well-mannered or educated as I thought."

"I meant no harm but if you can't get past it, well then, I won't sit here and try to convince you otherwise. But what about Steve Rockfish?" Jawnie interjected. If Annetta thought she had mis-stepped, Jawnie might as well get the rest of it out. "I've done my part here. Bring him out so we can leave all this behind us. You have what you came for."

Annetta's lips pursed, and a small vein popped in her forehead. "Well, aren't you just the topic jumper when you get flustered," Annetta replied. "Even in this moonlight, I can see the red spreading across your face. As for Mr. Rockfish, you don't think I'd be dumb enough to bring him here? Not our first rodeo, kiddo. What happens to your new-found friend from Charm City is entirely up to the Chief here." Annetta nodded at Ringle.

"You don't have to worry about him, he'll be alright and back home in Maryland before he knows it," Ringle said. "Come the morning, we'll out-process him, and my men will escort him across the Delaware Memorial Bridge with the firm understanding that there's a penalty for coming back here, let alone poking his nose around in my town. My men assure me that Mr. Rockfish fully understands the gravity of the situation now. And if he doesn't or has questions, Ms. Provolone here can call down to her friends in Baltimore to help him forcibly understand what his exact limitations are." Ringle interlaced his fingers and rested his chin on top, his elbows firmly on the table. He grinned, and Jawnie despised the man like no other.

She could only sit there and hope that Hasty's plan at the jail had gone off without a hitch. She felt helpless sitting here and didn't believe a word Ringle said. He would leave Steve to rot in that cell and with each reflection down that line of thought, Jawnie could feel the tension mounting inside her. She could feel sweat dripping down the small of her back and her legs were twitching.

"Now if you are done interrupting me, I feel the need to tell you that while you acted in good faith in coming here tonight, you've caused me and my associates some problems that cannot and will not be wished away. I require reconciliation before all parties move forward. And for you, moving forward means leaving this white trash hoedown still breathing and a debt that needs to be paid."

Debt? Paid? Jawnie wondered. She barely made enough cash to keep her parent's old house out of foreclosure. *If the Provolone family wanted free computer trouble-shooting services, what the hell was Chomo, Chenzo, whatever the fuck his name doing?* Her guessing was all over the place and interrupted only because 'sunglasses' finally spoke.

"What's gonna happen is that one of my men will show up every Friday afternoon and you'll hand him an envelope. Three hundred in cash. If you can't pay, we have other avenues of revenue we can explore with you. But it's better for all of us if you have the envelope ready."

"Much better on all accounts," Annetta added. "You like your shop; you don't want to take on a partner."

That threat did not go over Jawnie's head. Now, this movie, she'd seen. *Goodfellas* was her father's favorite, and they watched it too many times to count. Her mind immediately pictured Henry and Tommy inside her shop, late at night, getting ready to torch it for the insurance money. *That settles it,* she thought. *I'm never going home.* Jawnie needed to get back to Hasty's plan and get out of this situation. Anger with a dash of common sense now led.

"Yes, of course," she said. "Is there any denomination of bills you would prefer over another?"

The two mobsters looked at each other and then back to Jawnie. She had already dipped her toe in the sarcasm pool and went for it.

"Exactly what is the total I owe and is there a monthly statement your man will provide when he stops by?" By the look on Annetta's face, Jawnie knew she had run right up to the line. "What about taxes, can I deduct it?"

"Listen to me, you fucking cunt." Annetta brought out the index finger again. It slammed into Jawnie's clavicle with every syllable. "I've about had enough of you and that private dick and the trouble you're causing. I'm not sure what either of you clowns think can be accomplished by digging up dirt on something that happened last century. Television show, podcast, fucking sock puppet show, no one is going to watch that shit. But I'll let you in on a little secret. If the two of you keep digging into my current endeavors or even my ancestor's business, you'll end up like your relative."

The sideways mention of Edward McGee caught Jawnie's full attention, like a punch to the gut. Annetta's voice was substantially lowered after a brief pause, possibly for dramatic effect.

"The gist of this is, don't push me. I'm not the violent type, those days are over. It's not like my grandfather Julius is in charge." Annetta winked. "But sometimes people don't listen and you have to take action. Like in the old days. I understand he had a history with the McGees that didn't go so well for your side." She winked again.

The roller coaster of emotions that Jawnie rode the past hour rocketed off the tracks and crashed into the Ferris Wheel. In her mind, people screamed in pain, flames filled the night sky and those not grievously injured ran for the parking lot. On the outside, the tears flowed like a flash flood, fast and unexpected. She had let her emotions get the better of her, and Hasty's plan was in jeopardy because of it.

"I think we're done here," Annetta said and stood up from the picnic table. "We got what we came for and our points appear to be well taken."

The threesome quickly blended back into the crowd on the midway, not that Jawnie could have followed their path through her clouded vision. She remained firmly planted at the table, her head buried in her hands. She occasionally lifted her mask to wipe her eyes and nose with her sleeve, not giving a fuck at this point.

Jawnie's cell phone read 9:56, after she blinked half a dozen times so the numbers would come into focus. She wondered where Hasty was watching her meltdown from. She could really use a shoulder to get the rest of these tears out on, but he was a stickler for the plan and Jawnie knew she would be alone for a bit longer.

She sat for another ten minutes before finally rising from the table. Jawnie headed in the direction of the parking lot and with each step, her mind tried to plan some sort of revenge. What she hoped would be a large-scale Federal raid, arrest and trial was no longer enough.

****

Hasty watched the meeting break up from his vantage point alongside everyone's favorite 'Balloon dart game'. Jawnie remained seated with her head in her hands and he waited. He had the feeling something towards the end of the meeting didn't go as planned, and Jawnie's emotions may have taken over. For both of their sakes, he hoped she remembered the rest of the plan, especially since everything had gone expected, at least what he saw from his point-of-view.

He stood his ground, waiting for her to get up. The plan they had discussed and went over time and time again was for Jawnie to walk back to her house. The white trash carnival was less than a mile away, and it only made sense that was where they'd expected her to go. Hasty expected someone to follow her as she left and that was the reasoning behind her walking home and not him driving up into the parking lot and picking her up. Whoever was watching her needed to believe that she sulked the entire way back to her home after the meeting to cry her eyes out. Being back at her house would only reinforce the idea to the bad guys that in Jawnie's mind, there was no reason to hide anymore. The night was over. Whoever was assigned to follow Jawnie would be drawn into a false sense of security. Hasty wanted that, they needed that. The scenario would raise the least amount of suspicion.

Hasty watched as Jawnie finally pulled herself together and walked away from the picnic table. It didn't take Hasty long to identify the two men tasked with tailing her. *Amateurs*, he thought. They didn't try to conceal who they were or their mission. They followed her off the midway and out into the parking lot and Hasty did the same, although much more discreetly. He kept a good distance between himself and the two men, but not far enough away that he couldn't also have eyes on Jawnie. She crossed the parking lot and turned right onto the sidewalk that paralleled Lehigh Street. Hasty observed the men split up. One stayed on the sidewalk while the other jumped into a nondescript car that was parked on the side of the road.

Hasty kicked his pace up a notch, now that the car was slowly catching up to Jawnie. He could picture it pulling up alongside her and the three of them would be gone before he could do anything to prevent it. He held his breath as the car approached her, eventually sped past and then pulled over further up the road. The guy who trailed her kept his distance. The car pulled back onto the street as Jawnie and the man following her put a city's block distance between them.

This scenario repeated itself half a dozen times until Jawnie got within a block of her house. At which point the car picked up the other man and drove down the street, leaving Jawnie to walk the rest of the way alone. Hasty watched as the car pulled a U-turn before the next stop sign and eventually came to a stop directly across the street from Jawnie's house. It was amateur hour, and Hasty hoped to God that Jawnie had taken notice. But he also remembered how she looked when she got up from the picnic table just a little while ago. He hoped her emotions were not clouding her vision as to what was going on directly in front of her. Either way, the plan was for her to remain calm, eyes forward and keep moving until she was safely in the house with the door locked. She was killing it.

Hasty stepped behind a large oak tree on the corner of Avon Avenue. From here, he had an unobstructed view of the car idling across from the house. He watched as Jawnie proceeded up the walkway and through the door. No car door opened, nor did it budge as she proceeded through the first floor, turning on various lights. Hasty hoped that these guys weren't planning on spending the night. If they wanted to pick her up, they would have done so before she barricaded herself in the house. He laid odds they were only going to put Jawnie 'to bed' as they used to call it on the force. That entailed following someone until they were home, and you would know where to pick up the surveillance in the morning. Not that Hasty expected these clowns to stay the night or have another team relieve them at sunrise. He hoped that now that Jawnie had put some brick and a steel door between them, they would grow tired and drive away.

Hasty watched Jawnie backtrack across the first-floor and turn out all the lights one by one. A minute later, a bedroom light on the second floor flickered on and that was the car's cue as it slowly pulled away. He then broke into a jog and circled around Walnut Street where he had parked his car earlier. He ignored the car and cut between two houses and a backyard before ending up at Jawnie's back door.

She appeared ten seconds after he knocked, and they retraced his steps to the car and headed out to pick up Rockfish.

****

The moon was high in the sky and it had been two hours since Rockfish arrived at this recently harvested soybean farm. His legs still ached from the part walk, part jog, part crawl, three-mile hike. He loosened the laces on his shoes, hoping to lessen some of the pain from his swollen ankles. The days of acing the Presidential Physical Fitness Test were long gone. He collapsed in the one small section of ground where the tall weeds under the billboard did not grow.

Dear Lord, please tell me everything went as planned tonight and I won't wake up in this goddamn field in the morning, he thought. *All I can ask at this point is to get me home safely so I can spend some time with my dad. Oh, yeah and I don't want to end up sleeping with the fishes. Amen.*

Based on being right along the road, Rockfish figured this to be a prime spot for a patrolman to park before spending his shift writing tickets and filling the Township's coffers with fines. And if that didn't sufficiently sap the lower middle-class citizens of Elk Township of their hard-earned money, the billboard above Rockfish provided a fourteen-foot-high alternative. Apparently Hulk Hogan was still shilling for Rent-A-Center where you could rent a 42 inch RCA television for only $19.99 a week.

Or you could buy it from Walmart for $299, he thought, *and put some goddamn food on the table.*

Rockfish was still griping about everyone wanting to make a buck off the backs of those that couldn't even afford that dollar in the first place, when his little hidey hole was lit up by the umpteenth set of headlights he had seen this night. As he had done for each previous set, Rockfish moved into the brush and waited. This time, the car slowed, stopped, and then backed into the small clearing. Someone knew what they were doing.

"Appreciate y'all not forgetting about little old me," Rockfish said as he climbed into the back seat. "Nobody followed you?"

"Not a chance," Hasty replied.

"You sure?"

"I'm a cop, I think I'd know."

"Umm, used to be, and I think you would too, but you'd be surprised at the overstating of one's skill set I've encountered since I got to this godforsaken place," Rockfish said with a laugh and grabbed Hasty's shoulder and gave it a good shake. "Everything go as you hoped?"

"All according to plan," Hasty said.

"I was an emotional wreck and almost fucked it all up, but other than that, smooth sailing," Jawnie said.

"What's our next move?" Rockfish said.

"You want to have a catch-up strategy session right here under the Hulkster?" Jawnie said with a twinge of sarcasm.

"Good thinking," Rockfish said. "My first day of freedom. I'm still getting acclimated."

"Speaking of which, Willoughby texted me and said Ringle didn't stop by the jail. Your secret is still safe, at least until 6am when the shifts change."

With a decent head start, Rockfish knew what he wanted and didn't shy away from letting the others know what they needed to do.

"Swing back to my hotel. I need my car if they didn't have it towed by now. If it's there, I'll give you my address and meet you at my trailer in two hours. If Lana's locked up, I'll just hang here and give you directions from the back seat. I think the further we are from this place when the sun comes up, the safer we'll all be."

"Agreed," Jawnie and Hasty said in unison.

CHAPTER THIRTEEN

Annetta Provolone was in her happy place. The beauty salon smelled of lavender and the silence was music to her ears. Mrs. Choe always provided the professional courtesy of closing the shop whenever Annetta scheduled a day of beauty—half day or even a quick manicure—and that was what you called respect. Whatever small profit Mrs. Choe lost today, Annetta would more than make up for it by recommending the place to everyone she knew, spouses and goomahs alike. Most of all, Mrs. Choe also knew how to keep her mouth shut, and that was the primary reason for throwing business her way.

Sitting in the big recliner, Annetta leaned forward to watch as the little doctor fish swam around her feet and feasted on her dead skin.

Circle of life. Hakuna matata and all that shit, Annetta thought. She wondered if the little buggers could talk, what would they say?

Tastes like gabagool, she thought, and that made Annetta laugh out loud. She was in a good mood, and why not? Both her current problems were no longer an issue and on CNN this morning, the decaying turtle, AKA the senate majority leader, was quoted as saying, "No matter who won the upcoming presidential election, a second stimulus would be a top priority."

A noise caught her attention, and she turned to see her phone vibrating across the next seat. She leaned over and grabbed it before it slid off into the bucket of water.

Unknown Caller (856) 555-4251

Fuck that, she thought and tossed the phone back onto the chair. A second later, curiosity got the better of Annetta and she reached back over to pick it up. No voicemail notification, only one for the missed call. No sooner had she locked the screen, the vibrating started again.

Unknown Caller (856) 555-4251

Annetta readied her wrath and tapped the green answer icon.

"This better be goddamn important if you know what's good for you," She exclaimed into the phone.

"Annetta, Ringle here..."

"Shit," she said aloud and immediately took him off speaker.

"What the fuck, Scott? Do we ever talk on the phone? We have an app we use strictly to communicate. It's encrypted and safe. Need I remind you of the reason?"

"Sorry, Annetta, but I'm nowhere near my cell. This is my landline."

"To your house?" She didn't even wait for his reply. "Jesus Christ, just shut up. Don't say a word."

"Yeah, but it's important. Not to worry, my wife is out in the garage working on her car. She can't hear shit out there."

"It's not her I'm worried about, Einstein." Annetta's sarcasm was sharp, but Ringle continued on as if he didn't hear a word of it.

"We lost Rockfish last night, and I wanted you to hear about it ASAP. My men are on it and have assured me they'll have him back within our control before Leonard's stopped serving brunch omelets."

"I don't know who the fuck you are talking about, capisce?" *This guy,* she thought. *And on a freakin' open line.* She was at a loss for words.

"I know, but he ain't here no more."

"Ringle, listen. Because we know each other doesn't mean you can call me and fill me in on the screw-ups of your employees. I am not that shoulder people can cry on. Your employment problems are just that: yours. I'm sure there are procedures in place, some sort of cop manuals that can guide you through exactly what to do in a situation such as this."

"You have to listen to me!" Ringle said. Annetta could hear the strain in his voice. He was scared. He fucked up. Rockfish got out on his own. "Look, the place was empty when the day shift came on this morning. The overnight officer ain't here either. I'm not sure Rockfish and him are Bonnie and Clyde'ing it, or if Willoughby's a hostage. I'm losing my shit over here."

"Get off this goddamn phone and find your cell! The one I pay for!" Her glass of Pinot Grigio smashed against the far wall. She had enough of his breaking protocol. Annetta hoped the Government man in the middle listening in, was on their mandated fifteen-minute coffee break.

Annetta hung up on Ringle. The level of incompetence and stupidity of this man never ceased to amaze her. That call was the straw that came damn close to breaking her back, let alone the camel's. Maybe that Hasty guy wouldn't have been so bad to work around if he never played ball. She would have to give this some serious thought, but not until after the horse was found and shoved back in the barn.

Annetta's pampering day was officially over. Having paid Mrs. Choe in advance and knowing that she would be undisturbed within the spa, she decided to temporarily turn the space into her office for the rest of the late morning.

It took Ringle another twenty minutes before he messaged her with the complete story, and by that time, she had heard all she needed to hear from him. Next, she reached out to Bologna and told him to drop whatever he was doing and come join her for an angry mani-pedi, heavy on the angry.

****

Tony Bologna pulled up to the strip mall and guided his Audi into the handicapped space directly in front of Choe's Heavenly Spa. He sat in the driver's seat for a couple of minutes, building the nerve to go in. If she invited him for an angry mani-pedi, without even knowing his bad news, it would be more like a ballistic mani-pedi. Had she heard already? Fuck, he only knew about the girl slipping out of her house within the last hour. Did she somehow have his phone tapped? He made a mental note to have Chenzo look at it, then swallowed hard and went in.

Mrs. Choe met him at the door and escorted him to the walled off section to the right where Annetta was sitting. The chair was so large compared to her tiny frame that it looked ready to swallow her up at a moment's notice. She was swishing her feet back and forth in some sort of bucket and she seemed in a good mood. But you never could tell with the Boss. And even if she was, which he knew she wasn't, it wasn't going to last very long after he opened his mouth.

"Tony, come on in, the water is fine," Annetta said. "Actually, don't. I'm getting out. These damn fish creep me out, but they do one hellova job. Mrs. Choe, let Donna know that I'm ready for my manicure and that I'll be having someone join me."

Tony looked for a jumping off point, a place where he could squeeze his bad news in, but Annetta kept going as a small woman dried off her feet. He followed as they walked across the spa to the manicure area. Annetta sat and patted the chair next to her. Bologna did as he was told.

"I got a call from that jidrool Ringle. After our beautiful meeting last night, you were there. Everything was settled, and the seas were calm again. And then this stunod goes and fucks it three ways from Friday. Rockfish pulled a disappearing act and vanished." She pounded the arm of the chair. "Ringle claimed his men will have Rockfish back by lunch, but I don't believe that for a second."

Tony swallowed hard, harder than out in the parking lot. He knew the Boss was pissed off over something, but he didn't know that someone else had screwed the pooch as bad as he did. On the good side, it meant that he would only get half her wrath, instead of both barrels.

Annetta took a sip from her replacement wine glass. "I mean, Rockfish is gone. I expected someone to at least put the fear of God into the man before he ran home. That's if he even headed home. Now we gotta put resources into tracking him down and making sure he's on board like his little baldracca. I can tell you, that one won't ever give us a sideways glance again. She knows what's good for her. When the inevitable message from Ringle comes later today that his men have come up empty-handed, I'll call down to Maryland and see if Angelo can spare some guys to keep an eye out for Rockfish. Or not. Do you think that guy will be a problem any longer?"

By this time, Donna and another employee had slathering the two mobster's nails with cuticle gel before having them soak in the warm sudsy water.

Tony broke his silence and agreed. "Ah, I think he's going to hide out for a while. Scared like a cat. Plus, he knows that our friends in Baltimore won't hesitate to deal with him if he steps out of line or even tries to open his mouth."

"My thoughts exactly. Like I said, last night was perfect." Annetta said. "Now is there something you want to tell me? Your face looks like you haven't shit in a week. Now granted I've rambled on about that redneck asshole Chief, but you look like you're holding back on me, Tony. Please, for the love of fucking God, please don't tell me you've got fucked up news too."

He tried swallowing again, but there wasn't a drop of moisture in his mouth.

"Ahh, I-I-I lost the girl."

"Vaffanculo! I said please." Annetta's hand came out of the soaking water and backhanded him across the side of his head. She was fast, but even if Tony had seen it coming, he knew better than to move or even flinch. The left side of his face stung like a bitch, but he soldiered on.

"She's not at the house. My guys literally watched her go to sleep last night. I stopped by a little while ago to make sure she's still on the team, you know, abiding by what she said last night. People think too much at night, and I didn't want her making a rash decision because she was too wound up and over thought the situation." Tony lowered his head and rubbed his temples with his right hand. "Knocked, no answer. Banged, same deal. I had Chilly bust a window and wiggle through it. The place was empty. Nothing on the inside looked as if it changed since the day we took it apart."

Tony braced for the hand again, but it didn't come. The Boss' point was made the first time. Now it was time to explain how he would right this wrong. He knew she expected he would not have walked into the spa without a plan already being executed that would correct the problem.

"My crew is already pounding the streets with walk around cash if anything pans out. She got nowhere to go, no family close by, no nothing. Someone's going to see her or hear from her and we'll be there with some cash to make sure that information gets fast-tracked to one of my men." *I hope that settles her,* he thought. *At least until I can get the fuck out of here.*

"She's got something," Annetta countered. "I mean, she was somewhere before we met last night. She was somewhere when you trashed her house and shop. I would say that's exactly where she's returned to. You need to figure that shit out. That's your starting point, not sitting here trying to decide between Smoke Red and Bordeaux Lust."

Tony understood. He pulled his hands from the soak and stood up to leave. "I'll be in touch, Boss".

"Listen. You fucked up. Ringle fucked up. No reason for me to call down south. You f'd up, you call Baltimore. If Rockfish ran home, then they can verify. Might be a better than fifty-fifty the girl is with him. Find them both and put them in the goddamn well. What was good enough for her great grandfather is good enough for her. Goddamn it, should have listened to O'Hanlan."

****

"Yes. Yes, you should have," Bishop O'Hanlan said as Annetta walked through the rectory's front door, and Annetta wondered if he read her mind. It had been Annetta's idea to meet at the Holy Name of Jesus' rectory building. Partially because it would put O'Hanlan at ease but also, she had no desire to make the drive to Camden.

O'Hanlan was dressed in his best flowing kid-touching robes, and Annetta wondered what kind of impression he was trying to make. It had been a few decades since that get-up and tall hat put the fear of God into her, and longer since someone had tried to get handsy.

Maybe he has a Zoom call with the Pope afterwards, she thought. *Day-to-day business needed to continue, even during a pandemic*. He had spread himself out across the couch in the seating area, outside the hallway that led to the resident priest's living quarters.

O'Hanlan arched his back and relaxed back into his chair. "My sources tell me that both of your little issues are unaccounted for, despite your promises to the contrary on how well everything had proceeded last evening. Let me re-phrase that, *our issues*, I should have said, because we're partners and what is bad for you is equally bad for me. Maybe worse, I've got a reputation to uphold."

Annetta sat down in a chair opposite the couch and didn't say a word. As far as she was concerned, he could gloat and get it all out of his system before they actually got down to figuring out the next course of action.

She knew he would begin with the, 'If we had only done it my way, none of this would be a concern.'

"You don't think it's the slightest bit of a coincidence that our problem children vanished at the same time?"

Annetta shuffled in her chair. She wasn't able to hold her tongue any longer. *Damn robes,* she thought. *I'm not afraid of putting it all out there. What's he gonna do?*

"If you're asking me if I think that all of this is a big coincidence? If the strings behind the scenes are being manipulated by someone else? Neither of these two are that smart, nor are we aware of them working with anyone else. Two different fuck-ups fucked up last night. Nothing more, nothing less. Now, we as leaders need to come up with how we are going to fix it and, unfortunately, order these same fuck-ups to enact said fix. Unless you would like to bring some of your players into the game?" Annetta was getting sick of his little victory dance. It did neither of them any good to sit here and have Father Handsy recap the events of the last 24 hours. What was done was done, but apparently O'Hanlan had a different opinion and continued to drive it home. Like she had said, it wasn't as if he or his men were the ones out on the front lines. Monday morning quarterbacking, that's all it was.

"Well, in my world we don't believe in coincidences. Fate is the name of the game. Annetta, all signs point to you being played by these two mutts. Whether these two planned it, or someone else conducted the orchestra, it really doesn't matter. You were wrong this time, and you were wrong to question what myself or my team are capable of."

"Can we move past the berating—"

"So, she gave you a USB drive and shook your hand," O'Hanlan interrupted. "Did you even bother to check and see what was on it?"

Annetta gritted her teeth against the dentist's orders. "No, I put it in my pocket and then handed it to the rube running the basket toss game. It's probably been overwritten with child porn half a dozen times by now. Oh, I see, that's why you're so interested in it." Annetta could give far worse than she got. The Bishop should have known that by now. He was all talk and her team, the actionable ones.

"Don't patronize me Annetta with your worn-out stereotypes." O'Hanlan dismissed her attitude with a wave of his hand. "All I'm trying to do is protect the Church's interests here. It's a troublesome time now and any cash flow situation, legal or partially not, needs to continue. That is my priority here, not trading insults with you."

"It's all of ours," Annetta replied. "You think I would happily let all of this go to the dogs and send my men back to hijacking trucks and running numbers? This is true white-collar shit that takes little effort on the front end and pays off on the back."

"I'm just saying with recent events, someone needs to pay for these mistakes. It's the point I made previously and will continue to beat that dead horse when I know it was the right thing. I know damn well you'll let your men run every lead into the ground before their 'Come to Jesus moment'. Your aversion to breaking a few eggs has come back to bite us. I think it's time I act. The Church has sat on the sidelines observing, being a peripheral player for far too long."

Annetta grabbed the arms of her chair and stood, but thought better of it. *I'm here alone with no backup and who the hell knows what this clown is capable of,* she thought. She relaxed her grip on the chair and forced a smile.

As if right on cue, the front door opened and Annetta turned to see Ringle letting himself in without knocking.

"Sorry to barge in folks, but I heard you were having a meeting and I guess my invitation was lost in the mail. Thought I'd swing on by and see if y'all needed anything."

Annetta watched as O'Hanlan's face, above the face mask, turned beet red and steam rose from his ears. But from six feet away, she wasn't close enough to verify it. She turned to Ringle, watched him walk into the seating area, and pull up a chair.

"I miss anything?" Ringle grinned and sat down.

"Other than your face mask?" Annetta replied.

"Oh, I got one here," Ringle said. "I knew you'd have a conniption if I didn't bring it."

"We were discussing your men's running of Stalag 13," O'Hanlan said.

"Nice one. Hogan's Heroes reference. I won't say it wasn't uncalled for. But we'll find him. His car isn't at the Marriott anymore, so he's headed home. I mean, that's what you wanted, right? Problem solved. Not exactly the execution we all wanted, but mission accomplished nonetheless on my part."

Annetta cleared her throat and shook her head. She could tell whoever told him about the meeting failed to mention Jawnie McGee's disappearance. She pondered telling him at this moment, instead of pulling him aside afterwards, but a cough from the hallway behind Ringle's chair side-tracked her.

"Chief, Annetta, I'd like to introduce Father Busch. He's new to the parish, having arrived here in June." O'Hanlan said, and the priest waved from the hallway. Busch was the youngest in the room and, by the looks of his clothes, had just come from a workout. He leaned against the wall and it appeared to Annetta, the newest member of their group planned to take the rest of the meeting from that position behind Ringle.

"Chief, so you're saying that despite the jailbreak, Rockfish has left the state and we shouldn't worry about anything else?" O'Hanlan said.

"Exactly," Ringle replied. "The man is running scared and will no longer be a problem to us, trust me."

"If that's the case, then I'd say we're done here."

Annetta shook her head. *Done here? There wasn't a damn thing accomplished,* she thought as a blur came into her peripheral and a loud wheeze followed from her right. Her head swiveled to see what it was.

Ringle had his hands at his throat, and his feet desperately searched for traction. Father Busch stood behind him and pulled for all he was worth. Garrote, was her first guess. She watched in utter amazement at the unexpected move from left field being played out. O'Hanlan stood up from the couch and walked over to the flailing man.

"Through this holy anointing may the Lord in His love and mercy help you with the grace of the Holy Spirit. May the Lord who frees you from sin save you and raise you up."

Annetta recognized the last rites. A man dying in front of her wasn't something she had never seen, but the unexpectedness of today's sacrifice threw her for a loop.

Ringle continued to struggle for another minute, but the stench of urine let Annetta know the Chief was poorly hydrated and no longer a voting member of the group. *Well, that escalated quickly. Things are probably 50/50 now and I probably don't have the 51% I always thought I would in this situation,* she thought. *I need to walk out of here alive.*

When O'Hanlan finished with the last rites, he stepped aside and Father Busch dragged the lifeless body down the hallway towards the residence.

"Better get the actual winner of that election back on duty, before someone steals a cow and no one is around to investigate it," O'Hanlan said as he sat back down.

Annetta didn't change her expression over the piss poor attempt at humor, but was more concerned about getting back safely to her car before that ninja priest crept up behind her.

"Now Annetta, I don't expect you to exact that type of retribution upon the men under your scrutiny, but I'll expect you to hold someone somehow responsible as soon as that girl is found."

Both parties agreed, and the meeting ended. It wasn't until Annetta was back in her car, and the doors locked, that she pulled out her phone and messaged Tony.

add Hasty to APB & bring him to me - wheels r coming off

****

Day two in Maryland for Rockfish's guests was ending, and the cramped quarters were wearing on all. Rockfish had gotten off a call with his dad when he looked around and didn't see Jawnie.

"She said she needed some air," Hasty said. "Don't look at me that way. I told her."

"I'll go talk to her," Rockfish said. She had been through a lot the past week. Telling her she couldn't leave the small tin can they were all squeezed into had run her right up to the line, and she was close to falling over and losing it.

"Taking in that sea air," Rockfish asked Jawnie as he walked out and down the steps. She was sitting on the old wooden picnic table outside his trailer. While no one could see the table from the road, Jawnie was still taking a chance and at this late stage of the game Rockfish would have none of it.

"You are nowhere near the water. You lied."

"Near is a relative term. But you also agreed to stay out of sight for the time being. Lord knows who's watching this place. You met Annetta Provolone. While she runs South Jersey, her power doesn't stop at the border. These groups, no matter the family name, are intertwined. I'd be shocked if she hasn't already called down to the Marinis here in Baltimore to check on me and try to determine if you're here or not. I'd like to do everything in our power to have them fall on the 'not.'" He put his hand on her shoulder and gave a small squeeze. "I know how you feel. Yesterday, when I called my dad? He could tell by my voice that something was wrong. Said he had never heard me sound this way. Was it easy to tell him to stay away until I gave the all clear? No, but I had to do it. Look, this will not last forever. At some point they'll report back up north that they've seen nothing. Baltimore doesn't have a dog in this fight. They won't leave someone outside to watch us for any great length of time."

"You're right, you're right," Jawnie replied. "I'm sorry if I seem so loopy. I can't believe she flat-out admitted Julius gave the order for my great grandfather to be killed. How is this common knowledge in some circles but not in the ones that count?" The tears were welling in her eyes and Rockfish was prepared. He pulled out a tissue.

"People are paid to keep their mouths shut or do it out of blind loyalty. Pick one. They're both the same."

"They never found his body because they never really looked for it," Jawnie said. "He's in that well. How hard did they even try? Someone followed orders to kill him and those same fucks probably ignored the order to find him." She dabbed her eyes with the tissue again.

"You found time during this shit-show to read Tisha's diary?"

"Yes. I photographed every page and included it on those thumb drives. Do you think he's still there, with the others? I've spent my entire life thinking closure is a bunch of bullshit, but I'm rethinking that position. I need to know."

"He has to be, no reason he wouldn't, if everything we're learning leans that way. It's been all quiet for seventy-five years now," Rockfish said. "The well was most likely sealed soon after and covered in dirt. No one would think twice about someone moving a large amount of dirt around a farm. A normal everyday chore in most cases. Before all this started, I watched a lot of History and Discovery Channel shows. They're always hunting something buried and use ground penetrating radar to spot shit like that. It shouldn't be too hard to find. All you would need is permission from the current property owner and someone to run the equipment that can read the findings."

"When this is all done and over, I want to do that."

"If it's all done and we get the ending you deserve, I'd be proud to help you solve that last question. Would make for great TV," Rockfish said with a wink. "Now let's get our asses back inside."

Rockfish let Jawnie go up the steps first. He reached for the door but took one long look over each shoulder, as if it would be that easy. He shook his head, climbed the last step, and let the door shut behind him.

"Took you two long enough," Hasty said as Jawnie plopped down on the couch and Rockfish moved towards the kitchen area.

"We were just discussing what to do when this all blows over," Rockfish said.

"I got one for you," Hasty said. "Let's talk about how we're going to get there. How we're going to drag our asses across this finish line." He put his coffee mug down and sighed. "Two days of pretending to relax and not get on each other's nerves while having to say 'Excuse me' half a dozen times as I try to get to the can just ain't cutting it."

"No one's holding you hostage here, Champ," Rockfish said. "One of those strategy sessions might focus on finding you and Jawnie a place away from here where she can keep her head down and not worry about someone staking out the place. Might be the way to go."

"Can do, later this afternoon when the sun goes down," Hasty said. He left his car a couple of blocks over in a parking garage with the hopes that by keeping it away from the trailer, the odds were less likely someone watching the place would run the plate. As far as they all knew, no one had suspected Hasty's involvement, yet.

"Smart thinking and it might benefit all of us mentally for the time being," Jawnie said.

Rockfish walked back from the kitchen area and took a seat at his desk. There was still a pile of mail that Mack hadn't had a chance to go through while he was in New Jersey. *That could be one chore today,* he thought. *Stay busy and out of their hair.* And with the word 'chore' he remembered the other thing that he was avoiding.

"I've supposed to have one of those Zoom calls with that producer Davenport today, if you're heading out before dinner, I'll schedule it for then."

Davenport had been reaching out the past couple of days asking for any kind of situation update he could get, but Rockfish had been ignoring him since he returned home. He would fill the guy in today on most of everything, excluding they were hiding out from the mob.

"Also, on my end, speaking of contacts," Hasty said, "I heard from Willoughby. He got out of Dodge, booked it up to a friend's cabin in Maine, and plans on staying there to sit out the storm. I told him I'd throw up the all-clear sign as soon as I could."

"I thought our cell phones were off limits," Jawnie questioned. Rockfish could hear the disappointment in her voice as that had been her main vice before all this started, and Jawnie was in the running to earn her ten-day clean chip.

"I'm cell phone free, like the other founding members of the group," Hasty said. "I used an old trick to stay in touch with a confidential informant. We share the login credentials for an old Hotmail account. You log in and leave an email in the drafts folder. We told each other to check it at least once a day, when we first started talking about springing Rockfish."

"Learn something new every day," Rockfish replied. "I once had a client that—"

A loud knocking, damn near pounding, interrupted Rockfish mid-sentence. Each blow rattled the door in its flimsy frame.

Rockfish and Hasty both jumped up and took up position on either side of the door while Jawnie hightailed it towards the bedroom in back. Hasty pulled a gun from the small of his back, and Rockfish reached into a box of Captain Crunch on the counter.

WTF? Hasty mouthed. Rockfish answered by pulling his own piece from the bottom of the empty box, and then leaned to the right and looked through the blinds.

"Two suits. Look like Feds, or damn good imitators. Jawnie will be happy, they've got masks on. Hasty, grab ours before I let the virus in."

The woman at the top of the stairs stopped banging, pulled her credentials out and held them up to the window. The man standing on the bottom step did the same.

"Mr. Rockfish? Open the door, FBI Baltimore."

CHAPTER FOURTEEN

Hasty handed over his piece and Rockfish ditched their guns into the cereal box before opening the door.

"Steve Rockfish, I'm Special Agent Rhonda Thomas and this is my associate, Special Agent Matt Price, from our Philadelphia Field Office. Might we come in and talk?"

"It's a tight fit, but if you don't mind, I guess we're all good," Rockfish said. He moved out of the doorframe and the agents came in. The agents handed both men business cards and proceeded to take the couch. Rockfish sat down at his desk and Hasty stood in the kitchen. Once introductions were out of the way, Agent Thomas dived right into the reason for their visit.

"We're not here to waste anyone's time, so we'd like to know if you know the whereabouts of Jawnie McGee?" Agent Thomas said. Rockfish could see that he was facing a battle for the alpha dog role in the trailer. The agent's posture and attitude told him she knew the girl was fifteen feet away but wanted to give Rockfish the warm and fuzzy feeling that he was helping solve their puzzle. "We need to get a hold of her as soon as possible. Hers and possibly both of your lives are in danger."

"Tell us something we don't know," Hasty chimed in from the sink.

"That we could take you in right now for harboring a material witness. Probably come up with an additional charge or two if need be," Agent Price said. "But nobody wants to go that route."

With the threat of leaving the trailer in cuffs out in the open, whether or not there was anything to it, Jawnie emerged from the back bedroom. She presented her hands out front, palms up.

"Do what you want with me, but leave these men out of it," Jawnie said through her own mask.

"Ms. McGee, I presume," Agent Thomas said. "Could you just pull your mask aside for a second so that we can verify that you are who you say."

Jawnie complied and Agent Price stood up, allowing her to take his spot on the couch. Price then moved to the already crowded kitchen area with Hasty. "No one's taking anyone, anywhere, now that you've come out of hiding. Unless you'd rather talk in a less crowded area. In that case, I'd suggest we go downtown to our Field Office."

"We're good here," Rockfish said, answering for the team, and the other two agreed.

Agent Thomas explained the reason behind the visit was to talk about the manila envelopes Jawnie mailed to a handful of federal agencies in the Philadelphia and Southern New Jersey areas, not to mention the contents of said envelopes.

"So much for your attempt at anonymity," Hasty snapped. Jawnie shot daggers towards the kitchen but asked Agent Thomas exactly how they determined it was her behind the mailings.

"For starters, 2001 was almost twenty years ago, but anytime matching envelopes with identical contents are mailed to federal facilities, the first thought is terrorism. Could there have been some sort of anthrax or poison embedded on the paper, could the USB drives contain the next version of Stuxnet? You see where I'm going with this. Everything is meticulously reviewed, dusted for prints and checked for DNA."

Hasty immediately busted up laughing. "You tried so hard to hide your digital tracks, you forgot about your digit tracks. Common sense fail." He was the only one in the room to find it funny, but Rockfish mentally gave him points for the attempt to bring some levity to the situation.

Agent Thomas continued. "From there, it was simple dermatoglyphics to match what we found on the envelopes to your prints that were in our system."

Hasty and Rockfish looked at Jawnie. By their facial expressions alone, neither one could believe that Jawnie had a record. Traffic tickets, for sure, but an arrest, booking photo and fingerprints on file?

"College underage drinking?" Hasty guessed, not caring how his previous statement fell flat.

"I'll go one better," Rockfish said. "Picked up for protesting some granola, crunchy climate change issue."

"No, she was an applicant and part of the hiring process is being fingerprinted," Agent Price said.

"I applied for a computer scientist position with you guys, right out of college," Jawnie said. "But my offer letter was for the Oklahoma City office. You wanted to send a granola crunch Jersey girl like me to freakin' Oklahoma. I gave it two seconds of thought and turned it down. I'm an East Coast kind of girl, but the applicant coordinator in your office didn't want to hear it. It was OKC or the highway."

"Okay, enough with the sidetracking," Agent Thomas said. "Once we knew who you were, we tried tracking you down. An anonymous complaint of this level, with accusations against such high-profile individuals, we needed to talk to the source. About this same time, our organized crime squad from our Philadelphia office, that's Price's baby, acquired some information that came across a Title III —"

"Wiretap." Hasty added.

"Yes, Mr. Hasty, a wiretap." Agent Price said. "My team has been looking at the Provolone crime family and recently got a judge to sign off on the Title III intercept on a handful of devices and locations used by the organization's upper echelon participants. To date, the order hasn't been very fruitful. Annetta has her crew using encrypted messaging apps, but even a blind dog finds a bone every once in a while." Price cracked a smile and nodded.

Agent Price proceeded to vaguely tell what they had learned through the intercept, but Rockfish could read through the lines and he assumed the other two could as well. It appeared Annetta Provolone put it out across the family that she wants Jawnie and Rockfish found at all costs. These two were here to make sure that didn't happen.

"Nothing on you, Hasty. Sorry buddy," Price added. "But once Annetta finds these two, directions were for them to be brought to her shore house. She's big on watching, from what we gather. That gave us Rockfish's name, and we used that bit of information to come here. You can bet if we're traveling this route and checking the place out, Annetta's following those same breadcrumbs. Have you seen anything suspicious recently?"

"I'll take that one, Price," Rockfish said. "That's kind of the reason we're sleeping three to a bed here and only opening the door for federal agents. Since I'm the only one supposed to be here, and I'm middle-aged, I try to get out and take a walk around, a couple of times a day. Gotta get those steps in. And the malls aren't in the best neighborhoods anymore, or they've been abandoned. I make a mental note of any cars I've seen previously. But no, I don't think anyone's staking us out. Yet."

"Well, Ms. McGee, you are welcome to come with us and remain in protective custody. And actually, that is what we highly recommend." Agent Thomas held out her open hands.

Inviting, Rockfish thought. *But we've got other concerns.* "What about these two?" Jawnie said.

"You're our primary witness and with the Bureau operating under a continuing resolution, funding is scarce..."

"But I don't have to go? Right?"

"Of course not. You are free to remain here. Now that we've located you, we only ask you to reach out to either of us should you feel threatened or travel to another location. I will need you for formal interviews at some point in this investigation."

"Then I'm staying."

Rockfish watched as both agents shook their head in unison. *They want her on the team,* he thought. *I doubt they ever expected her to decline the big warm embrace of the Federal Government.*

"That's your prerogative," Agent Thomas said. "I'll have our surveillance guys do periodic sweeps around the area. That should scare anyone away. Keep your head down and please let us work through our investigation. At times, it may seem a slow and laborious process to you, but being meticulous and not rushing to the courthouse steps will mean these jokers do hard time. Federal time."

"You have our cards," Agent Thomas said, and they left. The remaining three looked at each other. Jawnie wide eyed, Hasty with the

'Told ya so' look and Rockfish wondering if he'd live long enough to ever get paid for this mess.

****

Annetta Provolone sat on the deck of her Ocean City shore house, the fall breeze coming in off the ocean and her whiskey sour needing a refill. The deck ran the length of the house and the stairway led down to the beach. Tonight, with Annetta unaware, somewhere two hours south of her, an FBI agent had recently talked about breadcrumbs. She had in fact followed those same breadcrumbs to Rockfish's trailer but had not yet called Baltimore for help. She assumed both were hiding out in the trailer and at least to her knowledge; they hadn't spoken to anyone. There didn't seem to be a reason to rush a solution. Her plan was to send her bumbling idiots down there to right their previous screw up.

With times like this Annetta wished she had listened to her consigliere, Giovanni Bianchi and traded Tony Boloney to Cleveland for a ball of fresh mutzadell. But at the time she balked at moving on from a potential problem child. Instead, she put more weight on Tony's loyalty than his actual job performance.

You only learn by experience, she thought. *Speaking of Bianchi, where the hell is he? He was supposed to be at the house over half an hour ago.* She wanted his input regarding reaching out to Baltimore and asking Angelo Marini to have some of his soldiers check out Rockfish and hopefully come across Dopey McGee in the process. If he balked at using his own men for this simple task, she would ask for permission to send a team down to do the find and pickup within his territory. Either way, the head of the Marini family would have to sign off on whatever her chosen course of action may be.

Annetta heard the sliding glass door behind her slide open and she jerked her head around.

"Sorry, Annetta. I'm late. Goddamn shore traffic. Remember when it wasn't even a thing after Labor Day?" He was dressed in a Phillies t-shirt and cargo shorts. He looked as if he was getting ready to put his kids on the carousel and not take a meeting with a Mafia boss. Annetta lifted her cheek and Bianchi kissed her and pulled up a chair.

"Fucking Pennsylvania assholes," Annetta added. "Every one of those cars that comes across the causeway has no license plate in the front. Do they think we're stupid? Go back across the goddamn bridge and vacation in the Poconos."

Bianchi waved them off with his hand.

"Agreed. But, while sitting in traffic before the causeway over the inlet, my guys let me know this Hasty character appears to be in the wind. His garage is empty and no action at the house. I sent Sally B to see if any of the neighbors saw anything and he could persuade some to talk."

"Be a darling, Gio, and make me another drink," Annetta asked. She kept quiet as he walked over to the small wet bar against the house. She had really hoped he had some good news she could benefit from.

"Here ya go," he said and handed her a clean glass and fresh drink.

"Let me see if I've got this straight, to see if I'm missing anything," Annetta said. She could even hear the sarcasm in her own words.

"Rockfish..."

"Gone. Presumed back in Maryland," Giovanni said.

"McGee..."

"Gone. Could be with Rockfish, could have bolted on her own. Nobody knows nothing."

"Willoughby..."

"Gone. Ringle's guy Sommers thought Rockfish might have taken him, hostage like, but the guy is presumed involved somehow."

"Hasty..."

"Gone. AWOL. Still trying to figure this one out."

Annetta breathed deeply and held it for a second. "Gio, I really think we're being played here. The more I think about it, the sorer my asshole gets. How is yours feeling?"

"Not good."

"What are the odds these fucking stronza are all somewhere, together. Laughing at us. That is what I think the more I hear. I'm actually second guessing myself. We should have jumped on Baltimore for help a day ago."

"All four are probably somewhere around Baltimore," Gio agreed with his boss. Annetta waited for him to say something in agreement regarding acting sooner, but it didn't come.

"It's been our starting point, has been for a couple of days now, while we've sat here and spun our wheels. I asked Tony, but he keeps complaining that either his calls aren't returned or he hasn't found the right person to talk to."

"He's tried, Annetta. I was with him the last time when he got the run around. Marinis claim some shit is going down on the docks and they're stretched thin resource-wise. Got no one to spare and aren't willing to cut someone loose just to sit and watch a trailer. Unless, we toss them some serious scharole their way and hope for the best."

She sipped her drink and put it back on the chair's built-in coaster.

"Gio, did you ever think you'd see the day where this thing of ours lacks the proper resources to take care of business, let alone work towards making a buck? Resource allocation? We sound like the freaking Federal government. Madone!" Annetta threw both hands in the air.

"Agreed. Since we're getting nowhere fast, I think we should elevate it."

"Okay. I'll deal with Angelo myself, and see if I can get him to see things our way, or at least give us free rein to drive down and do our own goddamn thing. It will take cash for them to come around, make a withdrawal."

****

Agent Price had returned to Philadelphia the same day he and Agent Thomas made their house call. Or was it a trailer call? Back in the office, Price had stayed late back-briefing his squad supervisor and checking for any recent information off the wire before driving home and collapsing.

Today's shift in the office was turning out to be no walk in the park either, and Price dragged as the afternoon wore on. The squad was shorthanded with a couple of vacancies that were not filled because of Congress' continuing resolution, which then turned into a hiring freeze. To make matters worse, three other members, Agents and Intelligence Analysts, were quarantined at home for an exposure which occurred during a meeting with another three-letter agency.

Thanks to COVID-19, he had picked up a second shift working the intercepts today and would be stuck in the office until 10pm, unless his relief took pity and came in earlier. Dinner consisted of half an Italian Wawa hoagie that he didn't have time to eat six hours ago during his working lunch.

The Bureau was up on Annetta Provolone six ways from Sunday. The rolling wiretap warrant covered identified electronic devices she used, along with hidden mics within her car, house and one on the back of a public bench further down the boardwalk where she would walk during pleasant weather and conduct any family business in person. Price wondered more about the devices she used that the Bureau didn't know about.

Tonight, he could put Annetta sitting on her back deck in Ocean City and most of what Price could hear was the clanking of ice cubes in a rocks glass. Sinatra, of course, it was always Sinatra, played over the speakers built into the pergola. Annetta was getting ready to tie one on, and Price was jealous. Annetta had the true work-from-home experience, with all the benefits, virus or no virus.

On the other hand, Price dragged his sorry ass into the office each day, for lousy GS-11 pay and worked alongside a clown that bragged about how he would use his car's heated seats to raise the temperature of his forehead, so he'd be sent home on days he didn't feel like coming in. *Dude, have the balls like everyone to call in sick. No need to MacGyver that shit and then brag about it,* he thought. The kids the Bureau was hiring these days couldn't critically think their way out of a wet paper bag if their lives depended on it. Sometimes the snowflake moniker was true. But Price believed in something. He was here to be part of a team working towards the dismantlement of this crime family. It would reward him with a promotion and perhaps even the choice of his next assignment.

He was halfway through the leftovers from lunch when the mic on Annetta's back deck picked up another person and the music dimmed, ever so slightly. The voice belonged to Bianchi and Price marked it in the logbook. If the consigliere made the drive to Ocean City on a Friday night, you could bet it wasn't for social purposes.

Price was correct in his assumption and he listened to the conversation, taking notes as names were brought up. The entire event would be electronically stored, but Price wouldn't have access to the tapes once he left the monitoring room. He needed to call down to Baltimore and speak to Thomas ASAP, but he also needed to make sure that when he called, he didn't gloss over any of the information said by either of the subjects.

Price slide his headphones off and picked up the phone when Old Blue Eyes was back to pre-meeting volume, and the rest of the exchange had turned to non-pertinent, half-drunk conversation

The Philadelphia Field Office switchboard transferred him to Baltimore and the person working the board there seemed to be as happy to be working a Friday night as Price. After identifying himself, Price asked to be transferred to Thomas' Bureau issued cell phone. She picked up on the second ring.

"This is Rhonda Thomas."

Price could hardly hear over the noise in the background. Annetta's ice clanking and constant Sinatra was easier to decipher.

"Hey, it's Price in Philly. I can barely hear you. Can you go outside or away from wherever you are?"

The thump, thump, thump of the bass told Price that someone wasn't on call this evening and had started their weekend off with a bang. Jealousy washed over him a second time this evening. The music slowly faded out and was replaced with the occasional honking horn and 'Where the fuck did you learn to drive?' Thomas had made it outside of the club.

"Is that better?" she asked.

"Tons. I'm assuming you're dancing six feet apart, per Directory Wray's memo. But listen, I picked up Annetta saying she's personally calling down to Marini to either ask him to pick up those four in the trailer, or to give his blessing for her to send a team down."

"Four?" Thomas said.

"Yeah. She's assuming Hasty is there and involved somehow. Like I said, just a guess on her part. A correct one, we both know, but she's throwing darts in the dark. Speaking of, she's claiming some guy named Willoughby is at Rockfish's too. Ring any bells?"

"Not on my end," Agent Thomas said. "I'll call my supervisor and we'll get over there and scoop them up."

"Perfect, I'm stuck here in the monitoring room until I'm relieved, but I'm going to make some calls and see if my supervisor can get this guy to come in early. Then I'll drive down. In the meantime, I'll see what I can find out about this Willoughby."

"Copy. Let me know when you get close and I can meet you."

"Okay. Hit me up if you get them all safe before I get there. Also, ask Rockfish about breaking out of a local jail up here. Annetta and her guest tap danced around actually saying it, but it sounded to me that he was picked up, held for a few days and then escaped. My chain's going to want some answers when they review the transcript of that conversation."

"Will do, see you later."

Price hung up the phone and dialed his supervisor's cell. If his relief could get here within the hour, Price would meet Thomas sometime between nine and ten that evening.

****

Rockfish pulled Hasty's car back into the parking garage at 8:30pm. He had left Lana at home in case Jawnie or Hasty needed to flee in a matter of seconds. Lana was a better option than having to sprint to the parking garage and up a few flights of stairs. He shut the trunk and didn't want to think about walking three blocks with six bags of groceries, but Rockfish was a stickler for the rules. He was adamant about not having Hasty's car identified anywhere near the trailer.

Rockfish was a couple of hours later than he had planned and hoped they did not wait on him to eat. He could picture Jawnie ordering DoorDash off of his laptop, enough food for two, but only ordering one drink so that in her eyes, anyone observing would believe all the food was for the only person supposed to be occupying the trailer: Rockfish.

He had spent the latter part of the afternoon and early evening touring cheap hotels. After the previous day when the FBI left, conversation in the trailer turned to Hasty and Jawnie heading out one night under cover of darkness and checking into a place of their own. The Feds showing up had put a spook into all three of them, no matter how good a front anyone had put up.

Rockfish couldn't be one hundred percent sure no one was watching them. He agreed that moving to another place and leaving him, alone, to stay in the trailer, served their situation, if anyone was watching. It made more sense than continuing to throw caution to the wind and hope that the other two might not be spotted. To get this ball moving, he grabbed a mask and sunglasses before slipping out of the trailer and taking one of his twice daily walks. This one followed a long circuitous route to the parking garage.

Rockfish knew the area so it should have been a quick errand, but like everything in this case, it had turned into a time-consuming nightmare of driving in concentric circles further and further out. It was at the third stop, The Preakness Inn, that the man behind the desk had warned him of the impossibility of his quest.

It's East Coast DomCon 2020 weekend. You should have booked your room months ago; you would have been closer to the Convention Center and all that nasty stuff.

Rockfish was middle-age, far from a prude in his own eyes, but the results surprised him when he Googled DomCon back in the car. His initial thought was how many people named Dominic could there be? How nasty are they and why do they feel the need to meetup? Especially in this shit show of a year? A second later, he learned DomCon was actually the world's premier professional and lifestyle domination convention. The West Coast Con was cancelled earlier in the year because of restrictions set in place by the Governor of California. East Coast version was still on, but with new attendance requirements in place regarding the pandemic. Still, the Internet reported planners expected close to seven thousand in attendance.

And they think Trump rallies are super spreader events, he thought. *Did Purell even work on rubber and leather, or was that more of an OxiClean situation? Ball Gags 4 Biden 2020. What the hell is my city coming to?*

Rockfish was finally able to rent a room for the next five days, in his old stomping grounds, all the way out in Laurel, Maryland. The Stage Coach Lodge had vacancies, and from the outside, Rockfish could tell why. The place was run down, too far off I-95 to be profitable, and the creepy old man behind the desk looked like he spent his spare time in the evenings looking through a two-way mirror. Rockfish knew it was perfect and put down a cash deposit for the stay beginning the next day. Creepy asked for a credit card, but some additional cash thrown his way made him overlook the motel's 'Policy'.

Rockfish's arms hurt from the groceries as he turned the last corner, and the trailer came into view. But that wasn't all he saw. Three large, black SUVs were parked behind Lana and he knew the Feds were back. Rockfish picked up his pace, but stopped ten feet short of the SUVs by what he could best describe as a stormtrooper. Except this one was five-feet-five, if that. He wasn't aware that they made SWAT gear that small, but now he was.

"Keep it moving, green grocer. Nothing to see here," the heavily armed man said.

"Where the fuck's your mask, Mini Me?" He replied. The man didn't say a word and stared through Rockfish. "This is my home, my property. Did something happen to the people that were staying here?" His voice raised with every sentence. *Why the fuck would all these people be here if someone had decided to put them all in protective custody?* He thought. *Unless they didn't come here with those intentions.*

"I ain't going any fucking place until I get a goddamn answer. I asked you if anything happened to the people in that trailer and all you can do is stand there with that stupid fucking look on your face." His heart was beating so fast, Rockfish expected to see spots any second. He stood his ground and looked over the man's head to the agents that milled around the trailer's front door. He spotted a face he recognized.

"Agent Thomas, Agent Thomas," he shouted with a wave of grocery bags above his head.

"Rockfish, that you? Schneider, let him pass," she called out and waved him over to where she and the others stood. They were all maskless, but for the moment, Rockfish didn't give a shit. He walked over to the front steps and put his groceries down to speak to Agent Thomas. Something caught his eye. The front door was half hanging off its hinges and more importantly, the fancy digital lock he had scammed from Strickland's was gone.

"Goddamn it. I just bought the friggin lock," Rockfish exclaimed. "Homeowners Insurance ain't never going to replace that."

"Please, Mr. Rockfish. If we can go inside," Agent Thomas pleaded.

He picked up the groceries and headed inside the trailer. They were back to sitting on the small couch like old times, as Rockfish filled in some of the missing blanks regarding his afternoon for Agent Thomas.

"...we took what you said last time to heart and figured it would be safer for Jawnie if she was not in the trailer. Hasty would go along to watch over her and I'd reach out to them if anything odd occurred here."

"You can't think of anywhere they might have gone? Any conversation you might not have remembered at first, where they mentioned plans? Could they have gone looking for you since you were gone so long?" Agent Thomas peppered Rockfish with questions he had answered the minute before. *She was borderline interrogation mode,* he thought.

"Gone? Have you seen that door? Taken is the word you are looking for. And you're wasting time here, talking to me."

"Now, I need you to stay calm. Yes, that door is fucked, but do you see any signs of a struggle here?"

Rockfish had to agree. The trailer looked dirty as normal, but not like Hasty had put up the fight he would have if someone had forced their way in. Rockfish was sure of it.

"Look, I told you I don't have a clue," Rockfish said and pointed out the window. "Do you think they hoofed it somewhere, cause that's my car you have blocked in out there. Not to mention that I had Hasty's since noon. Last time you were here, you and Price talked to us like human beings. But since I got home to find you here, going through my shit, it's been like I'm the bad guy here. Do you think I did something to them?" Rockfish stood up and paced the length of the trailer.

"Don't be ridiculous, Mr. Rockfish, and please sit back down." Agent Thomas said. "We need to know where they are. If you can't help us, then we'll move on and look elsewhere. We want your help. Anything you might remember?"

"What I can tell you is that the last time you were pretty straightforward with what was going on. Now all you can tell me is that you are working off a tip? Someone just happened to call up and say the people in the trailer were in danger? Is this tip credible or are you here feeling guilty because you didn't give it much of a try last time for Jawnie to go with you? I would if I were you."

"Now Mr. Rockfish, I understand completely that you're upset, but you need to understand that if my agency was half-assing it, as you're implying, I'd have called over and left a message on your machine when no one picked up." Agent Thomas' face shifted into stern mode and she crossed her arms.

"True, but you were here the other day. I invited you in. The door and now missing lock worked perfectly then. Someone barged the fuck in here and took them by force. These same people are putting miles between us and them, with every passing minute. We can sit here and talk about what might have been, what you think I might have done, or if the fucking Ravens will actually pull through in the playoffs this year, but it ain't gonna amount to shit. You. I. We need to be out there looking."

"If someone from the Marini or Provolone families did take them, we will do everything in our power to locate them. The same goes for if they voluntarily walked off. Which could have very well happened. A burglar or a bunch of kids could have done that to your door, after noticing the place looked empty. As for the place not being ransacked, that might have more to do with the lack of valuable items than an actual scuffle. It doesn't matter. What matters is that they are not here. I've already got their descriptions out to the Baltimore PD, surrounding counties, and all of our agents are checking in with their sources. Agent Price has analysts back in Philly reviewing the date from all their technical sources for any clues that may have been missed or deemed non-pertinent in the first review. Hell, he's in his own car, racing down I-95 to get here as soon as possible in order to help. But we're all half-assing it, right?"

"Are we finished here? I've got groceries to put away," Rockfish said.

"Do you plan on staying here tonight?" Agent Thomas said.

"Would you? Should I tape the goddamn door back in place and pull the covers up to my chin and think happy thoughts? Fuck that. I got a place. I'm fine. Worry about me as much as you did Jawnie when you left my house the last time," Rockfish said. *I've had enough of their Goddamn bureaucratic doublespeak,* he thought.

"Can you at least tell me where you'll be?"

"Small place, called none of your goddamn business. If you need me, you can call the phone on the desk over there," Rockfish said and pointed for emphasis. "You already said you have the number. I'll make sure to periodically check my messages. Good night, Agent Thomas."

Rockfish stood his ground until the last of the SUVs pulled away. He looked around the trailer. It didn't look like whoever did this was looking for something. They knew exactly the two things they needed to take. They must have been in such a rush, nothing was even tossed out of place to make it look like a robbery. Agent Thomas was right, there wasn't a damn thing worth stealing and trying to pawn between these walls.

Rockfish looked at the half put away groceries on the counter. He felt little like eating but didn't remember seeing a restaurant attached to the Stage Coach. What he needed to do was grab a bite here, no matter how he felt, pack some shit and head back to Laurel. He knew immediately where he would stay but wouldn't let Agent Thomas know. The less she knew about his location and movements, the better.

After a quick sandwich and some chips, Rockfish pulled out an empty bag and started packing. He grabbed some clothes, his laptop, and dumped in some toiletries. He walked back into the kitchen to get his gun. It hadn't made the trip to Jersey for what was to be a simple research and interview job, but now it would be a cold day in hell before he ever left home without it. At least for the remainder of this case. He stopped at the sink and looked out the window, while reaching to his left for the supposedly empty box of Captain Crunch.

As Rockfish scanned the street out front, his hand continuously came up empty. He finally turned his head and saw that there was no box to grab. It had always sat on the counter alongside the toaster. But that space was vacant. *Christ, they took that too*? He thought. *How would they have known?*

Rockfish looked over the small kitchen area and quickly located the box, wedged between the windowsill above the sink and the top of the faucet. Had it been any closer, it would have bitten him. He figured it to be empty, but when he picked it up; he smiled. The weight alone told him both guns were still there, and he thrusted his hand into the box. Out came his Glock and also a scrap of paper that he could never remember putting in the box. The paper wasn't folded, and he could easily read the flowing red ink:

GGRL-013 (MD)

That's my girl, he thought. *It had to be a license plate.* He had a starting point and just maybe Jawnie had a future as a PI.

CHAPTER FIFTEEN

Rockfish got little sleep on the Stage Coach Lodge's luxurious sleep mattress. One half tilted, as if Haystacks Calhoun slept on one side for a dozen or so years. He had spent a good portion of the night wondering if Jawnie and Hasty were even still alive, let alone somewhere in Baltimore before finally succumbing to exhaustion after 4am. He had barely settled into REM sleep when the sun's rays filled the room as the sun rose. Rockfish forgot to close the blinds when he finally got the key in the door and stumbled in last night, despite being stone cold sober this time.

The old creepy guy was gone when Rockfish arrived, looking to start the Hasty reservation one night early. Instead, there was a greasy young kid behind the desk, and he didn't have a problem moving up the reservation by one night. Along with the key, he also handed Rockfish a colorful promotional flyer detailing the nutritional benefits of the Stage Coach's continental breakfast spread. Rockfish stumbled out of bed and closed the blinds. He remembered the flyer and glanced at the time.

7:14am, he thought. *Breakfast had been rocking and rolling for the past fourteen minutes.*

Free coffee and food seemed to be the best way to start a day. If he was honest with himself, he wasn't sure what the hell he was doing after reaching out to Decker, his old Baltimore PD contact, later.

The kid with the deadmau5 t-shirt still manned the front desk when Rockfish wandered in from the outside. Rockfish had partially dressed for the occasion in a face mask, long sleeve Raven's t-shirt and shorts. He chose not to accessorize in the Stage Coach robe that hung in the closet, after giving it a closer inspection. His feet were bare and that kind of skeeved him out, knowing the clientele this place served, but his need for caffeine trumped all.

"Morning, Sir. How was your night?"

"Just point me towards the continental breakfast. Sorry can't do casual conversation this early."

"Oh," he said. "I haven't put it out yet, but give me a second. The coffee is almost done brewing."

"Flyer said 7am," Rockfish said. "It's now 7:24."

The kid didn't answer, but slipped through the row of hanging beads behind the desk. He emerged a couple of minutes later with a carafe in one hand and a box of Hostess powdered mini-donuts in the other. Rockfish didn't even try to hide his disappointment.

So much for the omelet station, he thought as the kid placed the advertised donuts and coffee on a wobbly, small folding table by the front door.

"There ya go," the kid said, waving his arms as if Rockfish didn't just watch him walk out from the back room.

"You know how this is going to go?" Rockfish said as he approached the table. "I better not hear a goddamn peep out of you," he warned as he picked up the carafe, box of mini-donuts and walked out the front door.

Back in his room, Rockfish washed his hands and bathed the outsides of the carafe and box in hand sanitizer before balancing the hijacked breakfast on the end of the bed, atop the shirt he wore last night. You can never be too careful with the bedspread in a place like this, or so an episode of Dateline had warned. Rockfish walked back to the door and hung the 'Do Not Disturb' card from the doorknob.

Time to set up the office, Rockfish thought. He pulled the chair and small round table that would be his office for the next couple of days over to the end of the bed so he could reach breakfast with his right hand without having to get up.

Rockfish plugged his laptop into the wall and powered it on. While it booted, he walked over to the television and picked up last night's pants, which lay in a pile on the carpet. He pulled the slip of paper from the front pocket and dropped the pants.

GGRL-013 (MD)

The paper stared back at him from the table. Rockfish opened his web browser and typed an email. His online sleuthing last night had failed to find out one iota of information regarding the license plate. Despite not wanting to ask for favors in a situation like this, he knew it was time to concede and reach out to Dan Decker. Rockfish doubted the Baltimore PD Lieutenant would be in the office on a Saturday, but he should be at least awake. He also didn't have Decker's personal cell number, as their relationship rarely ventured outside the bounds of professional. But what Rockfish had was an email address, and he hoped Decker would be one of those hard chargers that religiously checked their email while sitting at home, off the clock.

The email wasn't long or very detailed and meant to only trigger Decker's curiosity in order to get him to pick up a phone. And in case Decker didn't have Steve's cell number at the ready, Rockfish included it.

He sat at the small table for the next twenty minutes, not sure of what the next step would be if Decker didn't get back to him. Agent Thomas was an option but not one he wanted to use unless he was at his wit's end. While he waited for Decker to call, Rockfish's eyes rotated from the slip of paper to his inbox and then to his phone that sat on the table next to the laptop. Eventually the phone rang.

"Steve-O. What's the emergency, as if I didn't already have an idea?"

"Good talking to you too, Dan. I was hoping you could find someone to run a plate for me. I can pick up lunch at LuLu's once this damn pandemic is over."

"Steve, it's freaking Saturday, not to mention you already owe me Jimmy's Famous Seafood from the last favor I did for you," Dan replied. "And now that I think about it, there might be another one on top of that. Plus, you know I haven't pulled weekend duty since my Sargent days. I'm enjoying a nice relaxing day, getting ready to watch College Gameday. The Terps are at Michigan this afternoon. They're going to get killed, but I'm not at work so it will be enjoyable."

"You gotta know some new hire or old broad stuck working the radio that could run it and then lose the paperwork," Rockfish pleaded.

"All true, but I'm not sure I want to get involved with this," Dan said. "Be straight with me, Steve-O, because I already know the answer. Does this have anything to do with the people snatched from your trailer last night? Because you and I both know it does. The Feds are all over it and they've got pictures and descriptions out across the city and every county down to DC and west to Frederick."

Word traveled fast, Rockfish thought, but Agent Thomas had told him as much last night. Yet it still didn't stop Rockfish from putting on those well-worn tap shoes.

"Come on, Dan. You know me. I don't work open cases. I can't afford to get mixed up in police business, FBI cases, and end up getting my bonding or license pulled. I got a call this morning from a new client. Poor lady thinks her husband is stepping out with a Census worker that came to the house last weekend. I'm trying to stay busy and keep my mind off what happened last night. Guy's gotta make a buck even in these times."

"This lunch at LuLu's, drinks too, right? Because I'm keeping a tab," Dan said, but his tone told Rockfish he didn't need to break out the dance for this favor.

"Sure. Long Island Ice Teas for everyone. I'll even spring for one of those paper umbrellas."

"And you'll give me the whole back-story to this sorted mess with the Feds? Because we only got the abridged version last night. Sounds like you're involved in some deep shit, Steve-O. I'm worried that you're already in way too deep with some very dangerous people."

"Yeah, I can't seem to lose the FBI, no matter how hard I try. I'll fill you in on everything, Dan. I'll bring charts and graphs if I need to. You have my word."

"Okay, you got it. One lady working dispatch today owes me. I'll email you back with what we got."

"Perfect, knew I could count on you."

"I'm holding you to both meals you—"

Rockfish hung up without hearing the rest. The longer Dan stayed on the phone, the longer it would take for the results on the plate to come through, and time was a-wasting.

Rockfish finished the last of the powdered mini-donuts and said a silent prayer that tomorrow would be the chocolate-covered kind. He showered and returned the carafe and empty box to the front desk. The creepy old man was back at the desk and he gave Rockfish the what-for regarding hogging breakfast all to himself.

"Palmer told me you ran out the door with the entire spread. Said he tried to stop you, but Stage Coach rules prevent employees from leaving the front desk area unless it's an emergency. He weighed the situation and decided to stand down."

"Kid's name is Palmer? That fits," Rockfish said. "And don't say the entire breakfast spread. It's sad. Really. Plus, there is only one other car in the parking lot. You could have pointed them towards my room. Hell, the kid said it was ok. You know he's just covering his ass because he thinks he'd get in trouble. That's the problem with kids these days and the shitty work ethic they all have. Video games, man, video games."

"True that," Creepy said, nodding his head in agreement.

Rockfish walked back to his room and pulled up the office chair. A quick check of his inbox came up empty. He stayed in the chair, stared at the small laptop screen, and attempted to will Decker's email to come through. When that failed to get the response he needed, next up was pacing the small room. There were already a few paths worn into the carpet and he followed them 'round and 'round until the notification came in.

Ding

Decker's email was succinct, to the point and eye opening.

J - GGRL-013, white sprinter van, g&g laundromats, 8471 kellogg lane, towson. do me a favor and keep your head down and be safe - D 555-4055

It shocked Rockfish that Decker included what he assumed was the man's personal cell, and for a minute, he kind of wondered if their relationship had taken the next step. Rockfish also appreciated the kind words, but his eyes shot back to the first sentence. It hit the bullseye and blew his mind all at the same time.

G&G

Ginny & Gordon

Ginny & Gordon Reeceworth

Ginny & Gordon Reeceworth Laundromats, Van 13

His clients at the beginning of the shit-storm had come full circle. One was dead, and the other he presumed dead. That didn't give him much hope or much to go on being the official line was a murder suicide with the Gordon's body never found. The more he thought about it, the more none of it made sense. For the van to be registered to Gordon's business was way too much of a coincidence. Something didn't smell right with this, and he needed to get some answers. He had to figure out how his dead friend's business played a part in the abduction of Jawnie and Hasty. The lead was all he had. *Christ, I'd kill for a brain that works right,* he thought and slammed the laptop closed.

He grabbed his phone and opened his contacts. He dialed the number he had for Gordon, and to no one's surprise; the number was no longer in service. Ditto for Ginny's. But he had one other to try. Gordon had given Rockfish that number when he first hired him to locate Ginny and the money.

Use this if you absolutely have to get a hold of me. When I'm not around the office or the cell Ginny knows about, I'm available on this one.

Rockfish had forgotten all about it once Ginny's body was found, and the media reported that Gordon was presumed dead. He never thought twice about it after coming to terms with the lost income and finder's fee commission that he had banked on.

Rockfish had entered the number into his contacts under the name Alf. As in the television alien puppet from Rockfish's college years, Gordon Shumway. He tapped the phone number, and it started ringing.

"Stevie, buddy. It's about time this call finally came through. I was beginning to think you had forgotten about me."

****

The two old friends, one freshly found alive, agreed to meet at Oliver's Old Town Tavern, on Main Street in Laurel. It wasn't far from the Stage Coach and Rockfish figured that a dead guy would be happy to be out and about. Oliver's had quite a crowd on hand, and Rockfish second guessed his choice of venue.

Rockfish was finishing up his first drink when Gordon walked through the front door and scanned the crowed. Gordon looked damn good for a man who, in Rockfish's mind, had been resurrected by a phone call. Gordon was dressed sharp and looked like he had lost weight. *Death will do that to you,* Rockfish thought. As Gordon scanned the bar, Rockfish wondered if Gordon was looking for him or whoever he had gone into hiding from. Rockfish settled on a little of both.

"Hey, Stevie," Gordon said as he turned the corner of the bar and spotted Rockfish on the stool.

"Let's find a place less crowded so I don't have to watch what either of us has to say," Rockfish said. He stood up and led the way towards the back of the bar. Large glass windows separated the bar area from the outside deck and were lined with tables, that were spaced apart. Most of the patrons were out on the deck or had congregated towards the bar, leaving those tables free of busybodies.

Rockfish slid into a chair with his back to the glass and empty tables on either side. Gordon pulled out the chair directly opposite Rockfish and appeared to think twice. He pushed it back in and sat down to Rockfish's right.

"So where do we want to start?" Gordon said.

"How about starting with where's your fucking mask," Rockfish replied. "Just because you rose from the dead doesn't mean you aren't a spreader." He raised his hand to let the server know his dining guest would need a mask.

The two men made small talk until a disposable mask and a round of drinks were brought to the table.

"Gordon, I don't have a lot of time, and I may have already missed the boat on finding the timely information that I need." He had never stopped worrying if Jawnie and Hasty were still alive, or headed back to Jersey. As every second of the previous night ticked by, his imagination drummed up scenes where they were held at gunpoint in a car racing up I-95 in order for Annetta to get her rocks off.

"But right now, give me three minutes of how the fuck are you still alive," Rockfish said. "I've been out of pocket."

"You probably last saw the news when the murder/suicide angle was all the rage. So last time we talked, you told me that you had finally located Ginny. She was in that motel with my money, err I mean Angelo Marini's money. I hired you to find her and you did. Only problem was that I told Angelo that I had found her and the money and that I'd have it back for him. Unfortunately, they beat you to the punch."

"You're telling me shit I mostly already know and by the way, you still have an outstanding invoice with me."

"I know, I know. I'll make it right." Gordon said. "What Angelo did was hire a couple of meth-heads to do the job. Someone drops a dime on them a short time later, anonymously of course, and then big surprise—they both are found hung the day after being taken into custody." Gordon stared down into his drink. "That's my signal to come out of hiding with the bullshit story that I was in fear for my life. It's all bullshit, but no one questioned it because of the couple of dead guys in North Carolina. Case closed."

"And the cash? You know I still have nightmares about losing out on that finder's fee."

"Angelo's guys who dropped off the meth-heads at the motel immediately took the bag from them the minute they came out of the room. Angelo got his money back, and I learned I had to now pay for the sins of the dead. They told me in no uncertain terms that I would work off the debt of her crime. Long story short, I now have a not-so-silent partner in all of my business endeavors."

"I'd bet they would have had you whacked the minute word got back to Charm City that the briefcase was in their hands."

"Don't gamble, Stevie. Nothing good ever comes out of it," Gordon said, shaking his head. "There ain't no such thing as a sure thing."

"Not sure I believe any of it," Rockfish said, "but what I really need you to tell me about is one of your Sprinter vans. White, vanity license plate GGRL-013."

"Number thirteen," Gordon said wasting no time. "That's from our old maintenance warehouse, up in Towson. I don't own it anymore, it's one piece my 'silent' partners had me sell off but vans ten to fifteen were dispatched from there for maintenance calls. Now we contract out to some Mexican company on the south side for repairs and I'd bet my ass Marini has his mits into that company too."

"Don't bet, Gordon, nothing good ever comes out of it," Rockfish said with a wise-ass grin behind his mask. "They sold off the building but not the vans?" Rockfish said.

"The auction's scheduled but not for another month. The place is empty but hasn't gone to closing yet. Matter of fact, all six of those vans used by our service techs are still parked there as far as I know. Dispatch is trying to figure out what to do with them until the auction, so what's this about?"

Rockfish gave Gordon a very condensed version of the events that led up to his returning to a vacant trailer and when he finished, his happy hour friend didn't look so happy.

Gordon stopped staring at his drink and met Rockfish's eyes. "If Angelo's folks are involved, this ain't good. You ain't thinking about driving up to that warehouse, are you?"

"What I'm up against is a couple of goons that grabbed up my friends based on an ask from another low life piece of shit. Worried, yes. Scared, no. What, is Angelo going to have his entire criminal organization at this place standing around, watching two people, that is, if they are still there? And I won't know that unless I act on the only bit of information I have and, in fact, drive up there. I can't sit here waiting for something else, something less dangerous to react to. It doesn't work that way."

"Stevie, I didn't mean it like that," Gordon said, sounding as if he was trying to backtrack. "I just want you to know what you could be up against if you go nosing around up there."

"Look, this plate number is the only lead I have towards the disappearance of my friends," Rockfish said and jabbed the table with his index finger. "Forget that I found it in a cereal box. Don't look at the fact that they might be dead, and their bodies dumped somewhere out in the middle of the Chesapeake. There is a chance, no matter how slim, that they could still be somewhere in this warehouse. Or they could be on their way back to Jersey. The point is, I don't know. All I have is this license plate and where it's going to lead me to, and to sit here and play woe is me, well that ain't me."

They both stared at each other and the table filled with silence the next couple of minutes. Rockfish could see the wheels turning in Gordon's head. The man was weighing his exit from the game, or if he wanted to continue playing.

"8471 Kellogg Lane, Towson," Gordon said, repeating the address Rockfish already knew. "I'll go with you. If anything, I can get you inside. I'm sure the locks, if they are even in use, haven't been changed. If anyone sees me, I'm prepared to play the role of a dumb previous owner, checking on some widget that needs looking at before the deal goes to closing. Fuck, I might know one of the mooks if they are still there. That could help."

"Excellent. Let's get moving. And pick up the tab," Rockfish said as he got up from his chair. He was raring to go but would need to swap out cars before heading to Towson. A foreshadowing of giving chase or having to beat feet fast, lingered in his mind. And Hasty's little Toyota Camry wouldn't cut it. He had to call in the big guns. Lana.

"Stevie, I am sorry for pulling an end run on you over the whole Ginny thing. I owe you one."

"We're even when you pay for five days' work and incurred expenses. I filed your invoice back at my trailer. Speaking of which, I need to swing by there. Let's go."

****

The abandoned warehouse was cold and the small heating elements above Jawnie's head glowed red. But since heat rises, they weren't doing much good to her or Hasty. She glanced over at Hasty. He, too, wrapped himself in old moving blankets to starve off hypothermia. She had lost track of how long they had been in this cramped room and knew asking Hasty wouldn't accomplish anything other than making both of them feel worse than they already did.

Other than the cold, their captors treated their prisoners reasonably well. The food was fast, greasy, and non-vegan, so Jawnie spent a lot of time knocking on the door and asking to be walked down to the bathroom. But it was the waiting that played with both their minds. Jawnie wasn't sure for what and Hasty had settled on someone from Jersey taking their sweet time driving down. The longer this went on, the longer Hasty's opinion was that something smelled awry in the whole scenario. He had explained to her they were most likely being held until someone that worked for Annetta arrived on site to either take them back in order to face her, or to take them for the long walk off the proverbial short pier down at the Baltimore docks. But what drove the former Chief of Police crazy was that neither option appeared to be happening soon. The rush to do nothing ate at him and it was showing through his temper and the way he snapped anytime Jawnie spoke up.

"Jersey is less than a two-hour drive. They could have made the round-trip God knows how many times by now," was Hasty's constant refrain, but here they remained, shivering and Jawnie with an acute case of the runs.

Were the Provolone soldiers as inept as Hasty continually made them out to be, she thought?

For every moment Hasty said it was only a matter of time before their captors pushed them into the back of a car, Jawnie countered his default line of thinking with her own. Damn his attitude.

"Rockfish is on his way, you wait," was her standing reply. She never stopped thinking about the scrap of paper she had scribbled on and shoved into the cereal box, or her faith that he found it.

Jawnie thought it was dumb luck she was standing at the sink and looked up when the van's brakes squeaked. The van had come to a sudden stop alongside the trailer. She didn't have time to think or scream, she just reacted. Hasty was sleeping in the back and wouldn't be able to do anything in time. Whoever they were would be at the door and what did she have, thirty seconds, before they broke in? What was going to happen couldn't be stopped? Instinctively, all she did was leave a clue. For an instant she thought about grabbing for a gun, but five men piled out of the van and each had their own. She'd be dead before she could hope that she hit one of them.

That scrap of paper was her only shot. Rockfish would be the only person who would find it. But had he? If he saw it he'd know what to do. But what if he didn't return to the trailer, what if he was being held somewhere else? She wouldn't believe any of the negative scenarios that raced through her head. As long as they were held here, there was a chance-at least in her eyes-he would find them. That scribbled note was all she had to hang her hat on. *And damnit*, she thought, *I need that damn hat to keep in what little body heat I have left.*

"I spy with my little eye—"

"I can't. Not again," Hasty said, interrupting the game before Jawnie could get the hundred and fifty-eighth round started.

"Look, man, I'm trying to keep our spirits up. You can sit there and come up with a million different scenarios where you overtake one of these armed guards. Unless you can MacGyver some weapons out of these blankets or that old metal desk, we're going to sit here 'til the next set of orders come down. You've said as much yourself."

Jawnie could see how not being in a position of power or even an advantage weighed heavily on her partner. Hasty had spent his adult life being proactive, moving the ball forward so to speak, and keeping his fellow citizens safe. Now he had been reduced to sitting on a cold concrete floor, wrapped in an old, smelly blanket, and forced to play childhood games with a computer repair woman.

"How the mighty have fallen," Jawnie said mistakenly aloud.

"Huh? What are you talking about," Hasty said. To Jawnie, he seemed to pay attention to only half of what she said.

"Sorry, just thinking aloud." And with that, each retreated into their own minds.

Dinner and its inevitable diarrhea came and went. But it was when Jawnie was escorted back from the bathroom that she heard voices. She strained her neck to see over the railing to the empty warehouse below, but couldn't pinpoint where they were coming from. The place was cavernous, and the sounds bounced and echoed off every surface. She waited until she was back with Hasty and the shadow of the guard on the glass door moved out of frame.

"There are people down below. I heard them. More than one, so it's not a food run or the normal changing of the guard. What do you think it means?"

"Did you recognize any? Sound even remotely familiar?"

"No, but from what I made out, it sounded like two or three different people," Jawnie said.

"My guess is that someone's finally come for us, and that's probably not a good thing." Hasty's voice sounded as if he was ready to admit defeat. "Who knows anymore what they're doing."

Fifteen minutes later they both spotted the extra shadows on the glass door and could pick out a word here and there from the muffled conversation. The shadows shuffled back and forth and the now familiar sound of the key scraping the inside of the lock filled the room.

The evening's guard and fast-food delivery boy were the first through the doorway. The guard trained his handgun on Hasty and stepped to the side. Two more goons followed suit, each wearing the standard issue mafia tracksuit. One had a matching set of zip ties in his right hand. The last man through the door drew a reaction from Hasty.

"Sommers. I can't say that I'm shocked," Hasty said, acknowledging his former employee.

"Acting Chief Sommers, to you asshole," Sommers snapped back and ordered the other two men to secure the prisoners.

"Yeah, because this is definitely official Police business, you fucking Provolone hack," Hasty said and spit. "Which one of these two goons did Annetta send down with you to make sure you didn't fuck this up too? Amazing what a little GILF action does to a man."

Sommers waited until a henchman secured Hasty's hands behind his back before dropping the ex-chief with a wild haymaker. Jawnie dropped to her knees alongside Hasty before being violently yanked back to her feet.

"Get that mouthy clown up and moving," Sommers ordered.

****

It felt damn good to be behind the wheel of the Challenger again, but Lana wasn't the only thing Rockfish grabbed back at the trailer. He ran inside and took Hasty's gun from its hiding spot and gave it to Gordon as he slid back into the driver's seat.

"What the hell am I supposed to do with this," he asked. "Go to war with the goddamn Marini Family?"

"Just put it in your waistband when we get there. Keep your jacket unzipped. You never know, man. Better to be strapped than reach and find you weren't at some point."

Rockfish pulled out onto the street and hit go on Lana's GPS for directions. Next, he dialed Decker and put the phone to his ear. After three rings, the call headed to voicemail. *Fuck*, he thought. *The man gives me his number and then ignores me.*

Danny, it's Steve. I've got a lead on that plate and I'm going to check it out up in Towson and I'll ring you back if anything pans out. Pick up your goddamn phone next time.

The drive would be quick, half an hour barring traffic on I-695 as they cut through the suburbs towards the interstate. The interior of the car was silent except for the radio. The music kicked Rockfish's adrenaline in the ass, and he pressed down on the accelerator. Before he knew it, he signaled for the exit lane and it was almost go time.

"Let's lose these things," Rockfish said and dumped his mask in the back seat.

"Not so worried now?" Gordon said as he followed suit.

"No, probably more so. But if this is the end of the road, I'm sure as hell not dying with one of these goddamn things on."

"Agreed. It's up here on the left," Gordon said as Lana slowed and Rockfish turned onto Kellogg Avenue.

"Yeah, the lady on the GPS said our destination was coming up on the left," Rockfish replied. "But thanks, Tonto."

If Rockfish didn't know any better, the building looked occupied and still in use with the amount of lights on inside and out along with the row of Sprinter vans in the front parking area.

"You missed the entrance," Gordon said before the GPS lady could say she was recalculating. "You can't get around the back without going through the gate in the front."

Rockfish reached over and shut off the directions. "I'm going to make a couple of lefts and drive around the outside and see if I spot anything out of the ordinary before we just drive into an enclosed area. Just stay in your lane, Gordon."

"And what exactly is that?"

"Sidekick. Doer of things, not orderer of directions."

Lana slid through the first left-hand turn and as she drove alongside the short side of the building, Gordon immediately started again with his play-by-play.

"When you make the next left, that's going to be the rear of the building. About half-way down will be a door that leads to the back stairs and the offices on the second floor. I'll go in through that door and look around and see what's what before you barge in, guns blazing. Maybe I can resolve this peacefully."

By the time he finished saying what he was going to do, Rockfish knew it was time to rethink everything.

"Lane, Gordon. Mother fucking lane. You ain't doing shit," Rockfish said, pointing to the two idling cars parked in front of the door they planned on using for entry. The cars weren't trying to hide as both were well lit by a halogen light above the door in question. Not to mention one being a police patrol car.

Elk Township Police

Rockfish could read the side of the car as easily as if it had been daylight. *Please be safe, Jawnie and Hasty,* he thought. *If you mother fuckers hurt them... I will bring hell down on you!*

He immediately killed the headlights and took his foot off the gas. Lana continued straight to the next corner and had slowed enough that she took the left turn without needing her brake lights to announce their presence. Here, no longer in line of sight from the door or running car, Rockfish pulled over. He needed to re-think the dynamic duos plan for entry.

"That throws a monkey wrench in me waltzing in and getting the lay of the land," Gordon said.

"More like napalm," Rockfish replied. "If you bothered to glance at the side of that patrol car, it ain't Baltimore PD. Matter of fact, I've been in the back of that very car, harassed and jailed by its driver. Who I assume is inside that warehouse now."

Official police business. Nothing to see here, Rockfish thought. It would be clean sailing at 105 miles per hour up I-95 for Officer Sommers. *Not if I can help it.*

"I mean, I can still just wander in," Gordon said. "It's my building. I have every right to be there. With my dealings with Angelo, I might know one or two of the faces in there."

"Or it could as easily be your coffin. Cut the shit with you saving the day, okay? Tonto follows the Lone Ranger."

Gordon looked at Rockfish with a wide set of eyes and it was clear. The passenger didn't get the severity of the problem.

"Gordon, I think we confirmed my friends are there with what appears to be car loads of dirty cops and mafia goons. This late in the game, they wouldn't have a second thought about icing either of us on the spot. That's what those types of people do. Think back to your wife. Now shut up and lemme take another lap around and see what pops into my head."

Lana shifted into drive and crept forward again, still with her headlights off. They turned down the backstretch for the second time and Rockfish noticed something that made him question even more what could go wrong.

Tucked into an alleyway facing the back of the warehouse was the telltale black SUV. *Jesus Christ,* Rockfish thought. *The Feds are here and where there is one black SUV, there are probably half a dozen others close by. Don't fuck this up guys.*

Rockfish kept the car moving straight and made the next left. He stopped and backed into his own side street with a view and let out a loud sigh.

"Do you think they saw us?" Gordon said after Rockfish filled him in on the black SUV.

"If I spotted them this time, you can bet your ass they made us on the first go 'round. I think our plan is now to sit here and let the Feds do their job. We can be backup, should shit go sideways. Let the trained professionals handle it."

Rockfish picked up his phone and again hit redial for Decker, and this time, the Lieutenant picked up on the first ring.

"Yo, you ok man?"

"Hey, I'm here and it's the lead I thought it would be. Strange enough, the Feds are here, and that probably means Baltimore County PD ain't too far behind. I'll be sitting on the fifty-yard line watching." Rockfish hung up and placed the phone back in the cup holder.

"What do we do now?" Gordon said.

"We wait. It's called surveillance. You might have seen it on television. There should be some empty Gatorade bottles on the floor in the back if you have to take a piss. I'm going to listen to some tunes at minimal volume during this downtime. With those cars running, I don't think it will be long, but you can never be too sure."

Rockfish hadn't even pulled his right arm back from pointing towards the empty bottles when the warehouse door flew open. His pulse skyrocketed from seventy to most likely four digits, and his first thought was of the black SUV.

Had their collective pulses done the same? Rockfish thought. *Had they shifted down to drive and gunned the engine?*

Rockfish watched as they came out in pairs. Jawnie and Hasty were first, pushed through the doorway by a couple of guys he didn't recognize. Their heads were covered and hands restrained. *If you touch one freakin hair on their heads,* he thought. *You will wish you were never born.*

Sommers was next and last out the door was what Rockfish assumed to be a Provolone goon. Each brandished a weapon in case either of their prisoners thought about running. They each took Jawnie and Hasty by the elbow with their free hand and steered them towards the patrol car. Sommers popped the trunk. Rockfish noticed the two he didn't recognize were walking away, getting into the other car.

Angelo's men, he thought. *Their job completed it was time to clock out and head home.*

Rockfish swallowed hard as Jawnie and Hasty were pushed into the trunk and the goon slammed it shut. It would be tight quarters in there, but Rockfish knew it would not be for long. The cavalry was about to spring into action. He glanced over towards where the black SUV was and assumed it would have already squealed tires and smashed through the wire fence, like heroes ought to do.

But there it sat. Lights off, not moving.

"Fucking go!" he said, directed at the SUV, but Gordon instinctively reached for the door handle.

"Not you."

The driver of the black SUV obviously didn't hear so well, so Rockfish dropped Lana into drive and started doing the mental calculations on what speed he would need to get up to, in a short stretch, to get her through the fence. But before the computation completed, he watched the patrol car rolled out. Rockfish kept his foot on the brake as the patrol car rounded the far side of the building and then reappeared, heading down the street in front. The SUV's headlights flashed, and it rolled out in pursuit mode.

"I'd love to know what the fuck they are talking about in that damn car or on the fucking radio," Rockfish exclaimed and took his foot off the brake. Third in line, he raised the volume on his radio, and increased the speed until he was a couple of feet behind the SUV's rear bumper. It wasn't like they weren't previously aware of his presence.

Rage Against the Machine poured through Lana's speakers and Rockfish's adrenaline rose to meet the beat.

"What are you doing?" Gordon shouted. "This close and they'll know we're following them."

"I told you they saw us back at the warehouse. It's not them we're trying to lay the surprise on. Matter of fact, I want them to know we're here and plan to help crash the party."

"What about the other car back there?"

"If they're your Marini goons, you can make their acquaintance at the next meeting or business deal. I don't really care. I'm only interested in the cargo, two cars up. Not to mention they went in the opposite direction. Use your mirrors better, Tonto."

Rockfish stayed on the SUV's bumper but couldn't see around it. He gave a quick thought to swinging the wheel towards the center median to see exactly how far behind they were, but with his luck that would be the telltale clue to Sommers that he was being followed.

Half a mile later, Rockfish noticed their speed had slowly increased and was now hovering above fifty. He had ignored all but the SUV in front and guessed they had made their way out of the city limits and were officially in the 'burbs. He glanced down at the dashboard GPS, but it was absolutely no help.

"Gordon, where the fuck are we headed? You know this area better than me," Rockfish shouted over the radio.

Gordon reached over and lowered the radio's volume. "We're on East Joppa Road, but that don't mean shit to you. We've passed a couple of turn offs that would eventually lead to the Baltimore Beltway. Maybe the cop car thinks something's up?"

"Dude, I don't fucking know."

"But the next chance to jump on the beltway is coming up. Gonna be a hard right in a minute on Perring Highway and then under the beltway and the entrance ramp loop back thing is on the right. They get on there, they can really open it up."

"Well, for fuck's sake! Let's hope the Feds have some sort of plan to kick off before then," Rockfish said as he reached over and turned the volume back up. *And if they didn't,* he thought, *Lana's Hemi could keep up with the best of them.*

The right on Perring came without warning as the SUV took the turn without so much as a brake tap. Rockfish lost traction for a second before getting her straightened out and back up to speed.

"Ramp just ahead!" Gordon shouted.

This time the SUV hit its brakes and hard. Lana locked 'em up likewise, but still kissed the SUV's bumper. Both passengers didn't have time to contemplate the impending cases of whiplash when Rockfish noticed Sommers' cruiser speed past him going in the opposite direction.

"Motherfuckers!" Rockfish exclaimed and supposed Baltimore County Police had the ramp blocked off. He didn't hesitate or wait for permission from the Feds in front of him. He shifted into reverse and punched it. Three seconds later, he slammed on the brakes and spun the wheel. Lana performed a J-turn that any Hollywood stuntman would have given five stars. He shifted back into drive and Lana's engine roared. Rockfish had some catching up to do, but he was now the lead chase vehicle. As Lana lurched forward, Rockfish noticed two things. From the rear-view mirror, he could see the SUV had turned around, and those headlights were gaining fast. Also, Gordon struggled frantically with his seatbelt.

"Pussy," Rockfish said to no one in particular. He gripped the wheel tighter as Guns & Roses 'You Could Be Mine' filled the speakers. His eyes searched desperately ahead for any sign of the police cruiser.

Hollywood driving with a Rockstar soundtrack, Rockfish thought. *This is going to be fun, as long as I don't get anyone killed. Anyone that mattered, of course.* He was now in full T-1000 pursuit mode.

Rockfish squinted and focused on what he hoped were Sommer's taillights until a set of high beams in his rear view temporarily blinded him.

The Feds were back in the game and on Lana's ass. The SUV swung across the yellow line into the oncoming lane in an attempt to go around, but Rockfish wasn't yielding the lead. He sped up knowing no matter what cop engine was in that thing; the SUV was heavy as hell. Add to it the weight of all the people and gear inside, and the driver was fighting a losing battle. It would never get around Lana. He wouldn't let it.

Rockfish chuckled to himself as the SUV fell back in line and seemed to lose a little distance, too.

The chase continued westbound where they crossed under I-83 and Rockfish was now sold—these clowns had no plan, no idea where they were headed and this was going to come to an end, sooner rather than later. Jersey was in the other direction and he assumed Sommer's only hope was to lose both tails on these rural roads before trying to work his way north and east again.

Lana crested one hundred and ten miles an hour as Rockfish pulled close to Sommer's rear bumper. He ordered Gordon to take a shot and try to take out the cruiser's rear window.

"Aim high, top of the glass, way above the trunk!"

At the very least, Sommers might consider the jig is up and end this chase. Rockfish kept one eye on the bumper in front of him and the other on Gordon as he lowered his window and pointed Hasty's gun out the window and pulled the trigger.

Rockfish's eye on the cruiser let his brain know that Gordon missed.

"AGAIN!" He ordered. This time Gordon leaned the top half of his body out the passenger side window and fired again.

This time, the rear windshield shattered in an explosion of safety glass that made even Rockfish wince, despite having a windshield of his own between him and the shrapnel.

"Remember that one, asshole! Payback time!" Rockfish shouted.

Sommers slowed down the cruiser, and Rockfish tapped his bumper. For a second, he thought Sommers was doing the right thing, but when he saw the front wheel turn to the left, he immediately realized Sommers was trying to pull the same trick he did back at the blocked entrance ramp.

Fool me once, Rockfish thought. The SUV would surely block the cruiser's path this time, or he hoped it would. He wouldn't take that chance.

Rockfish pushed the gas pedal hard to the floor and turned his wheel. Lana t-boned Sommers' cruiser and pushed it across the shoulder into a roadside ditch. Rockfish slammed on his brakes and brought Lana to a screeching stop at the edge of the shoulder, her ass end sticking out into oncoming traffic. He and Gordon jumped out, guns drawn on the car that was now listing heavily on its right side.

"Outta the car, assholes!" Rockfish shouted, but neither man moved, their heads resting firmly on the deployed airbags.

"Gordon, if they move, shoot them," Rockfish ordered as he pocketed his own gun and slid down the embankment.

The damage to the driver's door told him it wouldn't open, but he tried for the hell of it. It didn't budge. But the window had spider-webbed with cracks, and a well-placed Macho Man Randy Savage elbow shattered the glass. Rockfish grabbed Sommers by the hair and pulled his head off the airbag. He reached across with the other hand and yanked the keys from the ignition.

Rockfish hadn't noticed the SUV pull up and was equally oblivious to the phalanx of Baltimore County police cars behind it. Their headlights lit up the entire area, but Rockfish didn't look up or back until he recognized Agent Thomas' voice screaming at him, ordering him to step away from the car and let them handle it. He looked back at her, lifted his hands, and pressed the trunk release on the key FOB.

He was at the back bumper before she could say another word and pushed the trunk fully open. He looked down at Hasty and Jawnie. They were doing their best imitation of big spoon little spoon, with their arms restrained behind their backs. He didn't see any blood or bones and immediately thought positive thoughts.

Rockfish pulled the hood off Jawnie's head, touched her shoulder, and her eyes opened.

"Come with me if you want to live."

"What?" came her groggy reply.

"You had to be there," Rockfish said. He reached down, scooped her up in his arms and lifted her out of the trunk. "Hasty, you're gonna half to hang tight till I get some muscle down here."

A muffled 'fuck you' came from the trunk and Rockfish laughed.

AMERICA NEWS NETWORK
Honest Reporting For Both The Red & Blue USA
*****BREAKING NEWS*****

Feds Takedown COVID-19-Relief Fraud Ring That Sought Millions - Diverse Criminal Group, Included Mafia Boss, Catholic Church Leaders and Bank Officials, Orchestrated Nearly $15M in Phony Loans

By Strom Wiggleston (email the author)
America News Network - Online Edition (ANN.com)

October 1, 2020 @ 3:45pm
Philadelphia PA - The United States Attorney, Hubert H. Lansing, along with FBI Special Agent In Charge William Gorham announced Thursday that the FBI had disrupted and dismantled a diversely structured and prolific organized crime group accused of defrauding the U.S. Small Business Administration's (SBA) Paycheck Protection Program (PPP).

The U.S. Department of Justice indicted fifteen Southern New Jersey residents by the U.S. on Thursday for allegedly attempting to fraudulently obtain more than $15 million in coronavirus economic relief.

Bishop Clinton O'Hanlan of the Catholic Church's Camden ArcDiocese, alleged mafia head Annetta Provolone and Farmer's National Bank President Leonard Putznoggle were identified in the indictment as coordinating the organization's fraudulent efforts and were taken into custody yesterday by the FBI.

All defendants were charged with three counts of conspiracy to commit bank and wire fraud, twelve counts of bank fraud and twelve counts of wire fraud. Annetta Provolone was also indicted for seven counts of aggravated identity theft.

According to the DOJ, all were allegedly "Part of a disaster relief loan fraud ring" centered in Gloucester County. Members of the ring submitted at least 35 fraudulent loan applications to receive funds from the SBA through the PPP and Economic Injury Disaster Loan (EIDL) program. In some cases, the defendants used false names. In others, they used their real names but submitted information about fictitious businesses.

SAC Gorham stated the defendants used this loan program as their own personal piggy bank.

When contacted at the Archdiocesan Pastoral Center, representatives for Cardinal Rattie declined comment.

Democratic Congressman Richard Fanucci, 2nd Congressional District, stated, "These crimes are the result of when the Federal Government rushes to throw money at a problem that wouldn't be half as bad if they had followed the Obama pandemic playbook. The lack of any planned oversight by government regulators in the distribution of the funds opened this program to fraud. Criminals lined up along with friends and family of this administration to steal money meant for hard hit Americans business owners and their employees."

Sources disclosed to this reporter that additional charges to include murder, attempted murder, kidnapping, false imprisonment, and others will be detailed greater in an amended indictment at the defendant's arraignment this coming Wednesday at the Federal Courthouse. SAC Gotham also indicated that additional arrests in this matter would be forthcoming.

All defendants are to make their first appearance in U.S. District Court in Philadelphia on Wednesday, October 7th.

EPILOGUE - MAY 2021

On a colder than usual May morning, Rockfish finally set foot on what was once known as the D'arnaud Farm. Nine months ago, Louie Sommers had prevented him from getting a lay of this old field, but today Sommers was a little tied up. Rockfish imagined the now federal prisoner was learning how to fashion lipstick out of Bing cherries and Vaseline for the rosy-red look his cellmate would go absolutely crazy for.

He stood before what was once Mary's farm, now littered with trailers and excavation equipment. As he walked across the field and closer to where the crew was filming, he spotted Jawnie sitting in her embroidered director's chair. She sat under a tent, behind where the cameras set up for the morning shoot. The day's filming was close to a wrap for Davenport's docuseries tentatively titled 'The Pine Barrens Stratagem'. Rockfish wasn't exactly enthralled with the name but his submission, 'The Jersey Devil Adoption Agency', never even made it to the drawing board, as Davenport was looking for something that encompassed the crimes of both 1945 and 2020; thus, the modern-day sequel's title would only need the required 'II' after it.

Yesterday's shoot was an emotional one for Jawnie and all it took was a phone call that evening, and Rockfish dropped what he was doing and made the early morning drive north to be on set for support.

Delsea Excavation and Grading did their part a few weeks ago in locating and uncovering the old D'arnaud well. Once it was visible, the production crew jumped through a few bureaucratic hoops and got the correct permits allowing Rutgers's University School of Forensic Anthropology to further excavate the location. After two days on site, the team officially announced that they had found what were presumed to be human remains at the bottom. From the way Rockfish heard it, that was the moment Jawnie realized she was unprepared for exactly what was happening. She shut down emotionally and raced home to her hidey hole. It had become her nest of positive emotions since Rockfish pulled her from the wrecked police car.

Today's shooting schedule called for both Jawnie and Gertie to be swabbed for DNA on camera, sitting next to the edge of the now empty, and slightly reconstructed for television, well. Angel Davenport had flown in to direct the shot, despite the continued COVID-19 spikes. Davenport was a proponent of having each woman swabbed on the actual location of where their lost relatives were located. That it would tug at the viewer's heartstrings much more than having it done at a sterile medical facility. He believed some of the remains located would genetically tie back to the two women.

As Rockfish walked into the tent, he could see Gertie, her wheelchair pushed alongside the well, talking with the local nurse that was hired to collect the DNA sample on camera. Truth be told, Davenport had ordered both women swabbed two weeks ago, the minute the old well was uncovered. Davenport wanted to make sure he had both women's genetic markers on file when the Rutgers's team validated his theory, because non-law enforcement DNA tests tended to be a low priority with most companies. Actually, it was everyone's theory, but he was the only one willing to take a chance and publicly declare it.

Today's DNA swab show was only for the cameras, while production continued to wait for the results on the remains and the comparisons to both women. They weren't the only ones, as both women eagerly waited for the closure that had always seemed out of their reach. In furtherance of that, Davenport had purchased a plaque that would be attached to the new well cap to honor those victims identified and those remaining unknown.

It upset Rockfish that no one would be charged in Edward's death but recently reinstated Elk Township Police Chief Ned Hasty promised Jawnie that he would give Edward's remains a proper burial with honors. Of course, the Davenport film crew would be there to tape it all, as a fitting end to the docuseries. Hasty had also recently presented Rodney

Jackson with an award for the valuable work his grandmother had done all those years ago.

Rockfish snuck up behind Jawnie's chair and placed his hand on her shoulder.

"How are you and Gertie holding up today, kid?"

"If you're asking if I still sleep under the stairs, you already know the answer to that," she replied. "Where do you think I called you from last night? And Gertie, I tell you that woman is ten times stronger facing all this then I'll ever be. Mark my words. Once Davenport finds a home for this series and it airs, that woman's going to end up being the star. I wish I could be as strong as she is and stop looking around in ten directions before I get out of bed in the morning."

Rockfish kept his mouth shut and gave her shoulder a squeeze. In the months after the arrests, they had spoken about this more times than he could remember. He tried to explain that those feelings, the constant looking over your shoulder, wouldn't go away. But life goes on and those people are going to be going away for a very long time. It's inevitable that someone is going to step into the power void created by Annetta going to jail, and technically that next Don owes you for the opportunity. Not that they will ever stop at your door and thank you in person, but what they will do is marginalize those loyal to the previous regime, those that might have an axe to grind.

"...like I said, the new boss will get rid of those types after the inauguration and no one will give a shit about us. So, relax. Sleep in a proper bed, you've earned it."

Jawnie didn't say anything, but Rockfish's hand felt the slight shrug of her shoulders.

"Hey, speaking of earning things, I hear Hasty's doing a hell of a job rebuilding the department." Rockfish said, hoping to elicit a verbal response this time.

"Yeah, from what I read when the mayor was indicted, the Township Board of Commissioners couldn't hire Hasty back fast enough. I need to reach out though, it's been a couple of weeks."

"I thought he might be here today. But he's probably busy hiring the right folks, and I hope he's cleaned a little house too," Rockfish replied. "Glad he brought Willoughby back into the fold."

"Betty Lou was the first to go, I heard," Jawnie said. "She's free to spend as much time as she wants on visiting day down at the Federal Correctional Institution at Fairton."

Someone unfamiliar to Rockfish and most likely part of the crew approached and leaned over to talk to Jawnie.

"Ms. McGee, they're almost finished with Ms. Roberts. We'll be ready for you in a couple of minutes. Take your time. Angel said he'll only shout 'Action', when you're ready to go."

"Hey, before you run out and get famous, I was thinking," Rockfish said. "If you need something to occupy your time and mind, now that we brought up Hasty, you'd make a damn fine digital analyst for them, if they have the spot and the budget. I can call and put in a friendly word, if you'd like. It's a better use of your old and newly found talents, than just wiping porn off old middle school laptops."

Jawnie looked up and smiled. It was a good sign and the first one Rockfish had seen today.

"I got my own thing I'm thinking about doing, now that you mention it. I'd like to run an idea by you before you bolt back down to Baltimore. Can I talk you into a Tofu burger and vegan fries as soon as I'm done?" Jawnie didn't wait for an answer, instead she stood up and headed out for her close-up.

As Jawnie exited the tent, Rockfish's phone rang. He looked down at the caller-ID.

Dad, he thought. *Checking in on me. Damn, he hates when I'm in Jersey.*

****

The angry man, formerly known as Father Abraham Renfield, parked his car across the street from the SugarHill Strip Mall and waited for the morning's festivities to begin.

At 10:30am he observed a caravan of cars pulling into the strip mall and the entire make-up of the Linthicum Heights Chamber of Commerce pile out of their vehicles. As they milled around and appeared to be waiting, one last car pulled into the lot. The black Challenger carried the Guests of Honors, so the others most likely didn't mind it being a few minutes tardy.

Renfield watched as everyone got into position for the man holding the camera. The chamber of commerce members formed a circle around the two late arrivals and cheered as they cut the ceremonial yellow ribbon with oversized novelty scissors. At the same time, a man in a suit off to the side pulled on a rope and the sheet hanging above the storefront fell to the ground.

Rockfish & McGee - Investigative Specialists

Renfield waited until they were all finished with the pictures and the crowd dispersed before putting his car in drive and slowly pulling out into traffic. Now that he knew the where, all he had to come up with was the how.

ACKNOWLEDGEMENTS

I have to start by thanking my awesome and extremely patient wife, Nicolita. From reading printed out scenes and chapters to being handed multiple three hundred-page, three ring binders, she was there to tell me what worked, what didn't, and when my inside jokes or witty dialogue fell flat. She was as important to this book getting done as I was.

My editor Ben Eads, who showed me how to better my craft in a very short period of time and had me realize how good a story this actually was.

Carson "Squeegie" Jenkins for the initial cover art idea along with his support and amazing skill in knowing exactly what would make a killer cover design during my self-publishing years.

I've had support from an amazing online writing community that has transitioned across a trio of message boards, especially Jason Little, Timothy Paul, and Brent Michael Kelley.

Jon Bradley for spurring me on with feedback for my self-published books that propelled me to this point. Without your words regarding *Huckleberry's Hail Mary*, I'm not sure I would be here today.

Thanks also to my beta readers, Val Conrad, Carlton James, John Hazen, Stephen W Briggs, Larry Karl, and Michelle Cyr. You input proved valuable and I learned from your edits.

I am grateful to Reagan Rothe and Black Rose Writing for their support in this endeavor and providing me the opportunity to accomplish a dream I've had since writing a story about two boys, a canoe, and a bear cub stowaway, in Mr. Bone's 4th grade class.

A large thank you to all those *e*-friends that spurred me on from the days of posting stories on the Rogan Board, to finding the resolve to self-publish.

Finally, the small town of Ewan, New Jersey and the surrounding areas, which I find myself turning to for inspiration time and time again. I couldn't think of a better town to base the large portion of my stories in.

ABOUT THE AUTHOR

Ken Harris retired from the FBI, after thirty-two years, as a cybersecurity executive. With over three decades writing intelligence products for senior Government officials, Ken provides unique perspectives on the conventional fast-paced crime thriller. While this is his first traditionally published novel, he previously self-published two novellas and two novels. He spends days with his wife Nicolita, and two Labradors, Shady and Chalupa Batman. Evenings are spent cheering on Philadelphia sports. Ken firmly believes Pink Floyd, Irish whiskey and a Montecristo cigar are the only muses necessary. He is a native of New Jersey and currently resides in Northern Virginia.

NOTE FROM THE AUTHOR

Word-of-mouth is crucial for any author to succeed. If you enjoyed *The Pine Barrens Stratagem*, please leave a review online—anywhere you are able. Even if it's just a sentence or two. It would make all the difference and would be very much appreciated.

Thanks!
Ken Harris

CPSIA information can be obtained
at www.ICGtesting.com
Printed in the USA
LVHW020330260122
709441LV00005B/575

9 781684 338719